Everyone watched as a towering confection was wheeled out of the kitchen. A golden heart suspended on shards and spirals of three kinds of chocolate hovered above a magnificent crème brûlée with fresh raspberries. It was an amazing dessert.

Flashes burst as several people captured the moment.

Mike looked up from the culinary marvel to its presenter and his thanks died on his lips. Patrice. His stomach clenched around its alcohol-soaked contents as all the guilt and desire of their past descended. He wasn't prepared to see her or to handle the mixture of feelings she always engendered.

"If this were Valentine's Day, I'd ask you to be mine." She smiled, laughter over their semi-private joke sparkling in her brown eyes. "But since it's not, I'll just say congra—"

"I'm not yours and never will be, and I don't want your damn heart." His inner turmoil over Patrice came tumbling out as anger.

Patrice's smile froze, breaking into a hurt "O."

Mike instantly regretted his words. He reached out in a misguided attempt to comfort her, but his aim was bad and his reflexes slow. He hit the top of the confection, snapping off the heart. He tried to grab it, to rescue it, but missed, bumping into the cart with enough force to tip it.

Mike watched in horrified fascination as the beautiful dessert slipped from the platter and smashed into Patrice.

She tried in vain to catch it.

Cameras whirred and bulbs flashed, capturing Patrice's stricken expression as globs of cream-colored custard, once perfect berries and raspberry sauce with chunks of caramelized sugar covered her hands, arms, and apron. A strangled noise came from her throat as she bolted for the kitchen.

Mike couldn't even apologize. At least not to her. She was gone before the initial uproar died down.

Gone before his mother caught his eye in a caustic glare.

Gone before Randy slugged him.

Author of *A Wish in Time,* finalist in the 2007 National Indie Excellence Book Awards.

A Wish in Time: "...had me glued to the pages from beginning to end. Bradley simply took my breath away with this captivating gem of a story..." Marilyn Rondeau ~ Reviewers International Organization

"I couldn't put the book down. I'll invite you to read this masterful work and enjoy its journey for yourself. You won't be disappointed." Jane Leopold Quinn, author of *Ancient Ties*

"*A Wish in Time* is an outstanding book, and I look forward to reading more from this author." Regina ~ Reviewer for Coffee Time Romance.

Crème Brûlée Upset

by

Laurel Bradley

Crème Brûlée Upset

Cover Art by *RJ Morris and Laurel Bradley*

The Wild Rose Press
PO Box 708
Adams Basin, NY 14410
Visit us at www.thewildrosepress.com

Publishing History
First Champagne Rose Edition
Print ISBN 1-60154-172-4

Published in the United States of America

Dedication

To Tom who makes everything sweet.
To Janet who always believed in me even when I didn't.
To Michelle for making this book shine like the top of the
Chrysler Building.

Chapter 1

Mike Tucker mingled, liberally sampling hors d'oeuvres from the groaning buffet at his surprise party. The food was beyond belief. The sweet, onion relish was a perfect contrast to the peppery edged roast beef. His housemates, Randy and Alex had obviously spared no expense.

The living room was steamy, and the buzz of conversation nearly deafening. Everyone he knew had been in on the secret—his business partners and their wives, the office staff, and friends from grade school on up.

He shook his father's hand and hugged his mother, smelling her spicy perfume.

"Did you call Patrice today like you promised?" his mother asked, brushing an invisible something from his suit coat.

He put on his expressionless courtroom face. He hadn't seen Patrice since she'd left for Le Cordon Bleu in Paris more than four years ago. "Yes, Mom," he said. And that was true. He had called Patrice. She just hadn't been home.

He scanned the crowded room, wondering if the call was supposed to have been the catalyst that would have allowed Patrice to attend the party. If so, it was better that he hadn't gotten through. He was no more ready to see her now than he'd been when she'd moved back to Chicago six months ago to take the job of head chef at Victor's. Still, part of him felt strangely disappointed when he didn't spot her. Maybe she'd be arriving later, with her parents. "Are the Wilsons here?"

His mother frowned. "Roy and Janice are in Cancun this week. Didn't you get their card?"

"Oh, yes, I did." She wasn't coming. He topped off his drink and took a long sip.

The Scotch was smooth and went down like water. Surprised to find that his world was a little blurry around the edges, Mike abandoned his tumbler and concentrated on his guests.

Moments later, Randy appeared at his elbow. "Having fun?"

"Yeah." Mike grinned. "This is a great party. You guys shouldn't have."

"Nothing more than what I expect from you when I make partner," Randy said as he led Mike to the far side of the room. "A word to the wise—be nice."

Be nice? Mike didn't get time to speculate on the meaning of Randy's comment before his roommate's whistle cut through the noise.

As heads turned in their direction, Randy's voice rang out. "Can I have your attention please?"

Patrice Wilson took a deep breath and opened the kitchen door. The surprise party was in full swing, and the air was thick with the sound of voices. Looking in the living room, she recognized a few of the guests, but not many.

Blocking the door open, she centered the serving cart in the passageway. This was it, the moment when she wheeled out her masterpiece and offered Mike congratulations on making partner. Still she hesitated, pausing to wipe damp palms on her crisp, white chef's apron. Maybe presenting this dessert wasn't the best idea.

Looking across the room, she saw her brother Randy had already positioned Mike where they'd agreed in front of the picture window. A single glance at Mike was all it took for her heart to skip a beat. His chocolate-brown hair had been recently trimmed and lay in sexy waves that begged to be touched. His navy suit was exquisitely tailored, emphasizing his broad shoulders and slim torso. But tonight wasn't about how good he looked. Tonight was about congratulating him, showing him she'd grown up, and moving on.

Everyone watched as a towering confection was wheeled out of the kitchen. A golden heart suspended on shards and spirals of three kinds of chocolate hovered above a magnificent crème brûlée with fresh raspberries. It was an amazing dessert.

Flashes burst as several people captured the moment.

Mike looked up from the culinary marvel to its presenter and his thanks died on his lips. Patrice. His stomach clenched around its alcohol-soaked contents as all the guilt and desire of their past descended. He wasn't prepared to see her or to handle the mixture of feelings she always engendered.

"If this were Valentine's Day, I'd ask you to be mine." She smiled, laughter over their semi-private joke sparkling in her brown eyes. "But since it's not, I'll just say congra—"

"I'm not yours and never will be, and I don't want your damn heart." His inner turmoil over Patrice came tumbling out as anger.

Patrice's smile froze, breaking into a hurt "O."

Mike instantly regretted his words. He reached out in a misguided attempt to comfort her, but his aim was bad and his reflexes slow. He hit the top of the confection, snapping off the heart. He tried to grab it, to rescue it, but missed, bumping into the cart with enough force to tip it.

Mike watched in horrified fascination as the beautiful dessert slipped from the platter and smashed into Patrice.

She tried in vain to catch it.

Cameras whirred and bulbs flashed, capturing Patrice's stricken expression as globs of cream-colored custard, once perfect berries and raspberry sauce with chunks of caramelized sugar covered her hands, arms, and apron. A strangled noise came from her throat as she bolted for the kitchen.

Mike couldn't even apologize. At least not to her. She

was gone before the initial uproar died down.

Gone before his mother caught his eye in a caustic glare.

Gone before Randy slugged him.

Chapter 2

Patrice's tears made brilliant stars of Chicago's streetlights and blurred the highway signs so completely that she almost missed her exit. Somehow she navigated the Monday night traffic to the safety of David Welch's lakefront house.

David was her best friend, the high school quarterback who had become Doctor Delicious, Chicago's ice cream guru. She and David had dated platonically all through high school. He knew all her secrets and she knew his. He understood about Mike.

Please, God, she prayed as she pulled into the driveway. Let him be home.

It was late. The Monday Night Football game featuring the Bears and the Giants in New York had just ended. Patrice hoped David hadn't flown out to watch his roommate Bubba Scott play.

She switched off her new Mazda, a welcome-back-to-the states/graduation gift from her parents, and slid from the car.

David opened the decorative glass door and stood, framed by the light, as he waited for her to run up the walk and into his arms.

"You poor baby, what did he do to you?" he asked, ignoring the gooey mess she was drenched in as he held her close and drew her into the marble-tiled entry.

For a long time, Patrice could do nothing but sob in the safety of her friend's arms. She was too upset to wonder why he'd been waiting for her.

David held her closely, smoothing her golden hair and murmuring all the things he'd do to Mike when he got the asshole alone.

The words slowly seeped into Patrice's emotion-clogged brain. "Skin him with a butter knife, huh?" she repeated his words with a soggy smile. "I think I'd like that."

"That's the least of it." David returned her tentative grin. "Then I'll rub him with those Cajun spices Bubba likes so much and set him under a sun lamp to broil. I don't suppose there's any call for slow-roasted skunk at that fancy restaurant of yours."

"No," Patrice laughed, wiping her tears with the handkerchief David handed her. "I don't think Victor's is ready for skunk—with or without Cajun spices."

"Damn."

David led Patrice to a leather recliner and sat, pulling her onto his lap. She rested her head against his shoulder and snuggled against his comforting bulk. Though he no longer played football, he still looked like he spent all day at the gym instead of at his designer ice cream store.

"Thank you for being here," she sighed, truly relaxing for the first time since she'd heard of Mike's party.

"Anything for you." He kissed the top of her head. "So tell me. What did the horse-apple do to make you cry?"

"It wasn't his fault." Tears welled up in her eyes once again.

"Bull." He wiped a glob of crème brûlée and raspberry sauce from her blouse and licked it off his fingers. "This is good. Did anyone else get any?"

"Only if they scraped it from the floor." Patrice frowned. "But, really," she continued, insisting on defending Mike. "I surprised him. He didn't know I was in town, and—"

"Not know you're in town?" David interrupted. "How the hell could Michael Tucker not know you're in town? Doesn't he read the papers? Just yesterday *Taste* called you 'the angel in Victor's kitchen.'" David snorted. "Does the man live under a rock?"

"He's been busy. He just made partner and—"

"Save it, sweetheart," David interrupted again. "You spent the last week planning and cooking every second you weren't at Victor's to put on a world-class party for this man, and he throws your masterpiece back in your face and tells you to fuck off. The man is shit on your shoe. Scrape him off and let's go shopping."

"How do you know what he did?" Patrice asked, her eyes wide with disbelief.

"You come here crying, smeared with dessert, smelling good enough to eat, and I put two and two together."

She narrowed her eyes and stared at the man she'd dated all through high school. "Liar."

"Okay." David shrugged. "Randy called."

Patrice slumped back into the chair. "So, then you know."

"What I know is that Mike isn't good enough for you—never has been, never will be. You can have anybody—always could, but you put yourself on a shelf for the one man who doesn't want you."

Patrice shook her head in denial.

"Hell, Pet. You dated a gay guy all through high school to keep yourself available for that loser."

"There's more to it than that," she protested. "I love you. You're my best friend—"

"And it doesn't look good if the quarterback is openly gay," he finished for her. "I didn't say I wasn't grateful. You saved me so much grief, not to mention beatings."

"Is your dad talking to you yet?" she asked, happy to focus on David's troubles instead of her own.

"Not since I bought the house with Bubba. My dad always hoped you'd convert me and that we'd get married and raise a bunch of grandkids for him. But we aren't talking about me."

"My life stinks. I'd rather talk about you right now." She laid her head on his shoulder and closed her eyes. "How's it going with Bubba?"

"Uh... he's got the highest sack record in the league. He couldn't be better."

Patrice opened her eyes and looked into David's. "What's up? I know Bubba's stats as well as he does, probably better."

"The media is starting to question his living arrangements."

"Oh, no," she moaned. In the good ol' boy world of football, homosexuality was frowned on. Gay players didn't get advertising contracts, they had a hard time getting roommates, and then, they found they had a hard time getting playing time. Being gay in the NFL was taboo.

"I was wondering if you'd... I hesitate to ask you when you've romantic problems of your own..."

Patrice laughed bitterly. "Since I have no love life of my own, I might as well date a big, black, gay defensive end." Tears welled up in her eyes. "It's not like I can turn anyone on anyway."

"That isn't like you, Pet. You need sleep."

"I'm not tired," she protested as David pushed her out of his lap.

"Of course not." He guided her to Bubba's bathroom. "But you do need to get cleaned up."

"I should go home."

"Don't be silly. You shouldn't be alone."

"But—"

"No buts, girl friend. Bubba's out of town tonight. Besides he wouldn't be using his bed if he were here." Ducking into Bubba's room, he pulled open a dresser drawer and took out an oversized t-shirt. "Here. Put this on."

When she came out of the bathroom, he took her dirty clothes and pointed to Bubba's bed. "You just crawl in there while I start the wash."

When she hesitated, David dropped the clothes by the door and ushered her to the bed. "Climb in, Pet, and let the doctor put you to sleep."

She laughed, but she let him tuck her in bed.

"I'll tell you about my exploits as quarterback before I blew my knee out," he wheedled.

"I know all your exploits. I was there, remember?"

"You might have been there, but you only remember what you saw, not what really happened. Now scooch over, and I'll tell you how I won the game against the Mounds View Mustangs my senior year."

"We lost that game," Patrice reminded him as he crawled in next to her.

"Not the way I tell it," he said, pulling Patrice close as a parent would a small child. He dropped his voice into hushed bedtime storyteller tones. "It was a crisp November night and the stadium was packed with screaming fans. The Lakeland Warrior cheerleaders were bouncing around, keeping the blood pumping in the straight boys' veins as the teams took the field for the division championship..."

Patrice never heard how David saved the day. By the time he threw the game-winning touchdown, she was asleep.

Chapter 3

All night the scene replayed in Mike's head. The stricken look on Patrice's face. Randy's fist. His parents' humiliated silence.

The party broke up pretty quickly after he dumped the dessert on Patrice. No one commented on how nice it had been. No one thanked anyone for a good time. And no one stayed to help clean up.

Both of his housemates were disgusted with him. Alex merely glared, but Randy was a bit more vocal.

"Tucker, you ass, she did all this for you. She bought everything, made everything, served everything—for you." Then Mike's two roommates each grabbed a bottle of booze and went to their separate rooms.

Mike scraped the dessert off the carpeting and tasted the top layer. Tears came to his eyes, but not because the taste was so heavenly. He'd finally done it. He'd destroyed any chance he may have had with Patrice.

He cleaned the entire house, putting away the leftovers—strawberries dipped in chocolate decorated with white-chocolate hearts, tender pastries filled with lumps of sweet crab, bite-size canapés decorated with salmon and caviar, paper thin roast beef topped with really good onion relish. There were even a few of the huge pink shrimp she'd spiraled around a dish of creamy red cocktail sauce.

She'd done it all for him. Guilt assailed him as private home movies played in his head.

Tonight's "If this were Valentine's Day, I'd ask you to be mine..." became a memory of when he'd been eight.

"Mine!" one-year-old Patrice had announced as she walked into the living room holding onto her mother's fingers.

He and Randy had been on the other side of the room, sitting on the rug playing Battleship.

Patrice had seen him, let go of her mother's fingers and ventured off solo, toddling unsteadily across the room.

Everyone—Mike and Randy, her parents, Janice and Roy, and his parents, Matt and Melanie Tucker—watched the tiny blonde's progress.

"Isn't she cute?" his mom commented to no one in particular.

Mike caught the look of jealousy on Randy's face as Patrice made a wobbly beeline toward him instead of her own brother.

"Mine," Patrice repeated excitedly.

"What's yours, sweetheart?" Patrice's mom asked. Moments later, Patrice made it to Mike's side. She grabbed his sleeve to steady herself and once again declared, "Mine!"

Randy exploded in laughter far more raucous than the situation called for. "It's you, Mike! She thinks she owns you!"

Neither Mike nor Randy had ever forgotten it.

He remembered everything about Patrice. How could he not when she was a part of nearly every memory he had?

When he was ten, three-year-old Patrice had chased after him like a delighted puppy. When he broke his leg at fifteen, it was Patrice who had sat at his bedside keeping him company while he was in traction. When he'd gone off to college, Patrice had begged him to wait for her to grow up.

Naturally, he'd laughed it off, saying that by the time she grew up, she wouldn't want an old guy like him.

But she had.

It wasn't until she'd begun to develop and he found himself attracted to her that he started getting mean, calling her "The Pest" and telling her to go play with her dolls. He told himself it was self-preservation. She was too young. Besides, their families were so close they were almost related.

He had told himself he didn't like the attention—that he didn't look forward to her letters and care packages filled with food, that he didn't count on her always being there for him. That's what he told himself, but whenever things got tough, it was the thought that at least Patrice loved him that made the hard times easier to get through.

He'd been quietly relieved that her high school romance with David hadn't seemed to change anything. Then again, why should it? After all, Mike was almost her brother.

He'd been both flattered and embarrassed when she'd asked him to take her to her prom. Of course, he couldn't take her. It would have been wrong. He knew he couldn't hide his true feelings from her if they were alone together that long. Besides, he was twenty-four to her seventeen.

At her graduation, he'd told her that it was a good thing she was going to chef school in France—maybe someone there could teach her to cook.

He'd really said that. He, Mike—the man who'd awaited the arrival of her boxes of baked goods with mouth-watering anticipation and shared the contents with extreme reluctance—the lying bastard.

And she'd laughed. He'd been an ass, and she hadn't taken it personally. She had still sent treats and weekly letters from France. And he'd written back, as he always had, every now and then.

She didn't know how he valued her letters, anticipated them, worried if one arrived a day late. And now he'd publicly humiliated her.

He carried the last armload of liquor into the kitchen and slid the bottles onto a corner of the counter.

Alex's digital camera sat in the middle of the kitchen table. Mike picked it up, intending to delete any pictures of the accidental dessert destruction.

He reviewed the photos inside Alex's camera. They had all been taken before the first guest arrived. There were some shots of the platters of food, but most were pictures of Patrice. The camera worshiped her. It captured her sparkling personality in her smile and flattered her trim curves. It made her neatly braided hair look as if it had been sculpted from spun gold. Alex had chronicled the step-by-step process she'd taken to create the masterpiece Mike had unwittingly thrown back at her. There was one picture of Patrice slitting the crème brûlée's caramelized crust while the shards and twists of dark, white, and milk chocolate lay on the tray at her elbow. Several frames captured the process of creating the caramelized heart by drizzling hot syrup over the chocolate frame. Mike's guilt grew as he viewed shot after shot, watching as she worked her magic with the candy thread, drizzling sugar strands on the framework and layering them until a glistening three-dimensional golden heart was suspended over the crème brûlée.

Randy's words came back to him. She'd done it all for him, and he'd thrown it back in her face.

Mike set down the camera and escaped to his bedroom. There were no mental images of Patrice there. No pictures. No memories of conversations or hours spent cooking haunting that room—just a cigar box of letters in the back of his sock drawer.

Chapter 4

"Leave ya alone for forty-eight hours and ya go straight on me, man. And in my bed too."

"It was kinkier in your bed. You know that I don't want anything perverted going on in mine," David laughed.

"Hi, Bubba," Patrice yawned in David's arms. "I guess we fell asleep talking. We didn't expect you back 'til this afternoon."

"I hear you had a rough night." Bubba sat on the end of the bed.

Patrice sat up and narrowed her eyes. "You heard what?"

Bubba dropped a newspaper in her lap. On the bottom half of the front page was a picture of Mike dumping her beautiful creation down the front of her. The caption read, "Bosworth's newest partner sends Victor's Patrice Wilson back to the kitchen."

"What is this—the *Enquirer*?" David asked, grabbing the newspaper from Patrice, who sprang from the bed and raced to the bathroom. "What's the *Herald* coming to?"

Bubba shrugged. "I guess some of the guests at the party were from the paper."

"Hell of a thank you," David growled.

The sound of Patrice retching behind the closed

bathroom door fueled David's anger. "I'd like to get my hands on that Tucker and teach him a thing or two about manners."

"I say we each take an arm and escort her to that Museum of the Arts Gala this weekend. There'll be media all over the place. We'll show everyone last night meant nothing. She doesn't need Tucker."

"I'd rather beat the crap out of him."

Bubba grinned. "There's no law says we can't do both."

Chapter 5

Mike wiped the steam off the bathroom mirror. Damn. He fingered the swollen tissue around his black eye. Randy had really gotten him good—not that he didn't deserve it. At least he wouldn't have to explain his eye at work. His partners, legal assistants, and secretary had been there last night. Everyone had seen Randy deck him.

He dressed and went to the kitchen, put a couple of slices of bread in the toaster, and poured a cup of coffee while he waited.

Alex and Randy ignored him until he was seated at the table next to them, and then Alex dropped the *Herald* on Mike's toast.

"You did her real good, Tucker," Randy said, pushing away from the table and standing. "Public humiliation is always best."

The picture, a black and white shot, showed the scene clearly. From the angle of the camera, Patrice's stricken face was caught in an astounded "O." The dessert she'd spent so long making was sliding through her arms. Mike was caught reaching over the cart, smashed heart in hand. Though he'd really been trying to rescue the brûlée, it looked as if he were shoving it at her.

"God," Mike moaned. "How was I to know you'd invited the press?"

16

"We didn't," Randy said. "I guess your mother thought it would be good for both your careers. What she didn't know was how much you hated Patrice. No one did, until last night."

"And now," Alex added, "the greater Chicago area knows."

"But I don't hate her," Mike moaned, dropping his head to his hand. "I love her." He froze. What had he said? He'd sworn he'd never admit that to anyone—not even himself.

His roommates stared at him in disbelief.

"You are so full of shit," Randy snarled, leaving the room.

"What did you say?" Alex demanded.

"Nothing," Mike mumbled into his hands.

"You said you love her?" Alex frowned. "Are you kidding?" He looked at Mike.

Mike ignored him, sitting like the poster-boy for dejection with his head hanging over the butter-smeared newspaper and cold toast.

"You aren't kidding," Alex said. "Why have you rejected her all these years if you supposedly love her?"

Mike shook his head and moaned.

Alex picked up his camera and laughed mirthlessly.

Chapter 6

Patrice walked into her one-bedroom loft apartment at nine o'clock. It was the perfect place for her. Close to the loop, with a bed and bath upstairs and a living room, powder room, and spacious kitchen down. It had everything she needed. She entered her beautiful kitchen to make a pot of coffee and sighed. She'd forgotten that most of her cookware, including her coffee grinder, was at Mike's house. She was used to cooking with the best utensils, cutlery, and cookware. She'd taken one look at the cheap bachelor-ware Alex and Randy had pulled out and had brought her own. Now her kitchen was empty, and she had to figure out how to get her stuff back without running into Mike.

The light on her answering machine was blinking. She hit the replay button and started water for tea.

"Pet," her brother's voice said. "Are you all right? I don't know what the hell is wrong with Mike, but I'm going to find out. I just want to make sure you're all right. Call me."

She listened to messages from Melanie Tucker, Victor, and some lady from the newspaper, before dialing Randy's work number.

While she waited for his secretary to forward the call, she filled the tea infuser and set it in the teapot. She poured the boiling water into the pot and frowned. She hadn't preheated the teapot with hot water. It was the details that made great food and great tea, she reminded herself. She had to focus or she'd be a wreck at work.

"How are you?" Randy's voice over the phone sounded concerned and edgy as if he were afraid she'd cry on the phone, and he knew he couldn't handle her tears.

Patrice smiled to herself. She never cried. Well...not counting last night, or the time Mike broke his leg running into a dock while water skiing.

Thoughts of Mike caused a sudden tightening in her chest and an accompanying prick of tears. She poured a cup of watery tea and took a scalding sip. It hadn't steeped nearly long enough.

"I'm fine," she lied, dumping the weak tea down the sink. "I need a favor, though."

"Anything," Randy said.

"I need..." Her voice broke and tears welled in her eyes. She closed her eyes, squeezing the tears down her cheeks. "I need..." she said again. This time her voice didn't betray her "...you to get my stuff from your house."

"What stuff?"

She could almost see Randy imagining her clothes and other personal items in Mike's room. It would have been funny had she not gone into Mike's room yesterday and imagined her clothes next to his in the closet, her hairbrush on his dresser, and her slippers beneath his bed.

"Cooking stuff," Patrice choked out before Randy could think anything else. "From the party, you know?"

"Oh, yeah." He sounded relieved and almost ashamed, as if he'd actually been thinking what she'd imagined. "Sure," he said. "Is tonight soon enough?"

"Tonight would be great. I'll drop off a key to my apartment on my way to work. If you'd put my stuff on the counters, I'd be grateful." Her voice was thick with repressed emotion.

"No problem."

"Thanks." She had to end this conversation. She was losing control. Backhanding the tears from her cheeks, she croaked, "I've gotta go."

"Pet?" Randy said gently. "It'll be all right."

"Yeah," she sniffed, unable to stop herself. "Bye."

She placed the phone in its cradle and tried to regain her composure as the tears dripped onto her spotless counter. She told herself that she shouldn't be this broken up. It wasn't as if she and Mike were anything more than family friends. Sure, she'd written to him every Wednesday of her life telling him about every important thing that had ever happened to her along with a whole bunch of unimportant things. And every now and then he'd written back.

It was all her own fault, she admitted. He'd never encouraged her, but he'd never come right out and told her to get lost either—not until last night, anyway.

It was time to grow up, to realize that her dreams of being Mrs. Michael Tucker were just childhood fantasies. It was time to stop the letters and the packages and move on.

The phone rang. Her hand jerked, knocking it to the counter.

"Sorry," she apologized to the caller. "Hello."

"Patrice?"

It was Mike. She swallowed hard. She couldn't talk to him.

Shaking, she hung up the phone and backed away from it as if it were alive and would attack.

It rang again.

She ran from the kitchen and up the stairs to the loft. She skidded into the bathroom as her answering machine picked up.

"Patrice? I know you're there. Pick up. I need to talk to you."

Patrice closed the door and turned on the shower to avoid hearing any more.

****

Mike hung up the phone and stared at it in disbelief. She wouldn't talk to him.

Maybe she didn't know it was me, he told himself, but he didn't believe it. He swallowed several times in the futile attempt to relieve the tightness in his throat and the sick feeling in his gut. He hadn't expected it would be easy to apologize. Okay, maybe he had. Well, not the actual apologizing maybe, but he had expected her to listen—to listen and understand and forgive. Her love was a constant in his life. It was something he could ignore and take for granted because it was always there. She'd always been willing to talk to him. More than willing. She'd always wanted more of him than he was willing to give.

There was an odd sense of pride and vanity in knowing that someone wanted you so much that they'd be happy with whatever bone you threw them. And now she wouldn't talk to him.

She's just mad, he told himself. She'll get over it. He'd call her later, and she'd listen. She'd listen, and everything would be fine.

He opened a drawer and pulled out the Yellow Pages. He'd send her flowers at work, just the same.

Chapter 7

Patrice stared at the flashing message light for a moment before hitting the eject button and throwing the cassette in the trash. She knew Mike just wanted to apologize and she should let him, but she couldn't trust herself to talk to him without falling apart. She'd wasted years mooning over him. That was humiliation enough. She didn't need to bawl on the phone to him too.

The buzz of the doorbell jolted Patrice out of her reverie.

"Yes?" she answered tentatively, every muscle prepared to run. Oh, please, don't let it be Mike.

"It's just us, Pet." David's voice came through the speaker.

Patrice buzzed David and Bubba in, wondering why they'd come.

"I told you I didn't feel up to lunch," she reminded the large men as she let them into her apartment.

"I know," David said, kissing her cheek. "It just occurred to us that you might want some moral support in case Tucker calls."

"I'm not a total emotional invalid. You don't need to baby-sit me. Besides, you're too late." She turned away from her friends.

Bubba noticed the answering machine with its open,

22

empty cassette compartment. "Got the machine, did he?"

She turned to smile at the big black man. "The second time. I hung up on him the first one."

"Good girl." David retrieved a suitcase from the hall. "So here's the plan."

"Plan? What plan?"

"Therapy, girl." He walked by her on the way to the kitchen. "You need therapy to purge the demon Tucker from your heart. Lucky for you, the doctor makes house calls."

"Since when?" She followed the men into her kitchen.

"Since it's you," David answered. "Now, I need a large bowl and a mixer." He put the suitcase on the counter and unzipped it.

Patrice stared in amazement as he pulled an ice cream maker and a variety of ingredients from the open case.

"I left my mixer at the party." Patrice blinked hard and managed to keep the tears from sliding down her face.

"You go ahead and cry, girl," Bubba encouraged, draping his arm around her shoulders, pulling her close. "David, you count them tears. I'm making Tucker pay for each one."

"I'm making a special flavor for him as well," David admitted, rummaging though Patrice's drawers for a spoon. "What did you do? Move your entire kitchen over there?"

"Pretty much." Patrice left the comfort of Bubba's arms to pull a large stainless stirring spoon from a drawer. "I can't cook with crap."

"I can," David smiled. "You haven't seen our kitchen."

Patrice smiled. "Yes, I have."

"If I buy some new cookware, will you move in with us and save me from the press?" Bubba asked, only half joking.

"No."

"Your mama wouldn't approve of you living with a gay, black man?"

Smiling, Patrice shook her head. "I don't think she'd mind the gay part."

"I know. It's like *Guess Who's Coming to Dinner*."

"'Fraid so," Patrice admitted.

"And here I thought a rich, black, professional defensive end was the stuff of every mama's dream," Bubba said in mock disappointment.

David shook his head as he mixed raspberries and three kinds of chocolate chunks into the cream and sugar. "Gotta work on that ego, man. No wonder you can't get a girl."

"Speaking of which," Bubba turned to Patrice, "could I take you to that Museum of the Arts fund raiser gala thing?"

"I'm in charge of the food at that 'fund raiser gala thing,'" Patrice said, "so I'll already be there. But I really won't have to spend much time in the kitchen. My job will be to wander around and be seen while I make certain everything is going all right. I have assistants to do all the last minute stuff, so I would be happy to—"

"Grace Bubba's arm and send him adoring looks while he gives you equally besotted ones?" David interrupted.

"Exactly," Patrice nodded. "What are you making there?" she asked David, leaning closer to look into the ice cream freezer.

"I told you—therapy," David informed her, elbowing her aside and snapping the lid firmly in place.

Patrice crossed her arms, frowning. "I don't think I like the sound of that."

"Quit whining." Bubba put his arm around Patrice and led her from the kitchen. "All ice cream is therapy. Give the man fifteen minutes and an unlimited supply of ingredients, and he could heal the world. He's not Doctor Delicious for nothing."

"I know," Patrice grumbled. "Gourmet ice cream at gourmet prices."

"Spoken like the chef of a five-star restaurant," David said, poking his head out of the kitchen. "Where do you keep your bowls? This kitchen is bare."

Fifteen minutes later David placed a large bowl filled with the ice cream equivalent of last night's crème brûlée in front of her.

"I'm really not hungry," Patrice insisted, hating the fact that her eyes filled with tears at the mere thought of facing the flavors of last evening's debacle. It might be therapy to eat them and disassociate the combination from the pain and sadness of last night, but she didn't feel able to taste them just yet. She didn't want to eat the ice cream. She didn't want to talk to Mike. She didn't want to do anything but bury her head in her pillow and feel sorry for herself. She stared at the ice cream sitting in her bowl.

"Therapy wasn't meant to be easy," David informed her.

"You'd know," Patrice grumbled, fingering her spoon. "How many of your customers have you bullied into eating whatever you thought they needed instead of what they ordered?"

"It's one of the draws of my store. Ice cream for what ails you. Now eat up before it melts. This portable ice cream freezer makes good ice cream, but it doesn't freeze it very hard."

"Just take a bite, Patrice, please," Bubba wheedled, eyeing his own bowl longingly. "You know the rules. The patient has to take the first bite, and I would rather not drink my ice cream."

"Fine," Patrice snapped, picking up her spoon. "Speaking of whining..."

"Just eat it," David insisted.

Patrice spooned up a glop of the soft ice cream and put it into her mouth. "There," she said around the spoon. "Happy?"

"Yes." Bubba smiled, digging into his own bowl.

"Swallow," David directed, watching her until she complied before eating a spoonful himself. "Good isn't it?"

"Not as good as the crème brûlée." Patrice frowned, taking another spoonful. Eating ice cream *was* therapeutic.

"Of course not," David smiled, indulgently.

"And you forgot the caramelized sugar."

"Damn, I knew I was doing this too fast. This whole thing must have rattled me more than I thought. I think it's the tears. I've never seen you cry before."

"I know. I don't like it either. I wish I could be mad instead, but I'm not angry, just incredibly sad."

"Buck up, sweetheart, he's not worth it." David stared into Patrice's wounded eyes and frowned. "Give me

25

a smile, and I'll make you another batch later at the store."

"With caramel?"

"It won't be true therapy until it contains caramel."

"Okay." She forced a grin.

"Damn pathetic."

****

Patrice walked into Victor's signature mahogany and cream foyer, running her gloved hand gently along the highly polished hostess's podium, and was greeted by Victor himself. He pulled her into a bone-crushing hug and bussed her cheek.

"You didn't have to come in today. I could have gotten Derrick."

"I told him I'd work for him," Patrice said, stepping out of Victor's arms. "Besides, with the gala Friday night, there's a lot to do. I need to finalize the menus, finish the ordering, and go over some things with Carrie and Johnny." She looked him in the eye. "I'll be all right, really."

"I know, Patrice." He patted her shoulder. "You'll be sure to come to me if you need a few days off or if there's anything I can do, right?"

"Right." She forced a smile and continued toward the kitchen.

"How did the onion relish on the shaved roast beef go over last night?"

She stopped, turning to face her boss once again. "Perfect. In fact, the entire party was a rousing success until dessert."

"I'd like to personally fillet Michael Tucker. And then the newspaper—God! We can stand the publicity especially on the heels of that *Taste* feature, but it really makes him look like the shit he is. You haven't forgiven him, have you?"

Patrice shook her head. "I don't want to talk to him just yet."

"Good, because he's *persona non grata* here."

Patrice offered Victor another weak smile before, once again, starting for the kitchen door.

Again, Victor's voice stopped her. "He sent you some flowers."

"What?" She stopped mid-stride to gape at her boss.

"Come." Victor led her into the kitchen. "I had them put in the cooler...in the back."

She followed him silently into the huge walk-in refrigerator.

A vase of pale pink roses sat eye level on a shelf. She stared at them in stunned disbelief.

Mike had sent her flowers? Now? Her heart clenched in pain. Why now? she wondered. Why not when it would have mattered, say...at graduation, or Valentine's Day, or her birthday.

Victor plucked the envelope out of the floral pick and put it into Patrice's hand.

She opened it automatically and read the card:

Let me pick you up after work so I can apologize in person. —*Mike*

"No," she said, handing the card to Victor. "When he comes, say I'm not here. I don't want to see him, and I don't want his flowers."

"Maybe you should send him a message so he won't come tonight," Victor suggested. "I've an idea."

"Do you?" She regarded him with wide eyes.

"Actually, I have several."

"You've given this some thought," Patrice remarked. "Had you read the card?"

Victor shook his head. "No need. A dozen roses are the standard peace offering. Most men will use red roses, though, as symbols of love. I'm not certain what pink symbolizes, but it isn't love. It's probably something lame like friendship."

"Maybe." Patrice shrugged. "I don't want even that from him right now." She took one last look at the large hothouse roses before turning her back on them and leaving the cooler. She paused at the door and said over her shoulder, "Mike won't get home until after six. We'll have plenty of time to work up something after I get the ordering done."

Victor smiled.

Chapter 8

It was nearly seven o'clock by the time Mike finally arrived home. It had been an incredibly long day. There had been a none-too-subtle air of disappointment and disapproval at the office. No one said anything to him about the party, but conversations stopped abruptly when he entered a room. His secretary was polite and efficient, but she met his eye with a look that dared him to look away.

Randy was sitting at the kitchen table drinking beer with Alex when Mike walked in. As it had all day, the conversation died as he entered. Uncertain of his reception, Mike hesitated to join them at the table, going instead to the refrigerator to get himself a beer.

"You're so damned smooth, Tucker," Randy sneered, breaking the silence. He shoved the distinctly marked "Made especially for you by the chefs at Victor's" takeout container toward Mike. "What did you do? Tell her you love her? Send her flowers?"

"What's this?" Mike asked no one in particular.

"Looks like Patrice has forgiven you after all," Randy said incredulously. "She sent you dinner."

Mike gave them a puzzled smile. She wouldn't talk with him this morning, and yet she'd sent him dinner. Could he be this lucky? Could the flowers have done the trick?

He opened the lid.

The remains of the roses clearly spelled out the answer: Nestled in a bed of mangled leaves and baby's breath sat an artistic arrangement of green rose stems and severed pink buds forming the word "No."

There was no doubt this dish had been prepared especially for him by the head chef at Victor's.

"No?" Randy read aloud, chuckling. "After all these years, she finally told you no. Way to go, Patrice!"

"Thanks," Mike said under his breath.

Alex and Randy exploded with laughter.

"You sent her flowers?" Alex laughed, tears of mirth rolling down his face. "What did the card say? 'Will you forgive me?'"

"No," Randy interjected. "Remember this morning? He loves her, right? And after his obvious show of affection last night, the card said, 'Will you marry me?'"

Mike glared at Randy.

"I still can't believe you claim to love Patrice," Randy taunted, turning to Alex. "Have you ever heard such a load of shit? You'd better never tell her that." His eyes raked both of the men in the room. "Either of you. You know she'll believe it and take it the wrong way, thinking he meant 'in love with her.'" He turned to glare at Mike. "You love her," he snorted. "What did you say something like that for? Hell, you can hardly stand her."

Mike shrugged, but his heart clenched. Was that how Patrice saw things now? Is that what he'd finally accomplished? His stomach felt as if he'd eaten the roses—thorns and all.

"I don't hate her," Mike offered lamely.

"I know," Randy said. "You've just pushed her away for so long that it's become a habit. She's the closest thing you've got to a kid sister. I know what it's like. She *is* my sister. The kid sister adores the big brother, and the big brother despises the kid sister. It's classic. And that's the way it's supposed to work with kids. But we're all grown up now. You need to realize that she's not 'The Pest' any more. She's an adult. And so are you...most of the time." He smiled wickedly. "You don't need to shove her aside. She's not going to follow you around Chicago spying on you like she did when she was young. Make peace with her. Apologize for being a world-class ass and get on with your life."

Get on with his life. Mike frowned. He'd been trying for as long as he could remember to forget Patrice and get on with life, but he'd never been able to do it. She haunted him. On the other hand, he couldn't bring himself to admit his true feelings to her. She'd always been the closest thing he had to a sister. It was just that he didn't feel very fraternal toward her.

The guys loaded Randy's SUV with Patrice's cookware before Alex plopped in front of the television to watch Tuesday's line-up.

In the kitchen, Mike popped another beer and handed it to Randy. "You want last night's leftovers?"

Randy nodded, and Mike pulled the leftovers from the refrigerator and put them on the counter. Removing the lids, he peered inside. "Looks like Alex beat us to them, but I think there's still enough." He put several containers of cooked hors d'oeuvres into the microwave and carried the cold hors d'oeuvres to the table.

Randy looked at the arrangement before him. "She really outdid herself, didn't she?" He fished a jumbo shrimp out of its container. "Man, these are huge. They must have cost a fortune."

"Rub it in a little more," Mike grumbled. "I don't feel bad enough already."

"Sorry," Randy chuckled, sticking the shrimp in his mouth. He chewed it silently, savoring it. "So when are you going to try to apologize again?"

"As soon as she'll let me."

The microwave's buzzer rang. Mike brought the steaming Tupperware to the table and sat down.

"If I were you, I'd wait a day or two," Randy said, helping himself to the food. He sampled several items. "This stuff is too good. Did you taste these little shaved beef sandwiches with the sauce? Pet has got to bring these Christmas Eve." He glanced at his friend as he reached for another one. "Sorry."

"I don't think I'm going to be able to eat this after all," Mike said, pushing away from the table.

"Suit yourself," Randy shrugged, "but she's not going

to be any less angry for your not eating it. And it really is good." He waved a bruschetta invitingly under Mike's nose.

Mike snatched it from Randy's hand and shoved it into his mouth, spraying crumbs everywhere. "Why does she have to be such a good cook?"

Randy laughed. "Just to torture you."

"For years I thought so, but now I'm not so sure," Mike admitted. "Now I think she is all the things she is because that's the way she is."

"Very deep, Tucker, very deep." Randy swallowed his mouthful.

"Hey, you want some wine or something to go with this. This is way too good for beer."

"Sacrilege!" Randy guzzled the last of his beer. "Well, maybe wine would be better." He eyed the selection of food on the table. "Make it a red, if we've got it."

"Oh, we've got it." Mike opened the closet door where several partially consumed bottles of wine lined the floor. "Merlot or Cabernet?"

"Mm, Merlot."

Mike found a corkscrew and coaxed the cork from the bottle. He reached high into the cupboard for wine glasses.

"Did you know she even had glasses brought in?" Mike asked over his shoulder as he poured the wine.

"I know," Randy said. "I was in on planning this party, remember?"

"Where do you think they're from?"

"Victor's catering department."

"Maybe I'll take them back there tonight and see Patrice."

"Do you think that's a good idea after the flowers and all?" Randy asked.

"I left a message on her machine this morning saying that I'd be there. I have to show up."

"Well, if you're certain. But I bet she isn't counting on you." Randy bit his lower lip and shook his head. "If it were me, I'd still wait a few days, and then maybe go to that Art Museum Gala. It would make your mom happy as well. She's on the board, you know."

"I know. She's been pestering me about going."

31

"So go." Randy sat back and sipped his wine.

"I don't know if she'd want me after last night."

"She'll want you. She's your mother." Randy set down his wine glass and looked at the selections again. "Go. It'll get you off her shit list and maybe you can make nice to Patrice. She'll be there. Victor's is catering it, and she's in charge."

"Maybe."

"It'll be in public, and Patrice won't do anything to harm Victor's reputation," Randy pointed out.

"I'll think about it."

Randy wiped his mouth with the back of his hand. "That was good, but I could use something sweet. Didn't Patrice make anything for dessert?" A wicked grin played at his lips.

Mike groaned, dropping his head into his hands.

Chapter 9

Mike pulled into Victor's parking lot with a trunk full of glassware. The car's vents poured warm air into the idling vehicle as Mike stared out at the parked cars in the brightly lit lot. He knew from experience that the kitchen of this popular restaurant generally stayed open until nine on weeknights. Patrice was sure to be there, putting the finishing touches on the last few meals and overseeing the final clean up.

Slowly, almost reluctantly, he turned off his car and stepped into the brittle coldness of the night. Doubt assailed him. Maybe this wasn't a good idea. Maybe he should wait before trying to apologize. Maybe he should have let Randy take the glasses to Patrice's apartment.

Taking a deep breath of frigid air, he pushed aside his reservations. He was here. At least he could return the glasses.

He pulled open the massive oak doors and let two laughing couples out before he entered. He banged the parking lot slush from his shoes and approached the unmanned hostess's podium. It was a few moments before a waitress spotted him.

"I'm sorry, sir. We're not seating anymore this evening. The kitchen has closed."

"That's all right. I really just need to know where to

33

return some glassware from a party."

"Oh," she said, really looking at him for the first time. "Wait here. I'll get some bus boys to help."

Two minutes later, three young men came from the kitchen, zipping their coats and pulling on gloves.

"Where are you parked?" the tallest of the three asked.

"Near the back, by the kitchen," Mike replied, leading them into the night.

Once the glasses were gone, Mike contemplated leaving as well. He'd done what he'd set out to do. Well, some of it at any rate. Maybe he should heed Randy's advice and give Patrice a chance to cool off.

No. He was here. He'd told Patrice's machine he'd come. He couldn't let her down anymore than he already had. He'd just go in and get it done with. Then, when his mother called to grill him tomorrow, he'd have an answer for her questions.

He walked resolutely back into the restaurant.

Victor himself stood behind the podium, waiting.

"You're not welcome here, Tucker," he said across the entry room. "I thought Patrice had made it clear that she doesn't want to see you."

"I just need to talk to her."

The coat-clad bus boys returned to the entryway, rubbing gloved fists and looking more like thugs than the clean-cut kids that had just taken the glasses from his trunk.

"She doesn't want your apology," Victor continued. "Just leave her be. You've done enough."

"I see." Mike pulled himself up straight. "You wouldn't be trying to intimidate me would you, Victor?"

Victor shrugged. "Take it as you like, Tucker. Just leave and don't let me hear that you've been bothering her."

"I suggest you take out your hearing aid then, my friend," Mike said, wearing false bravado like a coat, "because I intend to talk to her."

The waitress Mike had spoken to earlier poked her head into the entry. "Victor, do you want me to call the police?"

"No, Marie," Victor said, though he continued to

34

watch Mike. "Mr. Tucker was just leaving."

Mike inclined his head to Victor in acknowledgement and backed out of the restaurant. He didn't start shaking until he'd pulled out of the parking lot. Maneuvering his car into a nearby gas station, Mike raced to the bathroom.

He stared at his pale visage in the mirror before cupping cool water in his hands and splashing his face. Had he hurt Patrice that much? Had Patrice known and approved of Victor's actions or had her boss taken it upon himself to scare the crap out of Mike? He didn't know. Either way, now it was even more imperative than ever that he talk to her soon.

Chapter 10

Patrice crawled between her flannel sheets. The weight of the down comforter felt heavenly on her tired limbs. It was good to be home and have the day over. Everything was back to normal. The new normal. The cookware and knives Randy had returned were clean and in their places. He'd even returned the glassware to Victor's.

The party was officially cleaned-up and over. She just wished she felt better about it. There wasn't any of the usual post-event satisfaction. No feeling of accomplishment or knowledge of a job well-done. There was just loss.

Had Mike found someone else, someone pretty and accomplished or really nice, Patrice would have been able to move on with her self-esteem intact. She would have been able to tell herself that he loved this other person. She could have been big-hearted and generous as she tried to be happy for the couple. The death of her romantic dreams would have been the result of someone else's triumph instead of what it was—a personal rejection.

It was hard to feel good about yourself when you knew that your dream man wasn't in love with someone else. He didn't want another person above all others. He simply didn't want you.

A sob caught in her throat.

Personal rejection was what made last night hurt so badly.

She closed her eyes and tried to get comfortable.

Impossible. Without her dreams of a happily-ever-after, her personal safety net lay in tatters. Without Mike to fill her thoughts, she was alone as she'd never been before. She sniffed. Well, lonely, but not quite alone. She had said she'd go out with Bubba.

Patrice sighed. There she was, back to dating a gay man. Was that better than being alone?

She flipped from her right side to her left. Who was she trying to fool? Bubba was David's. And even if he wasn't, she wasn't his type.

She turned back to her right side.

Maybe she should get a kitten. She'd prefer a puppy, but not without a yard... Pet or no pet, she would be okay. She was still young. There were plenty of fish in the sea. Dating Bubba was just a favor to a friend, not a preview of coming attractions. Eventually a straight guy would ask her out. She was fine, would do just fine. Heck, she'd lived through the humiliation of the newspaper and the shock of the flowers.

She turned onto her back and stared at the ceiling. Flowers. From Mike. Tears leaked into her ears. How many times would she have died to have received flowers from Mike? And when did she finally get them? After he'd told her once and for all to bug off.

Fine.

Patrice punched her pillow and flopped on her belly. The important thing was she'd lived through it and hadn't let it distract her too much. She'd been able to concentrate on cooking and hadn't ruined anything. In fact, now that she thought about it, work as a whole had gone surprisingly well. She'd chatted with several customers who loved their meal enough to call her to their table, and no one even mentioned the morning's picture.

Of course, it helped that no one ordered crème brûlée.

Like a video loop, Mike's hateful words and dessert destruction played over and over in her head.

"I'm never going to get to sleep!" she sobbed into her

pillow.

****

Mike lay on his back and stared at the darkened ceiling of his bedroom.

"Damned brûlée," he muttered, turning over to pummel his pillow into shape. He caught sight of the glowing red numbers on his clock radio and groaned. He was going to be worthless all day if he didn't get to sleep.

He closed his eyes and tried to will his mind into silence. But, as often happens in such cases, his mind would not shut up. "I'm sorry," he told Patrice in dozens of different scenarios to dozens of different responses.

It wasn't long ago that he felt certain that he knew what her response would be no matter how he apologized or what exact words he said, but no more. After today, he didn't know how she'd respond. He only knew that he'd have to keep after her until she responded correctly, until she loved him again with that comfortable consistency like she used to. He couldn't understand why he hadn't realized how much he needed her love until he'd thrown it away.

He was still watching the clock when it flipped to five.

Maybe if he were able to talk to her first thing in the morning before going to work today, he'd be okay. He rushed through his morning rituals, skipped the breakfast he knew he wouldn't be able to eat, and left the warm, sleepy silence of the house for the chill of the predawn.

He pulled into a donut shop for coffee. He ordered two cups and a bag of mixed fancies to go, wishing that he knew which donuts she preferred and how she drank her coffee. It bothered him that he didn't know if she even drank coffee. Maybe she preferred tea—or hot chocolate. Didn't they drink chocolate for breakfast in France and eat croissants? Damn. He hadn't gotten any croissants. Or maybe she was a thoroughly modern girl who drank Diet Pepsi to start her day.

Hell, he didn't even know if she were a health freak who didn't start the day with a jolt of caffeine. Maybe she started her day with a run. He shuddered. He played racquet ball twice a week and hit the gym once or twice more, but never first thing in the morning. He was a try-to-get-another-couple-of-minutes-of-sleep guy, not an up-and-at-'em guy.

It was almost six by the time he pulled in front of her building. He hadn't had to look up her address. He'd known where she lived since she moved there. The fact that he hadn't spoken to her until two days ago didn't mean he hadn't kept an eye on her.

He scanned the listing outside the door for her name. P. Wilson lived in apartment 409. He pulled on the door, but it was locked. Of course, she would live in a building with security. This was downtown Chicago after all. Still he mentally kicked himself as he tried to think of how to get in. He could call up and try to mimic Randy's voice. He could see if anyone else would let him in, though the chances of convincing a newly awakened stranger to let him into the building were slim. He leaned against the wall and groaned.

It shouldn't be too long before someone left to go to work. He'd just wait. He settled back against the wall and scalded his lip trying to sip coffee.

A black Hummer pulled up to the curb, and a big black man who looked suspiciously like Bubba Scott, the Bears' All Pro defensive end, walked up to the door and buzzed someone.

Mike tried to look casual while he prepared to slip into the building before the door closed.

"I'm here," Bubba said into the intercom. "You ready?"

"Yes," a female voice answered. "I'll be right down."

Mike thought the woman's voice sounded like Patrice's, but decided he was delusional. How would Patrice know Bubba Scott?

"Better just let me in," Bubba said. "There's a shady-looking character hanging by the door, and I wouldn't want him bothering you."

"Oh." The discomfort in that one word was clear.

"I'm an okay guy, really," Mike defended himself. "It's just that my girlfriend and I had a fight, and I wanted to surprise her with breakfast."

"But you don't know if she'll let you in, huh?" Bubba asked, sounding as if he understood.

"That's right." Mike nearly sagged with relief. This

Bubba Scott look-alike was going to let him in after all.

"I don't know, Pet," Bubba said, facing the intercom again. "What do you think? Should I let him in?"

It was then that Mike noticed what number the man's finger rested on. Damn!

"No, Bubba. Absolutely not."

It was definitely Patrice's voice. Patrice's voice—firm and resolute. And she had just heard him lie to this other guy.

The door buzzed.

Bubba pulled it open and entered, pulling the door closed behind him before heading for the elevator.

"Patrice?" Mike rang her apartment. She'd let in that other man—a black guy named Bubba who looked like Bubba Scott. Where the hell had she met him? "I've got to talk to you. Please, Patrice." She'd let in Bubba Scott.

Only silence answered him.

The morning felt colder than it had moments ago, and the sun, rising in the distance, did little to brighten the day.

****

"Is he gone?" Patrice asked, watching Bubba look out the window.

"He's pulling away from the curb...okay, he's gone."

Patrice let go of the breath she'd been holding.

"I can't believe he came here."

"Honey, I saw him. His was not the face of a man who's gonna give up easy. He ain't gonna leave you alone until you talk with him."

"But I don't want to talk with him yet." She looked at Bubba in desperation. "I can't, Bubba."

"I know, Pet." He opened his arms and folded them around her. "He's gonna be knocking at your door, though, until you let him have that talk with you. And if you're not ready, why..." He tipped a hand palm up to show he was helplessness to stop Mike from coming. "That's why I think you need to move in with me for a while." He grinned to let her know he was teasing.

She smiled, shaking her head. "Oh, yeah, great idea, Bubba. Let's say I move in with you and give my mother a heart attack."

"Maybe not," he conceded. "Now get your coat if you

40

still want breakfast. I'm hungry and practice starts at eight-thirty."

****

"I've become a stalker," Mike moaned, plopping onto the leather couch in his living room.

"I doubt it's that bad." Alex folded the evening newspaper he'd been reading and put it on the coffee table.

"No, it is," Mike insisted. "I tried to sneak into Patrice's building this morning. I followed her to breakfast with Bubba Scott. I—"

"Bubba Scott? The Bubba Scott? As in Chicago's very own leading sacker, Bubba Scott?"

"Yes, the very one." The sarcastic tone in Mike's comment was wasted on Alex.

"Patrice knows Bubba? I didn't know she knew Bubba. Did you know she knew Bubba? Do you think she could get me an autograph?"

"Who cares?" Mike shouted, surging to his feet.

"Well, I do," Alex said quietly.

Mike groaned his way to the kitchen and wrenched the refrigerator door open. His stomach growled in anticipation of a long-awaited meal. He'd dropped the bag of donuts somewhere before he'd had a chance to eat one and had sipped tepid coffee outside the diner watching Bubba consume everything on the menu. Patrice had a waffle and a cup of coffee with cream.

At least he knew this much: she ate breakfast, and she took cream with her coffee.

What he didn't know is why she was out with Bubba. How long had they known each other? Were they dating or just friends?

Yeah, right, a man was "just friends" with someone who looked like Patrice. Mike swore softly.

He had told her to quit chasing after him when she was dating Bubba Scott. The irony choked him.

"You gonna clean it, too, or just defrost it?" Alex asked, walking into the kitchen.

"What?" Mike looked blankly at his roommate.

Alex nodded to the refrigerator door.

"Oh, yeah." Mike grabbed the milk. Cereal would be good and fast. He poured a bowl of Cheerios and sat at the

41

table.

He hadn't eaten lunch either. After spending most of the morning calling Patrice's apartment and listening to her phone ring, he'd called his mother and asked about getting a ticket to the art museum's Gala. The call had eaten his lunch break, and the memory of it was now ruining his supper.

Melanie had begun scolding as soon as he'd asked about the Gala. "If you are planning to go to try to humiliate Patrice, you can just stay home, mister."

"Mom, I don't want to humiliate her. I never wanted to in the first place. I was just surprised to see her and acted badly. If there hadn't been the media there—"

"Don't try to blame me for this, Michael Tucker. If you had called her like you said you had, none of this would have happened."

"I did call her, Mom. I told you that. She wasn't home."

"Likely story. I can't understand why you hate her so much."

"I don't hate her." He was really getting tired of saying that.

"You shouldn't. She's such a nice girl, and she always doted on you." She was silent for a long moment.

Mike was about to ask if he should buy his ticket elsewhere when his mother chuckled softly.

"What?" he asked. His level of irritation was rising again.

"Never mind." Her voice still contained remnants of mirth.

"All right," he relented, not wanting to continue this conversation any longer. "About the ticket, should I—"

She interrupted him. "There was a time when Janice and I thought you and Patrice would fall in love and get married."

"Are you kidding?" His stomach clenched in regret. Really? Had they honestly felt that way? Why hadn't he seen it? Had he truly been that blind?

"But that was a long time ago," she continued as if she hadn't heard him. "Long before it became clear that you couldn't keep a civil tongue in your head around her. Long before we knew how stubborn and unforgiving you could be. What is it she did to you anyway?"

"Nothing." He felt sick and defeated, beaten by his mother's words and his own stupidity. Patrice had never done anything but love him.

"That's what we thought. Janice and I went over and over your childhood, trying to come up with something that Patrice might have done to make you despise her so, but we could never find anything. She was always so sweet to you."

He could almost see her shake her head.

"Well," she continued on a brighter note. "If you are truly going to make nice to her and apologize, then I guess I'll let you buy a ticket."

"You're all heart. How much?" He felt oddly reluctant to go to the Gala now. He needed to talk to Patrice, but an apology in a crowded hall wasn't what the two of them needed. At least it wasn't what he needed.

"I'll take it out of your inheritance."

"No, Mom. I want to pay for it." That way if he decided not to go, his mother wouldn't have the price of the ticket to hold over his head.

"Fine," she snipped. "The price is on the ticket. I'll leave it at the door in your name. If you insist of paying for it, you can give your father the money at the Gala and explain to him why he can't pay for his son's ticket."

"Mom," he sighed in resignation. She'd beat him again. "Why must you make everything so difficult?"

"I could ask you the same thing, Michael." Her tone was as sad and resigned as his. "Have a good day, dear," she said, ending the call.

Now, the cereal was soggy in Mike's bowl. He pushed it away.

Alex watched him, shaking his head.

"What?" Mike glared at his roommate.

"In the twelve years we've been roommates, I don't think I've ever seen you like this." Alex grinned. "You were always the confident, strong guy. The guy the girls loved, but never got to. The one with no relationship troubles of his own, who could see exactly how to solve everyone else's."

"You're enjoying this, aren't you?" He wanted to wipe the stupid smile off of Alex's face.

"Just a little." Alex pulled a chair from under the table and sat down. "She'll calm down after a day or two, and then she'll let you apologize."

Mike said nothing. He looked at the unappetizing bowl of soggy cereal. So different from last night's menu.

"I hear she spends Sunday afternoons at Doctor Delicious hanging with the Doctor himself."

Mike raised his head. "How would you know?"

"Well," he shrugged, "I've met her there before."

"You've met her there?" Mike's eyes narrowed dangerously. Wasn't it Alex who'd taken all those pictures of Patrice? Mike frowned. His roommate had better not be involved with his...well, with Patrice.

"Calm down, buddy," Alex smiled. "It's where Randy and I met her to plan your party. And before you ask, the Doctor is David Welch."

"I know who the Doctor is. Everybody knows who the Doctor is. I just didn't know she was still seeing him."

"Maybe they're friends. I was with her, and I'm not dating her...yet."

Mike sat up and glared at Alex. "Yet?"

"Well, David was there first, and we can't forget about Bubba." His eyes twinkled. "You know, it's probably a good thing you don't want her."

"Who said I don't want her?" Mike asked through clenched teeth. His muscles coiled, ready to spring across the table and throttle Alex.

Alex's smile widened. "Well, you did—very publicly, in fact." He slid his chair back. "And it's a good thing too. It looks to me like her social calendar is pretty full."

Mike stood abruptly, knocking his chair to the floor. "You'd better shut up, Masterson. The more you talk, the more I want to punch someone."

"Sounds like premeditated assault."

"Damn right."

"From a man with well-publicized poor anger control—"

"Keep talking," Mike said, picked up his chair and set it on its feet under the table.

"—I think I'd have a pretty good case against you, counselor."

Mike looked Alex in the eye. "I don't give a damn."

Alex sprang from the chair and was out of the kitchen before Mike rounded the table.

Chapter 11

Patrice was stirring sauce in a large pot at the restaurant Wednesday afternoon when one of the other chefs took the spoon from her hand and gently elbowed her out of the way.

A protest died on her lips when Victor draped his arm around her shoulder and led her out of the kitchen. "Go home, Patrice. You aren't scheduled until Friday morning."

"I know." She read the concern on Victor's fatherly face. "But it's Wednesday."

"I know. You don't work Wednesdays."

"That's not what I meant." She stopped and faced her boss and friend. "I write Mike on Wednesdays."

"You still can." Victor smiled. "Hate letters can be very therapeutic even if you don't send them."

Patrice smiled for Victor's benefit.

"Do you want to talk about it?" He gave her a squeeze around the shoulders.

She shook her head. "No, I'm fine."

Victor raised an eyebrow.

"Really."

He narrowed his eyes in disbelief, but didn't push it. "All right then. Go home and don't come back until Friday."

She shuffled her feet along the icy sidewalks as she walked to her apartment. She couldn't write Mike just as she couldn't talk to him. Victor had meant well with his comment about writing Mike a hate letter, but she didn't hate him. She wasn't even mad at him. She was angry with herself. For years—for all her life really—she'd been in love with Mike. And all that time Mike had made it very clear that he didn't love her.

She'd written him every Wednesday so that every Friday he'd get a letter from her. She deluded herself into thinking that he wanted to hear from her, that he looked forward to her letters and packages, when the truth was that he couldn't have cared less. He probably hated Fridays because of her letters.

She'd been a pest. No wonder he'd blown up at her Monday night. She'd driven him to it with her constant unwanted attention.

She should be the one apologizing. But she couldn't. She couldn't talk to him. Not now. Not ever. It was too humiliating. She'd thrown herself at him for years, finally forcing him to reject her publicly. Now she understood. He didn't want her and wasn't going to change his mind in the face of letters and bakery. It had taken years and a public rejection, but she finally got it.

Tears blurred her vision as she fumbled her key into the apartment building's lock.

Pests are rather dense after all.

She wouldn't write Mike today. Not even the apology letter she owed him. She wouldn't bake anything for him or send a jar of her latest creation packed in ice. She would finally give him what he wanted even if it killed her.

She'd leave him alone.

Chapter 12

On Friday afternoon, Mike grabbed the pile of mail off his secretary's desk and rifled through it. Nothing. No letter. Nothing but legal correspondence.

"Can I help you find something?" his secretary asked.

"No." He went into his office and closed the door.

He'd gone home for lunch as he always did on Fridays, but there hadn't been anything from Patrice in the mail there either.

It wasn't as if he'd been expecting there to be. He'd hurt her and embarrassed her after all. But somehow, he'd hoped there would be. Even an angry letter, blasting him for what he'd done, would be better than this silence.

He stared blindly at the folders on his desk, contemplating the bleakness of a Friday without a letter from Patrice. It was the only day of the week he ever went home for lunch, and he did it so he could read her letter. It was a ritual he'd been performing since the early days of college. Friday lunch meant Patrice to him as much as a package in the mail meant culinary heaven. This was to have been his package Friday as well.

He hid his face in his hands.

What had he done?

****

Friday night the art museum's atrium was humming

48

with conversation and chamber music. Waiters and waitresses bearing plates of beautiful hors d'oeuvres and trays filled with glasses of wine and champagne wound through the crowd of beautiful people in tuxedoes and cocktail dresses.

Patrice checked the buffet tables, exchanging a word with the servers in chef hats and white aprons who manned the silver service trays of sliced beef and ham. Everything was as it should be. The roast was juicy and the ham succulent. The garlic potatoes were perfect little shells piped into individual potato pastries ready to be popped neatly into hungry mouths. Everything was designed for easy eating so that the guests could wander and nibble or sit and dine at one of the small tables set under lit paintings.

Victor came up behind her, touching her elbow.

"You've outdone yourself again, Patrice. You keep this up, and I'm going to have to give you a raise."

"Give it to her anyway, so someone doesn't hire her out from under you," Bubba said, joining them.

"Victor DiMagio, Bubba Scott." Patrice introduced them automatically.

"Ah," Victor smiled, "a performance bonus."

"Exactly."

"Is that what's keeping you in Chicago?" Victor asked. Bubba looked appreciatively at Patrice and smiled. "That along with other things."

Victor's grin grew.

"Would you mind if I took your head chef and got her something to drink?"

"Not at all. In fact, Patrice's job for the rest of the evening is to be visible and mingle. How better to do that than on the arm of Chicago's own Bubba Scott?" Victor bowed out. "Enjoy the party."

"Nice guy, your boss." Bubba plucked a potato-filled pastry from the tray behind Patrice and put it into his mouth.

"I like him," Patrice said.

"These are good." Bubba snatched a couple more.

"Thank you. Would you like to fill a plate? I think you'd like the roast beef, and the honey-glazed carrots are quite nice."

"Have you eaten?" he asked, taking a plate.

"A good chef tastes everything."

"Which is why good chefs are often round. How do you stay so slim?"

"I just taste—I don't eat."

"Like a winetaster tastes?"

"No," Patrice laughed. "I swallow. I just don't have more than a taste." She looked across the table at the server. "Carl, he'll want some caramelized onions with that."

They collected two glasses of wine and made their way to a vacant table beneath a pastoral painting.

"It feels so good to sit," Patrice sighed.

"Long day, huh?"

"Just a little."

"Schmoozing at a party you've catered has got to be like giving interviews after a big game."

"I thought you guys liked that."

Bubba shook his head. "Some of the young hotshots do, but me—I'd rather just hit the showers and crack a cold one."

"I'm more of a chilled Riesling and a bubble bath kind of gal."

"We could skip out, grab a bottle, and hit the hot tub at home."

"Don't tempt me. I need to stay here for at least another hour. My folks are here with some family friends and so is my brother, Randy. Besides, I thought the purpose of tonight was to be seen."

"We've been seen," Bubba told her. "At least three different photographers have snapped our picture since we sat down."

"No kidding." Patrice looked into the room and saw a photographer take a shot of them. She also saw Mike watching her. The smile froze on her face, and she turned back to look at Bubba.

"I know, Patrice." He covered her small pale hand with his large brown one. "He's been here for a while. Can't seem to keep his eyes off you. I'm surprised you hadn't noticed before."

"I was busy." Patrice took a shaky sip from her wine glass. "Is he coming this way or just watching?"

Bubba ate a bit more, glancing casually over Patrice's shoulder. "Just watching, but pretending not to. He's talking with an older couple that looks like they could be his parents." He looked Patrice in the eye and smiled. "I used to love playing spy."

Patrice laughed. "Me too, but I'd rather not do it anymore, especially with Mike. Let's talk about something else or mingle. There's a dance band in one of the galleries."

"Just a minute." Bubba continued his visual reconnaissance. "The woman is motioning for someone to join them."

Patrice started to turn her head to look.

"Don't look now—they've been joined by another couple, and they're headed this way in perfect wedge formation. Should we run for it?"

Patrice grimaced, wishing she dared to run. She knew when she'd told Bubba she'd help him that her parents weren't going to like her dating a black man, but she'd foolishly hoped to delay their finding out until tomorrow or the next day. She didn't want to deal with the burden of their silent disapproval now.

"No. It'll be my—"

"Patrice?" a woman asked, interrupting Patrice's low comment.

"—mother." Ordinarily she would have been happy to see them, but the presence of Mike and Bubba made the situation awkward and edgy. Patrice tried to hide her discomfort behind a pasted-on smile as both she and Bubba rose to face her parents. "Dad, when did you two get back?" Patrice hugged both her parents, getting a kiss on the cheek from her father.

"Last night. We called, but your answering machine must be broken."

Patrice's answering machine was unplugged, and everyone knew it.

"I'd like you meet Bubba Scott. Bubba—my parents Roy and Janice Wilson, and Melanie and Matt Tucker with their son Mike, whom you've already met. I've known the Tuckers all my life. They're like family." She avoided looking straight at Mike. She was painfully aware of his presence. She could feel him staring at her.

Bubba seemed to sense Patrice's discomfort. Moving closer, he draped his arm over her shoulders.

Patrice felt her parents stiffen, though their expressions remained politely interested.

"I'm a big fan," her father said, offering his hand to Bubba.

"Thank you, sir," Bubba said.

"I didn't realize you knew my daughter," Janice commented as the men shook hands. She looked to her daughter for an answer.

Patrice watched the two men stare into each other's eyes, silently taking measure.

"Can I borrow my daughter for a moment, Mr. Scott?" Janice hooked her daughter's arm and led her off without waiting for his answer. Melanie brought up the rear, causing Patrice to look around her as she peered over her shoulder to see Bubba.

Bubba looked away from Mike long enough to smile at Patrice.

He's enjoying this, Patrice realized, taking in his twinkling eyes and genuine smile. She nearly laughed at the absurdity of the situation as she followed her mother through the crowd.

"What is going on?" Janice asked her daughter in the privacy of an out-of-the-way restroom.

Patrice purposely misunderstood her. "I'm hiding in a bathroom with you and Melanie when I'm supposed to be mingling and doing PR work for Victor's."

"I don't mean that." Her mother frowned. "What is this with Bubba Scott?"

"Oh." Patrice smiled innocently, happy to relieve her mother's fears with the simple truth. "Bubba needed a date for tonight, so I volunteered."

"Come on." Melanie folded her arms across her chest. "A star like Bubba doesn't lack for girls to date. I'll bet they're on him like flies now that you aren't there. This has to do with Mike, doesn't it? You're mad at Mike, so you're dating someone high profile to get back at him."

"That's not true," Patrice protested. "But even if it were, would it be so bad?"

"Normally, no," Janice told her daughter. "Your father and I just don't want you rebounding with the wrong sort of guy. Football stars are notoriously loose. We wouldn't want you to get in trouble."

Patrice's eyes narrowed. She didn't like the insinuation. She also knew that her mother didn't mean "football stars," but was too conscious of public opinion to get caught saying something blatantly racist where there was any chance of being overheard.

"I won't get into any trouble. I can take care of myself. And Bubba is a truly nice guy."

"I'm sure he is, honey. He's just not what your father and I want for you." She meant "not white," and Patrice knew it.

Patrice shook with rage and humiliation. Gone was her intention of soothing her mother and Melanie.

"I don't know," she snapped, glaring at the two women. "I think Bubba is exactly what I need right now. And I know I'm just what he needs."

"But," Janice protested.

"But nothing. I'm tired of being unloved and alone," she said on the verge of tears. "Now if you'll excuse me, I think I'll go find my date." She elbowed Melanie and her mother aside and stalked out.

Despite having conversations with half a dozen other Gala-goers en route, Patrice was still upset when she found Bubba.

"Has it been an hour yet?" She winced when she realized what she'd said. "I'm sorry, Bubba. I didn't mean—"

"Don't worry, Patrice," he said, guiding her to the coat check. "I don't blame you for wanting to leave. If it were me, we'd have been long gone. If my mama had even tried to drag me off for a talk, you'd have seen some tricky moves." He retrieved their coats and helped her on with hers. "How'd you think I got so good at getting around people that want to pin me down? My mama would make yours look like a bantamweight, and I ain't just talking size neither. Let's pick up a bottle of Riesling and go sit in my hot tub."

Mike had just gotten his own coat when he'd heard Bubba's voice, and he ducked into the hall leading to the restrooms. He watched as Bubba helped Patrice into her coat and held the door open for her.

Bubba was taking her home—his home—not her apartment. Jealousy rose thick and green in Mike's eyes. He knew he shouldn't care. After all, wasn't this what he had always said he wanted—for Patrice to fall for some other guy and leave him alone? He wasn't so sure any more.

He followed the couple into the parking garage, noting that the elevator they'd entered went up. Mike's car was on the ground floor. If he hurried, maybe he'd see them drive down the ramp. Why? He stopped himself from going into the elevator. What was he planning on doing if he spotted Bubba's Hummer? Follow it? No. He would not stoop to following them on another date. Once was enough. He didn't know what he would do if he saw Bubba kiss her. He didn't know if he'd be able to control himself if she seemed to enjoy it or if they went farther than a kiss.

Dinner churned in his stomach at the thought of Patrice with somebody else. She was meant to be his.

Damn it! He had to stop thinking like this. He had to talk with her soon. He was becoming obsessed.

****

Bubba shifted his Hummer into park in front of Patrice's apartment.

"Are you sure you don't want to go to the house? We could soak in the hot tub, and David's sure to have a Riesling in the wine cabinet."

"I'm sure," she said, unbuckling her seatbelt. "Thanks any way." She looked at her mountain of a friend and smiled. "I just need to be alone to sort things out."

"I think you're alone too much, but who am I?"

"Don't. You're great. You and David are all that's getting me through this."

"And work," he added.

"And work," she agreed. "But work can't dry my tears."

"And neither can David and I when you won't come over."

"All right," she sighed her acquiescence as she opened the car door. "I'll go get my swimsuit."

"And your jammies and toothbrush."

She crossed her arms and looked over her shoulder at

him. "I am not spending the night, Bubba."

"Please, Baby," he wheedled in his best fake get-the-girl-to-say-yes voice. "I'll be the perfect gentleman."

Patrice narrowed her eyes at him.

"Come on, Sugar. I'll be good to you, and I promise I'll respect you in the morning."

Patrice shook her head and laughed. "Sounds like a well-used line, Bubba. Does it ever work?"

"Like a charm—with good girls that is. And I only use it with good girls. No come-on line can scare off them bad girls. They want into your pants, and nothing you say is gonna change their mind."

"Especially not an invitation for sex."

"You got that right." Bubba nodded. "But seriously. I'm not going to feel like hopping into a car and driving you home after a couple of drinks in the hot tub. And you, sure as hell, won't be in any condition to drive. So it only makes sense that you stay over."

"Or stay home," Patrice suggested.

"I thought we went through that. You need a shoulder, and me 'n David have each got two big ones." He flexed his arms and squared his shoulders, turning to show them to their best advantage beneath his coat. "Mine are bigger, but we all like it that way, don't we?"

Patrice laughed despite herself. How could she not give in? "Okay. I'll pack a bag."

****

One glass of wine and a half hour in the hot tub were enough to turn Patrice into warm porridge. She flowed down the hall into Bubba's room, crawled between the cool sheets, and was asleep in moments.

Bubba and David stood in the doorway, checking on her like loving parents.

"I wish we could find her someone," Bubba said, watching Patrice sleep. "Someone straight who'll love her like she was meant to be loved."

"I've been wishing that for years," David whispered, drawing Bubba back and gently closing the door. "But it's not going to happen until she gets over Tucker."

"Why does she love that guy anyway? He's ignored her forever."

David shrugged. "Who knows what attracts anyone

to anybody? I love you, Bubba, but if I had my choice, I wouldn't be gay. I'd marry Patrice and show her how a man should love her. She would never even think about Tucker again. But as it is, she just confuses me. I love her, but only as a friend."

"I know," Bubba admitted. "Life would be easier all around if I just wanted to jump Patrice's bones instead of yours."

Chapter 13

A beam of bright winter sunlight inched across Patrice's face. When it hit her closed eyes, she stirred, greeting Saturday morning with a yawn.

Rolling over, she squinted one eye at the alarm clock. Bubba would be up and gone by now. Saturdays in the season meant breakfast meetings and light workouts in preparation for the game on Sunday.

Patrice dragged herself out of bed and into the bathroom. She caught a glimpse of herself in the mirror as she undressed for the shower and cringed. Her hair had been damp from the hot tub when she'd gone to bed. Now it looked as if it had been styled by mousse-carrying monkeys. Tufts stood up on one side, and the other was plastered to her head.

"No wonder you can't get a man, looking like you do," she told her reflection.

Twenty minutes later, looking and feeling like a different person, she made coffee in the kitchen.

David dragged himself in wearing a t-shirt and boxers. He was unshaven and wonderfully mussed, like a G.Q. model ready for a photo shoot. Patrice barely glanced at him as she pulled another mug from the cupboard and filled it with coffee.

"Thanks," he mumbled, accepting the cup and

cradling it in his hands. He took a noisy slurp and sighed. "Why are you up so early?"

Patrice joined him at the table with her own steaming mug before looking at the clock and shrugging. "It's nearly seven-thirty."

"On a Saturday," David added. "And you were up late."

"You were up later, Dad." Patrice smiled over a sip of coffee. "If it's so early, what are you doing up?"

"Bubba got me up," David admitted. Patrice felt a pang of jealousy, not that she wanted either David or Bubba, because she didn't. She wanted what they had—a stable, loving relationship. She wanted to be part of a couple, to wake up in her husband's arms and know that it was forever.

"What?" David asked.

Patrice looked at him, puzzled, not realizing she'd sighed.

David frowned, misunderstanding. "Quit sighing over Tucker. He's not worth it."

Patrice shook her head. "I wasn't even thinking about Mike. I was thinking about you and Bubba. I want what you two have."

"A hidden, gay relationship that you can't admit to friends and family? You want that?" David smiled. "I know a dyke or two; I'll see what I can do."

"Not the hidden, gay, or frowned-on part—the love part."

David nodded, his silly smile fading. "Me too. I don't want the hidden or frowned-on part either."

"I'm sorry," Patrice said. "Here I am watching the two of you, envying the way you are together, but still just thinking about me. I don't really see what's going on with you."

"Or maybe you see the way it would be in a perfect world where everyone accepted gay love like you do." David shook his head. "I wish my dad would look at Bubba and me and see what you see, but all he sees is his failure to make a man out of his son. He sees me as an abomination. He sees the frailty of his own masculinity and fears that homosexuality is contagious and that he'll catch it from me."

"Oh, David." Patrice rose to wrap her arms around her friend. "I'm so sorry. I didn't mean to bring it up."

"It's okay, Pet." David dashed the tears from his eyes. "You're the best person I know, and I wish I could love you like my dad wants, but..." He shook his head.

"I know," Patrice soothed, smoothing his bed-rumpled hair. "But I don't have the right parts."

David chuckled damply into her chest.

"They're nice parts, but they make me think mother and not lover." He cushioned his head on one full breast. "They make nice pillows, though. I'll give them that."

"Gee, thanks." She shoved him out of her arms. "Watch yourself, David. Your sweet talking might just turn a girl's head."

"As long as it's away, I won't mind."

Patrice smiled. David never stayed down for long. If she didn't suspect it was all an act, she'd consider taking a page from his book. No, it was better to face her feelings instead of hiding behind humor. Maybe she'd get over Mike while she was still young enough to have children. The smile on her face faded.

"So what's on the agenda today?" she said, a bit too brightly.

David acknowledged the tone with a quick look.

"Today's the day I fill you up with sugar and saturated fat."

"You're making my ice cream?" Her smile was back.

"And doing it right this time."

"Caramel," she sighed extravagantly.

"Yes, my dear." David rose from the table to pour himself another cup of coffee. "While the doctor prepares for surgery, his lovely chef will prepare him an omelet using whatever she can find in his ill-stocked refrigerator."

"She will, will she?" Patrice smiled, playing along.

"Of course. She is captive after all."

"Which reminds me," Patrice ended the game. "I need to be to work at four."

"The doctor cannot think when he's hungry."

"Or in need of a shower," Patrice added.

David placed his open palm on his chest, giving Patrice a look of open-mouthed surprise. He sniffed in mock pain, and then sniffed again as if he'd caught a whiff of something foul. He lifted his arm slightly and sniffed again. Gasping for breath, he fled the room with his coffee.

Chapter 14

Mike called Patrice's apartment at six-thirty Saturday morning. He knew he was running the risk of waking her, but actually that was what he was counting on. He hoped that she'd grab the phone too groggy to think of checking the caller I.D., and then he'd get the chance to quickly apologize before she recovered enough to hang up.

It was a mediocre plan that might have worked had she been home and had the answering machine still been disconnected.

"You've reached Patrice's place." Bubba Scott's voice greeted Mike.

"Bubba, stop," squealed a high-pitched voice that might have been Patrice laughing, but Mike was too stunned and the voice was too far in the background for him to tell for sure.

Bubba's voice continued. "She can't come to the phone right now so leave a message, and we'll get back to you."

Bile rose in Mike's throat. He dropped the receiver in the cradle with a shaking hand. They're living together. Oh, God. He closed his eyes against the tears that burned there. Oh, God.

****

David waited until after Patrice had made him breakfast before admitting what he and Bubba had done.

"Your car is in the garage next to mine," he said as proof.

She didn't believe him and ran to the garage to check.

"Give me the phone," she demanded, quivering with anger.

She snatched it from David's hand and dialed her apartment.

"You've reached Patrice's place..."

She listened with mounting anger and frustration.

"I've got to go." She slammed down the phone and glared at David. "What were you thinking? If my parents hear this, they'll think Bubba and I are living together." She yanked her coat from the closet and shoved her arms in the sleeves. "David, how could you do this? You know my mother."

David didn't look her in the eye. "It was stupid, I know. I just... Bubba insisted and I..." He winced. "Maybe she hasn't called yet," David suggested hopefully.

Patrice glanced at her watch. It was nearly eight-thirty. Maybe if she called her mother first.

"Give me the phone," she ordered.

David scrambled to put it into her hand.

Patrice hit the numbers and prayed.

"Patrice!" Her mother's voice exploded over the phone, causing even David to wince.

"It was a joke, Mom," Patrice rushed to explain. "Bubba and David did it as a joke. I didn't know about it until David confessed at breakfast."

"Why weren't you at home?"

"David and I went out for breakfast." Patrice glared at David as if daring him to contradict her.

"At six-thirty in the morning?"

Patrice stared daggers at the sheepish David.

"Bubba's car wouldn't start this morning, so David drove him to work, and then, since he was in town, he came over and got me up to go to breakfast."

"At six-thirty?"

"I was probably in the shower then and didn't hear the phone ring. How come you were calling so early anyway?" Patrice hoped a change in the focus of the conversation would help her.

"I didn't. Mike called you, hoping to have a chance to apologize and got the machine. He called Randy in a panic. I didn't call you until eight."

"Randy called you to tell you about my answering machine message?" she asked incredulously, silently imagining how she'd get back at her meddling brother.

"Of course not," her mother grumbled. "He never tells me anything unless I ask explicitly. I didn't find out that Mike had called him until I called him after I heard your message. Did you know he was sleeping at his girlfriend's apartment?"

Patrice didn't answer. There wasn't time anyway as her mother rushed on.

"Where did I go wrong with you two?"

Patrice closed her eyes and shook her head at the rhetorical question, knowing that her mother would blame MTV as always.

"I knew I shouldn't have let you watch MTV, but that's beside the point. Where did you go after you left the Gala last night? I sent Randy and his girlfriend to check on you, but you weren't home yet."

This was why she didn't live at home anymore. She was too old to play twenty questions with her mother.

"Mom, I'm an adult," Patrice insisted, not sounding very adult at all.

"You are a girl who has had a misunderstanding with an old friend and is now rebounding all over the place."

"I am not rebounding," Patrice insisted.

"And what would you call dating a black man?"

"Bubba is a good friend."

"And are you kissing this 'good friend'?"

Patrice slid down the wall to the floor, wishing she could just disappear.

"What is it you want me to do, Mom?" she said aloud. It wasn't her fault Mike dumped dessert down the front of her.

"I want you to go out with Mike," her mother instructed. "Let him apologize properly. Kiss and make up so that you stop this foolish and dangerous game you are playing."

Patrice's hackles rose.

"I am not playing a game. If there's a game in town, it's the one you're asking me to play with Mike. He doesn't want me, Mom." Tears flowed down Patrice's cheeks. "He wants to apologize because his conscience is bothering him, not because he wants to make things right with me. He'd just as soon he never saw me again, and right now I'm quite happy to grant him that wish." She took a shuddering breath. "I'm the innocent one here. All I've done is help out a friend. Bubba needed a date last night, and I was available. He's a good friend, Mom, a good friend and that's all."

"Patrice." Janice's voice grew gentle and comforting. "Honey, it's past time that you and Mike talked. He needs to see you as an adult—a friend, not a child or a pest. You need to settle things between the two of you, and you can't do it if you won't talk to him."

"Fine, Mother," Patrice choked out. "I'll do it, but in my own time."

"I'd like it done by Thanksgiving. That's what—five days from now?"

"Forget it, Mom." Patrice got back on her feet. She wouldn't let her mother stomp all over her. She was an adult after all. "I can't do it. We aren't even going to see the Tuckers on Thanksgiving. They always go to New York to be with Melanie's mother and watch the parade. We aren't getting together until Christmas. I'll see him and talk to him by then."

"When should I tell him to call?"

"Tell him not to call," Patrice insisted. "I'll call him when I'm ready. I don't want him bothering me before. Got that?"

"You're getting a little cheeky, girl," her mother warned although humor softened her voice.

Patrice frowned. "I get it from you, Mom." It didn't matter that her mother meant well; she was still meddlesome.

"You'll be here tomorrow for dinner?" It wasn't really a question.

She was tempted to say no, but she restrained herself. Fighting with her mother wouldn't help anything. "I'll be there at noon as usual," she said. "Can I bring anything?" It wasn't the kind, considerate suggestion she made it sound like. Sunday dinner ill-prepared by her mother was a family tradition. It bothered Janice to no end that Patrice could prepare culinary masterpieces with seemingly little effort when she struggled to create something merely palatable. Normally Patrice said nothing, having learned young that her mother didn't want the help, but today she couldn't resist a little dig.

"I can make a perfectly delicious roast myself," Janice said defensively.

"I know," Patrice lied, feeling a twinge of guilt. None of this was really her mother's fault, but some of it was David's. David—who knew the true quality of her mom's cooking. "Can I bring someone?"

David frantically shook his head, eyes widened in horror.

"Let's just have it be family this time," Janice said, mollified. "Randy's girlfriend is going to visit her parents and won't be able to come, so it will give—"

"It'll give you a chance to read Randy the riot act," Patrice interrupted, still testy.

Janice cleared her throat. "It will give us an opportunity to enjoy a Sunday dinner as we did when you were kids."

"As I remember, Mike was frequently at those family dinners," Patrice reminded her mother.

"But he won't be at this one," Janice insisted. "This one will be just family."

Patrice wasn't certain how much she trusted her mother to keep her word.

When Patrice finally hung up the phone, David raised his eyebrows in question.

"She believed me. I think," Patrice answered the silent question.

"Do I have to go to dinner?"

She made him squirm a moment then shook her head.

David sighed in relief.

Patrice stared at him intently until he looked at her again.

"What?"

She gave him a nasty smile. "But I'm not off the hook

and neither are you."

"I'm not?"

"Not by a long shot. I have to make friends with Mike before Christmas, and you have to help me."

David furrowed his brow. "How?"

"Help me get over him by then. Find me someone else to fall in love with."

Chapter 15

"I wish my mother would call the people she wants to talk to instead of going through me," Randy complained to Mike over a Chicago Red Hot.

They sat at the end of the crowded counter, eating big beef dogs with everything and guzzling Pepsi. The sky outside was slate gray and spitting little snow pellets. Mike's mood was nearly as bad as the weather, and he had a feeling it was about to be made worse.

"What did she want?"

"She's convinced Patrice to 'kiss and make up' with you." He noticed the arch of Mike's eyebrows and quickly added, "Mom's words, not mine."

Mike nodded. "So when do I see her?"

"Mom said she promised to let Patrice make the first move. But I am also to suggest that you plan to run into her someplace. Mom suggested Victor's, but that's because she doesn't know Patrice goes to Doctor Delicious every Sunday around four. If you feel the need to corner Pet someplace, Doctor Delicious would be the place."

"Four, huh? She must not be eating much of your mother's pot roast if she's hungry for gourmet ice cream by four."

Randy shrugged and smiled. "No one eats much of Mom's pot roast. You've tasted it enough times to know that Patrice became a chef out of self-preservation. I don't know why Mom still insists on making a roast on the cook's day off. Surely there're some leftovers in the fridge." He shrugged again. "I'm about to lobby Mom to change family dinner day to Monday. Her cook works Mondays."

Mike laughed. "Good luck. I don't think your mother knows she can't cook, just as my mom doesn't know she can't sing."

"The hills are alive..." Randy sang a painfully good imitation of Melanie's singing voice in a tremulous falsetto.

Mike elbowed Randy to stop.

"What do you think of my chances with Patrice?"

"Chances of what—being her friend?" Randy took a bite of his Red Hot.

"Yeah, and maybe a bit more." Mike took a bite of his hotdog for show. He hadn't been very hungry lately. Thinking about how things stood between him and Patrice always killed his appetite.

Randy stared suspiciously at Mike. "What sort of a bit more? You weren't serious about that 'I love her' crap, were you?" When Mike didn't answer, he swore. "She's like your sister, Mike. Are you sick or what?"

"She's not my sister, Randy. She's your sister."

"And you're like my brother. It's just too gross to even imagine."

"Well, try."

Randy chewed silently for several long moments before shaking his head. "It's no good, Mike. You've spent too many years trying to avoid her to want to be with her now." He picked up his napkin and wiped mustard off his lips as he spoke. "She's 'The Pest', remember? She knows what you look like in Batman underwear, and it bothers you." He looked up at Mike.

Mike smiled sadly, remembering the fuss he'd made in law school. He'd been trying to convince her that he was too old for her when she pulled out the picture she had of him as a little kid in Batman underwear. "You're not that old, Bruce Wayne. Seven years may seem like a long time when I'm fifteen and you're twenty-two, but the gap is closing. By the time we're in our thirties we'll be the same age. Besides," she grinned at the picture, "you look pretty young here."

Randy continued, oblivious to Mike's inattention. "You couldn't wait until she graduated from high school and went to France so that you wouldn't have to look for ways to tell her you couldn't be her date for prom."

Mike shrugged. "And how would that have looked—a twenty-four year old at a high school prom?"

"That's not the point," Randy argued. "You've never wanted to be around her even when you should have. You hid from her at her sweet sixteen party and wouldn't dance with her at her graduation dance. Hell, Mike, you trained Alex and me to tell her that you're not home when she called."

"That was prom avoidance, and you know it."

Randy rolled his eyes. "Whatever. So now she's grown up, but she's really just the same as she's always been. And you're the same as you've always been. She's still as thoughtful and as caring. She'd still rather lie to our parents and spend the night holding our heads while we puke our guts out than let us get in trouble."

"If you're trying to convince me not to pursue her, you're doing a crappy job."

"What I'm trying to say, smart ass, is that she still has a weakness for you, and you still treat her like shit." Randy shook his head. "It scares the hell out of me that you think you might be interested in her as more than just a friend. She'd do anything for her friends and even more for you." He set down what remained of his hot dog. "Mike, she loves you as much as cooking. But I don't think you love her. I think you just miss the trip of having someone worship the ground you walk on. Your ego is stinging because for the first time in twenty-two years, you're afraid that you won't see the adoration when you look in her eyes.

"I think you're sorry that you've hurt her. And don't make any mistake, Mike. You have. She cried about what you did at that party, and you know she never cries. But I don't think you feel any more for her than that."

"Are you done yet?" Mike asked with barely leashed anger.

Randy glared at Mike. "No. It might be nice for you to

get yourself back on that pedestal, but you wouldn't be doing her any favors. She loves you. You can't casually date her. You'll break what's left of her heart when you decide she isn't really what you want."

Mike clenched his fists to keep from punching his best friend in the nose.

Randy continued, oblivious to the danger. "You can't tell her that you think you might feel something more than friendship for her unless you are truly in love with her. And you aren't."

"What makes you so certain?" Mike asked. All this stuff about how big, bad Mike would come and break sweet, wonderful Patrice's heart was really getting to him. "Okay, maybe it wasn't obvious that I was a fan of Patrice."

"Maybe?" Randy smirked. "I'd say it was clearly. Clearly you haven't been a Patrice Wilson fan."

"Shut up, Randy," Mike growled. "I let you have your say, now you let me have mine." He took a breath and repeated, "I haven't been an obvious Patrice Wilson fan because I tried to deny it—even to myself. I didn't mean to hurt her, and I'm not planning on hurting her in the future."

He glared at Randy to forestall any possible interruptions. "What makes you think you know what has gone on between us or how I feel about her? Did you know she's written to me once a week since I left for college or that I've kept every one? Do you have any idea how I felt when this Friday there wasn't a letter?"

"No," Randy spat out. "How did you feel, Mike? And how many letters have you written my sister? Tell me that, Mike? I've seen the box she keeps them in, and it isn't a big box. How many weeks went by when she didn't hear from you, huh? And how do you think she felt?" Randy stood up, facing his friend as he put on his coat. "Don't tell me how you want more than a friendship with Patrice. You've had your chance for years—years, Mike. And now that you've thrown it and the world's best damn crème brûlée in her face, you want to pursue her? Forget it, Mike. It's shit.

"Tell her you're sorry you've been such an ass for years, and leave it at that. Don't pursue it. Don't tell her you might have feelings for her. For once in your life, Mike, think of her and her feelings instead of you and yours."

Chapter 16

David called Alex at lunchtime.

"I need a favor," David said after he'd identified himself.

"Oh, what can I do for you?" Alex asked suspiciously.

"It's not what you can do for me," David said. "It's what you can do for Patrice."

That caught Alex's interest. "For Patrice? Really? What?"

"You know that she's had a crush on Mike for years?"

"Yeah."

"Well, that party for Mike really did a number on her. She's doubting her appeal with guys. She needs some male attention to help her get over this thing with Mike."

"Male attention? What about you? What about Bubba?"

"Well, if you'd rather I called Bubba..."

"Uh, no," Alex stumbled. "I just thought that she was dating Bubba."

"He's the wrong kind of guy for her right now—too pushy. She needs someone safe to rebound on."

"And I'm safe?" Alex asked, insulted.

"You're not the kind of guy who would take advantage of a girl in Patrice's position. You'd take the time to build a relationship. I've seen the two of you together. She laughs with you, and you had that interested-but-not-acting-on-it look in your eye. You want her, but you're holding back. That's what she needs—a guy who's interested but can restrain himself. I just called to tell you that maybe you've got a shot with her. She'll be here Sunday at four."

Alex paused, excited about the prospect of being with Patrice, but hesitant as well. "I don't get it, David. Why are you calling me? Why aren't you hitting on her yourself?"

"I'm involved with someone or I would be. But hey, maybe I made a mistake here. Maybe I shouldn't have called. You obviously aren't interested, and Patrice would die if she knew we had this conversation."

"Who said I wasn't interested?" Alex asked, panicked.

"You've got reservations. I respect that. I'll let you go. All I ask is that you don't tell anyone I called—especially not Patrice."

****

At four o'clock Sunday evening, Alex arrived at Doctor Delicious and was handed a bowl of orange sherbet mixed with swirls and chunks of chocolate.

"What's this called?" he asked, almost afraid to hear the answer.

David grinned. "Today it's Screwing Your Roommate. Tomorrow, who knows? She should be here any minute."

"Why do you think I'm here to see Patrice? I could be here because I like the ice cream with or without the psychoanalysis."

"After my phone call? Get real. You've obviously put aside whatever reservations you had that day and decided to try your luck. Since Mike is out of the picture, why shouldn't you pursue her? You're here to see Patrice. I'm the doctor. I know."

Alex shook his head. "You're just a little too sure of yourself, 'Doctor.'"

David beamed. "I know. It's part of my appeal." He punched the sale into the cash register. "That will be sixteen bucks."

"Sixteen? I thought a medium was eight."

David raised his eyebrows. "You didn't want to pay for Patrice's?" He shrugged. "Okay, it's eight."

Alex pushed a twenty across the glass counter. "You're right. It's sixteen."

David nodded, handing Alex the change.

Less than five minutes later, Patrice walked in.

"Hi, Pet," David greeted her. "How was lunch with the family?"

"Grizzly, but that might have just been the pot roast." She hung her coat on a blue wall hook shaped like a human hand.

"Hi, Patrice," Alex said, rising in greeting.

"Alex bought this for you," David said, handing her a bowl of orange sherbet with chocolate swirls and chunks identical to the one Alex had left sitting on a table.

"Thanks, Alex. What's it called?" Patrice asked.

Alex glanced quickly at David and then back to Patrice. "For you, it's Expanding Horizons."

"That's good." David grinned at Alex. "That's very good. I think I could give you a part-time job if you're interested."

"Thanks anyway," Alex said, guiding Patrice to his table. "I think I'll stick with advertising."

Once seated, Patrice ate a spoonful. "Ah, this is good," she said loud enough for David to hear.

"Of course, it is," David called back. "And just what you need too."

"Of course, it is," Patrice laughed. "I never doubted that for a moment." She put down her spoon and leaned conspiratorially toward Alex. "So, Alex, what did he call it for you?"

"Expanding Horizons, of course," Alex answered, straight faced.

"Of course," she repeated, grinning. "You aren't going to tell me what he really called it, are you?"

"Not a chance."

"All right then," she laughed. "How was your week? I haven't seen you since Monday."

"And I was having withdrawal symptoms, so here I am."

"You're smooth, Alex. You could sell ice in Alaska."

"One of my biggest accounts," Alex grinned. "Actually, I have been thinking about you a lot. I kind of got used to seeing you with planning the party and all."

He winced, remembering the party. "Sorry, I didn't mean..."

"Don't worry about it. After lunch with my family, it's a topic I am well used to. My mother wanted a dish-by-dish account of what was served, all the while I'm sitting with a slice of cracked shoe leather on my plate and getting hungrier and hungrier." She shook her head. "Did you know it was possible to make lumpy potatoes from a box?"

He laughed.

"Anyway, don't worry about mentioning Mike's party. I'm over it."

His smile became brittle. "I guess that means you've forgiven Mike then."

"Not quite yet." She stiffened perceptively. "You aren't here on his behalf are you?"

Alex shook his head and relaxed. "No. No. I'm just here to see you and eat ice cream." He took a spoonful in demonstration.

She smiled. "Good. I don't want to see him just yet or hear anyone else sing his praises either."

"Who's he got singing?"

"Just my mother, but she's a diva."

"Scary."

She laughed. "You're telling me."

"How do you think he got your mother on his side? After all, it was her baby girl he dumped on."

"I don't think he did anything. My mom just wants Mike and me to kiss and make up so that there's peace when our families get together."

"I think I'd skip the kissing if I were you," Alex said, hoping he wasn't crossing the line. Oh, what the hell. David had nailed it on the head. He was screwing his roommate.

Patrice choked back a laugh. "Don't worry. I don't intend to do any kissing. And I think Mike would rather have dental work than kiss me." She shook her head in wry amusement.

Alex hid his guilt behind a spoonful of ice cream. He knew Mike wanted Patrice, but he wasn't going to let him get her. At least not without a fight.

A woman at the next table got up to put on her coat,

bumping Patrice's elbow in the attempt. Ice cream slid from Patrice's spoon to dribble down her sweater.

"Oops," Alex said.

"I'm so sorry," the woman said, handing Patrice a wad of napkins.

Patrice dabbed at the dribble. "Don't worry about it. Casualties of eating," she said, rising. "I'll just go to the ladies' room and wash it out real quick. It'll be fine."

She had just left when Alex glanced out the window and saw Mike cross the street, heading toward Doctor Delicious.

He shoved an over-large spoonful of ice cream into his mouth in surprise. His eyes watered as he swallowed and the cold froze the air in his sinuses. He rose and walked quickly to the counter where David stood.

"Do you want to spit that out?" David asked. His eyes were wide with amusement over the pained look on Alex's face.

"Too late," Alex gasped, wincing in pain.

"Ice cream headache." David grinned knowingly. "What did you eat it that fast for?"

"Tucker." Alex didn't have a chance to say anything else before the door chimes rang. Pretending not to see Mike enter, he walked down the hall to the bathroom—the ladies' bathroom.

Mike didn't notice Alex. He scoured the room looking for Patrice.

"Is *she* here?" Mike asked David.

"I don't know, Tucker. It all depends on who the she is. Did you mean: Is the woman who has given you more love and attention than your mother only to have you publicly throw it back in her face here? Or, did you mean: Is the woman who spent countless time and money trying to give you the best party of your miserable life here? If you did, then the answer is yes. But if you meant: Is the woman who is going to rush into your arms and accept whatever lame excuse you offer her here? Then the answer is no."

"That's enough, David."

"That's Mr. Welsh to you, fucker," David said, coming around the coolers.

Mike held up his hands. "Cool it, David. I didn't come

here to fight."

"Then leave." David raised his fisted hands.

"I just want to talk to her." Mike stood firm, faking a bravado he didn't feel. David might not be a professional athlete anymore, but he still looked like one. Somehow Patrice had attracted a lot of big, strong, and physically threatening protectors. It would have made him feel good about her safety if they weren't all trying to pound him into the ground.

"She's not ready yet," David insisted, pulling his arms in toward his chest so that they were ready to punch.

"Then let me hear it from her." Mike hoped his voice sounded strong. He was used to stiff competition and mind games in the courtroom, but until lately, nobody had threatened to punch his lights out.

Patrice was opening the ladies' room door as Alex reached for the handle.

"The men's is the next one." Patrice smiled at Alex's mistake.

He pressed her back into the restroom.

"What are you doing?" she protested.

Alex pulled the door closed behind him. "Mike's here."

"Oh." Patrice froze for a moment. "I'm not afraid of him, you know."

"I know. I just thought you wanted to avoid seeing him for a while." Alex still blocked the door with his back.

"I did. I do, but I'm not going to let him chase me out of places like some scared seventh grader. I was here first. I can eat my ice cream here if I want to." She looked at Alex who still blocked the door. "Unless you'd rather he didn't see us together."

Alex looked distinctly ill at ease. He opened the door and held it open for Patrice. "No. I just didn't want you walking into a situation that would make you uncomfortable."

"Thanks," she said, touching Alex's arm. "You're sweet."

"Sweet," Alex repeated under his breath as Patrice walked by him. He shook his head.

Patrice entered the serving area in time to hear

David tell Mike to leave.

She read David's stance in an instant. He was coiled and ready to fight. Mike watched him, standing his ground, not flinching or cowering or even raising his hands in defense as David silently threatened him.

Adrenalin coursed through Patrice's veins. She wanted to throw herself between David and Mike to protect Mike. Stupid, she scolded herself. How could the very thought of Mike cause her stomach to clench, yet she still wanted his safety and happiness above all else? She wasn't ready to see him.

"I just want to talk to her," Mike was saying.

Her heart paused in panic. No! It was too soon. She was still too much in love.

"She's not ready yet," David told him, looking as if he was ready to back up those words with his fists.

Still, Mike didn't relent. "Then let me hear it from her."

Oh, God! I'm not ready for this.

"I'm not ready yet," Patrice said. Her voice sounded a little shaky, but not too bad. At least she wasn't crying.

Alex's arm came around her shoulder in sympathy.

Sympathy. She swallowed hard. She could handle anything but sympathy. Yell at her, scream at her—anything—just don't be sympathetic when she was fighting tears. And she was fighting. And losing.

Calm, she ordered herself. Be calm.

Her words had no effect on the tears that filled her eyes.

Alex turned her into his shoulder. "Oh, great," she whispered. More sympathy. The tears came in earnest now. She shoved herself out of Alex's arms and raced for her coat.

Mike grabbed her.

"Patrice." His voice was full of remorse and regret.

"Not now, Mike." She struggled out of Mike's arms, pausing only long enough to snatch her coat from the wall before fleeing into the cold.

Mike took a step in pursuit before Alex and David grabbed his arms.

"Let her go," Alex advised, dropping his arm before Mike could shake him off.

"I told you she wasn't ready," David snarled, dropping Mike's arm as if it might foul him. "Damn it, I wish you'd have left before she saw you."

"Why?" Mike asked. "Why was she crying?"

David shook his head. "You're even dumber than I thought you were, if that's possible."

Mike looked at Alex. "What's going on?"

Alex shrugged, returning to his table. He wished he had some kind of a claim on Patrice before confronting Mike, but it looked as if that wasn't possible now. She saw him as sweet. It was the kiss of death—right up there with, "I think of you as a good friend" or, worse still, "I see you as a brother." He scooped the remaining ice cream from Patrice's bowl into his and began eating.

Mike sat down in Patrice's vacated chair.

"Alex, what's going on? Were you here with Patrice?"

Alex ignored him, calling across the room to David instead. "David, bring Mike something."

David nodded. "I have just the thing."

"You know what I like about this place?" Alex asked Mike.

Mike shook his head.

"It's that the Doctor always gives you what you need, no matter what you ask for."

"What are you eating?" Mike asked, peering into Alex's bowl.

"It's called Expanding Horizons amongst other things," Alex said.

"Is it any good?" Mike asked.

"It's exactly what the doctor ordered."

Mike stared at Alex with one brow raised. "What?"

Alex didn't answer. He watched David come from behind the counter with a bowl, smiling in anticipation as the Doctor placed it in front of Mike with a deliberate bang.

Both Mike and Alex looked into the bowl.

It was filled with what looked like a large pile of frozen shit.

"It's what you deserve," David said, walking back to the counter.

Alex laughed. He laughed until tears streamed down his face. He laughed long after Mike had gone.

****

Mike did not drive home after leaving Doctor Delicious. He went looking for Patrice. This had gone on too long. He missed her. Okay, maybe he hadn't really talked to her in years, but he'd always known that he could and, damn, he missed that. And maybe he'd been a shit to her, but he was trying to apologize. Didn't that count for something?

Surely she knew he really hadn't meant to dump the dessert on her. Besides, he was trying to make amends. Couldn't she see that? Why was she avoiding him?

He felt sick when he thought of Patrice's tears. Were those really his fault? Shouldn't she be angry with him, not sad?

By the time he pulled up to Patrice's apartment building, he was resolved. She'd listen to him if he had to break down her door. But she wasn't there. Her car wasn't in its reserved spot. He decided to wait for her and turned off the car.

Long, slow minutes passed. He watched her building until his breath frosted the windows of the cold car. Where had she gone? He shifted uneasily in his seat, finally starting the car to clear the glass.

A few cars passed in the slow, late Sunday afternoon traffic while the heater blasted warm air. Flipping on the radio, he searched for something he wanted to listen to. There was nothing. He flipped off the radio, letting the engine idle.

The sky darkened and the streetlights came on.

He checked his watch. Six-thirty.

He'd gone to Doctor Delicious at four-fifteen, four-twenty. She left, say four-thirty. It took fifteen minutes, maybe a half an hour, to drive to her apartment. That made it on the outside five o'clock. Maybe she stopped for groceries or dinner. That was reasonable. She hadn't eaten most of her ice cream. She would be here any time now.

Again, he turned off his car to wait. She wouldn't be looking for him to be here, but she might look at the car if it were running.

Lights had come on in several of the apartments in her building, but not hers, of course. She hadn't parked somewhere else and gone in without his seeing her. Unless she was sitting in the dark, watching, waiting for him to leave.

He shook his head. She wouldn't do that, would she?

The car grew cold again. His warm breath fogged the windows, making it hard to see. Starting the car, he lowered his windows an inch to let out the moisture and then turned off the engine again.

Slowly the windows cleared.

His watch said seven o'clock.

Where was she?

He'd give her another half hour and then he'd go. He was cold and hungry, and he had needed a toilet for the last hour.

At seven-forty five, he started his car again for the last time.

At eight o'clock, he pulled away from the curb.

He called her when he stopped at a gas station at eight-fifteen. The message on the machine was one of the prerecorded ones that came with it. He didn't leave a message.

He drove through McDonalds and then made another swing past her apartment, even though it wasn't on his way home.

Her spot was still empty, her windows still dark.

He checked Victor's parking lot and swung by Doctor Delicious looking for her car. Nothing. She wasn't at her mother's either. He wished he knew where Bubba lived.

At ten-thirty he decided that he'd check at her apartment one last time before going home for the night.

Nothing had changed.

His house was dark and quiet when he unlocked the door and let himself in at eleven. Alex and Randy had obviously gone to bed.

Mike tossed his coat on the couch and walked into the kitchen without bothering to turn on the lights. He bumped into a chair that hadn't been pushed under the table. His hands shot out to steady it before it fell. Pushing it under the table where it belonged, Mike slammed the chair into the table's legs.

The outline of the bottles left over from the party was slightly darker than the darkness of the counter on which they sat. Mike felt his way amongst them, fumbling for something that felt like Scotch. Muttering a curse, he left the bottles, groping for the range light.

"What the hell are you doing?" Alex growled as he stomped into the kitchen. The dim light revealed his finger-tangled hair, black Bears t-shirt, and striped boxers.

"Getting something to drink." Mike returned to the cluster of bottles on the counter.

Glaringly bright light filled the kitchen as Alex flipped the switch for the overhead light.

"That should make it easier and quieter. You were making enough noise to wake the dead." Alex smiled as Mike cringed from the light.

"Sorry." Mike was too focused on wondering where Patrice could be and too wrapped up in his own feelings to notice Alex's tone.

Alex turned to leave.

"Do you know where Patrice went after she left Doctor Delicious?"

Alex turned back around and shrugged. "Home, I'd guess."

Mike shook his head.

Alex shrugged again. "She didn't come home with me."

That caught Mike's attention. Why had Alex been at the ice cream store in the first place? He'd discounted it as coincidence until now.

"Were you there with Patrice by design or accident?" Mike asked.

Alex hesitated, and then shrugged. "I knew she'd be there, but she didn't know I would be."

Mike was silent for a long moment. "Did she say she'd get Bubba's autograph for you?"

Alex laughed, breaking the tension. "I didn't ask her."

"Sorry...guess I scared her away before you had a chance." Mike finally found the Scotch. He lifted the bottle and tilted it toward Alex in question.

"Sure, why not." Alex waited in silence while Mike poured the drinks and accepted a tumbler from Mike before continuing. "Actually, Mike, I wasn't there to get

Bubba's autograph. I hadn't even thought of that. I was there because I like Patrice, and David called me."

"David called you? Why?"

Alex took a long sip before answering.

"Because Patrice needs someone other than you to be with."

"And so you went?" The knuckles on Mike's right hand whitened around the glass.

Alex nodded once. "I like her, Mike. I have for a long time. I've seen her devotion to you through the years, and I've wanted it for myself. And now she wants someone else to focus on. I want it to be me. So I plan to be there for her even if it's only someone to rebound safely with."

Mike took a healthy swallow. "So how's this going to work, Alex? We share a house, but I'm not going to share Patrice with you."

"In case you haven't noticed, Mike, she's not yours to share."

Mike glared at him.

"But let's not fight about it. I say we leave it up to her," Alex said.

Mike laughed mirthlessly. "And the loser gets to be best man at the wedding."

"Deal." Alex offered his hand in agreement.

Mike clasped it in a healthy grip. "She loves me," he warned.

"But she answers my phone calls." Alex grinned.

Mike ended the power play with a sobering thought. "But she's dating Bubba Scott, and she didn't go home tonight."

Alex frowned. "You don't know that. She just went home after you left."

Mike knew better, still he nodded. "Maybe."

Chapter 17

Bubba arrived home to find Patrice in the driveway, sitting in her car.

He opened the passenger door and slid in beside her. "Did you forget the code?" he joked. Then he saw her face, and his smile faded. He opened his arms. "What happened?"

"I'm such a wimp," she cried. "Mike came into David's store, and I burst into tears. And I'm still crying." She sniffed with disgust. "What is wrong with me?"

Bubba held her closely and kissed the top of her head. "You're in love, Pet. When girls have trouble with love, they cry. When guys have trouble with love, they drink. And when fags have trouble with love, they get into fights. Ever noticed the number of black eyes and fat lips in a gay bar?"

Patrice shook her head.

"I guess you wouldn't have. Come to think of it, I don't know from experience either." He shrugged. "But I believe it. If David were to say he didn't love me anymore, I'd have to rip his head off."

Patrice smiled. "David worships the ground you walk on."

Bubba shook his head. "No. That's me."

"That's both of you," she corrected him. "I was telling

84

David the other day how jealous I am of you two."

"You are?" Bubba grinned. "Good. Then move in with us for a while so I can ruin your reputation, and you can straighten out mine."

"That reminds me," Patrice said, wiping the last of the tears from her face. "I'm still mad at you for that stupid answering machine stunt. You got me in such hot water with my mom that I had to promise to make friends with Mike to calm her." Tears welled in her eyes at the thought. "And I don't think I can."

"Oh, baby," Bubba soothed. "Of course, you can. David and I will mediate. You can sit on one couch, and David and I will sit on Mike on the other. He'll croak out his apology. If it's good enough, you'll forgive him, and we'll let him live. It'll be fun."

Patrice chuckled.

"There's my girl." He ruffled her hair. "Now let's get inside and get some food. I'm starving."

Patrice turned off the car. "Good. I brought groceries."

Bubba grabbed Patrice and gave her a big kiss. "I love you."

She smiled. "You love that I cook for you."

"That too." Bubba got out of the front seat and opened the back. "Ooh, look...salmon and greens and cream and French bread and those little caper things." He peeked into the bags before picking them up. "I think we'll wait a while before making Mike apologize. You can cry on my shoulder anytime for this."

"I always cook for you, and I never cry." She frowned. "Except lately, that is."

"I know. Still, we've seen you more this week than before this Mike-thing began, and I kind of like it. Maybe I should thank the turd."

****

"I think you should let Mike apologize and get it over," Bubba suggested as they cleaned up after dinner. "It isn't going to get any easier with time."

"But what if I make a fool of myself again?"

"You won't," Bubba assured her. "You both know the score. He sees you as a sister, so act towards him like a sister. Think of him as a little kid."

85

"He's seven years older than I am, Bubba. I've never thought of him as a little kid. He's always been so big and strong and in control. I was in awe of him."

"Didn't he ever do anything dumb as a kid that you can remember when you talk to him? Stuff that a sister would know—like lighting his farts on fire, or belching Happy Birthday, or dressing up like a super hero?"

Patrice laughed as she wiped off the table. "I think I need to talk to your sisters. What super hero did you like to dress up as?"

"The Black Marvel."

"What was the costume?"

"He wore a cool black suit with a hooded mask, yellow gloves, boots and belt, and a red cape. I wore shorts and a hooded sweatshirt over black long johns with a bath towel cape safety-pinned to my shoulders."

"I'll bet you were adorable."

"Goofy is more like it." Bubba pushed the dishwasher door closed to start it. "Mama's got pictures."

"I'd like to see them sometime."

"Don't hold your breath. But that's the type of stuff you need to think of when you talk to Mike. You've got to think of him as goofy and young, not the object of your infatuation."

She thought about it for a moment as she leaned against the counter with the dishcloth in hand. What goofy thing could she remember to think of when Mike sat across the table from her looking hunky and unobtainable?

She remembered the picture Melanie had given her of Mike in his Batman underwear with a bath towel cape. She'd never thought of it as anything but cute or maybe a wistful vision of the kids she'd have with him someday.

Maybe it would help if she got out that photo and looked at it. Somehow she doubted it. Likely it would just depress her more—looking at a future that would never be.

"You're right," she told Bubba. "Not about picturing him as a brother—I don't think I can do that any time in the near future—but the part about it not getting any easier with time. I promised my mom that Mike and I would be on amiable terms by Christmas, and that isn't going to happen if I run away and hide every time I see him or hear his voice." She rinsed the dishcloth and hung it to dry. "I have to face him and move on. And the sooner I do the first, the sooner I can do the second."

She dried her hands and walked to Bubba.

"Thanks, Bubba," she said, giving him a big hug. "I'll give Mike a call tomorrow."

"Tomorrow?" Bubba winced. "So soon? Wouldn't you like to stay here and wallow in self pity for a few more meals—I mean, days?"

Patrice laughed. "There's leftover salmon in the fridge, and I put two quarts of soup in your freezer just the other day."

"It was last week."

"Poor baby. I don't work tomorrow or Tuesday. I'll do a little cooking for you and fill your fridge."

He gave her a hug. "I think I'm in love."

She laughed. "I won't tell David."

"Let me give you some money for groceries." He pulled a wad of bills out of his pocket and peeled off several fifties.

Patrice raised her eyebrows. "Just what were you hoping I would make? Lobster Newburg for ten?"

"I was hoping for your bouillabaisse," Bubba said, handing her the money. "But I think I owe you from last time too."

Patrice laughed. "Bouillabaisse and what else?"

"Blackened catfish? And maybe red beans?" Bubba asked, salivating. "You sure you don't want to just move in?"

"I'm sure. If I moved in, you'd keep me so busy cooking for you that I wouldn't have time to work at Victor's."

"You wouldn't have to," Bubba told her.

"I wouldn't have to what? Cook for you or work at Victor's?"

"Work at Victor's," Bubba replied. "Do you think I'm gonna let you get away? Hell, no. You're the onliest one I know who can make Cajun that makes me sweat."

Chapter 18

Patrice got up with the sun Monday morning, looking forward to a day of puttering in the kitchen. She loved cooking at Victor's, but this was even better.

After breakfast, she turned on some New Orleans' jazz and stood smiling happily in front of her opened refrigerator filled with the fresh produce and seafood she'd selected last night. The shellfish were perfect, and the red and green peppers were beautiful. She caressed their shiny, brightly colored skins as she took them out of the refrigerator and set them on the counter beside the plump tomatoes, onions, and garlic.

The phone rang as she peeled the garlic.

"Don't hang up," Mike said, when she answered.

"I won't," she said, though her stomach tensed.

"I am so sorry about the party. I didn't mean what I said, and I didn't mean to spill the brûlée."

"I know," she said, peeling an onion so that the tears she was afraid might come would have another explanation.

"I want to apologize."

"You just did, and I accept." She felt good—strong. Talking with him on the phone wasn't that hard after all. The onions probably hadn't been necessary. Patrice increased her chopping speed.

"I want to apologize in person."

"No need. We're fine." She blinked back the tears—induced by the onion, of course—and kept chopping.

"I want to talk to you in person. Take you out for dinner."

"No need. We're fine. Really. Mike, you don't need to take me to dinner. I understand how you feel about me—finally." She gave a single self-deprecating chuckle that ended in a moist sniff.

"I don't think you do." He paused. "Are you crying?"

Patrice heard the guilt in his voice and smiled as she finished the last onion.

"I'm chopping onions." She covered the phone and cleared her nose.

"At seven-thirty in the morning?" He sounded skeptical.

"If you chop onions before you do yoga, you'll always have clean nasal passages."

Mike was silent.

"Okay," she relented. "I promised a friend I'd make some Cajun dishes for him, and I thought I'd start early."

"Him?"

Patrice laughed as she drizzled olive oil into a warmed pan and added the onions.

"Who are you cooking for?"

Patrice laughed again. "Geez, Mike, you sound like Randy."

"I do not," he snapped. "I'm not your brother, and I never have been."

"Fine," she said, confused yet pacifying. Isn't that what he wanted? Wasn't she supposed to think of him as a brother?

"We need to talk about this. Can I take you out for dinner tonight?"

Dinner—an hour, maybe two, across the table from Mike. Tortured bliss. Unfulfillable temptation. Not a step toward getting over him and moving on. "I can't. I'm busy."

"Drinks then?"

Would that be any easier? It could be shorter, but there'd be alcohol involved and...

He broke into her thoughts. "Just say yes, Patrice.

We're going to talk. You can put it off if you want to, but why? I won't go away. Besides you promised your mother that—"

"Okay, fine," she snapped. She didn't need to be reminded what she'd promised her mother. She snatched up a spoon and attacked the sautéing onions. At least he hadn't said that he knew she wanted to. "I'll meet you at Victor's at five."

"Not Victor's," Mike insisted. "The Blue Moon Lounge down the street from you."

"Okay. The Blue Moon at five for one drink."

"Or two," Mike suggested.

"I can't."

"That's right. You have plans. What time is he picking you up?"

It sounded to Patrice as if Mike didn't believe she had plans and was making fun. The fact that she didn't have plans, yet, didn't help her growing anger. She'd have plans by tonight even if they were just a long soak in the tub. "Six."

"Maybe you'd better have him meet you at the Blue Moon."

"So you'll believe I have a date or so you can pass judgment?"

"Uh, neither," Mike stumbled.

"Screw you, Mike. You can wait at the Blue Moon until...until...the moon turns blue, and you still won't see me."

"I'm sorry, Patrice."

Her hands shook. It was ridiculous to meet him for drinks when they couldn't even have a civil phone conversation.

"I didn't mean it like that." He sounded contrite almost desperate. "Say you'll still meet me."

"I can't." She wanted to say no, but couldn't do that either.

"It's just that I get a little jealous where you're concerned, is all."

"Yeah, right. You liar." Patrice grabbed another tissue. She wasn't crying. It was the onions.

"I really am sorry, Patrice. Please say you'll come."

She still didn't say no, but she knew she should. "I've

got to go now before you make me burn the onions."

"Then say you'll be there."

"I'm hanging up now. Good-bye, Mike."

"I'll be waiting for you at the Blue Moon at five," he said as she clicked off her phone.

She should have told him no.

****

The bouillabaisse was simmering gently when the phone rang again.

Patrice answered it, half-hoping it was Mike so she could tell him to drop dead. It was Alex. She smiled. She liked Alex. He was a nice guy—a nice, safe, non-threatening guy.

"If you aren't working tonight, I was wondering if you'd like to go to dinner with me."

She silently cheered. Plans for tonight that would make her meeting with Mike short. "I'd love to." It felt as if a weight had lifted from Patrice's shoulders.

"Great." He paused. "Where do world class chefs go when they go out to eat?"

"I haven't had good Chicago deep dish in a long time."

"Great. Pizza it is. I know just the place. I'm through work at five. I can come get you at five-thirty."

"I have a meeting at five. Can we make it six?"

"Six? Uh, sure. Will that give you enough time for your meeting?"

"More than enough."

"Good. Then I'll see you at six."

Chapter 19

Alone at a small table in the darkened lounge, Mike shredded the cocktail napkin that had come with his beer. He checked his watch. It was still ten minutes to five.

He shouldn't have gotten there so early. He should have stayed at the firm longer and worked on something. Not that he could concentrate on anything.

He checked his watch again.

Would she come? She hadn't said that she would, but she knew he'd be waiting. Two weeks ago, he'd have had no doubts. She would have been the one there early, waiting. But that was two weeks ago. Would she come now? She said she'd forgiven him, but then he'd put his foot in his mouth again. What would he do if she didn't come? And what exactly would he say to her if she did?

He peeled the label off his Samuel Adams and watched the door.

Precisely at five, she entered the room. Mike immediately rose to greet her.

"I'm so glad you came," he said.

For a moment Patrice looked at him like she always had, with appreciation and approval clear in her beautiful blue eyes. Then she swallowed and jerked her gaze from his. When she turned back, the warmth in her eyes had cooled.

"I have a table over here." He put a hand on the back of her waist to guide her. She flinched at his touch.

Flinched? At his touch? He cursed himself and that damned dessert. How was he ever going to fix this? He held his face courtroom still as she sat and slid off her leather jacket.

Mike signaled the waitress.

"What would you like?" he asked Patrice.

She looked at the waitress instead of him. "White Zin."

Mike touched his empty bottle. "Bring me another."

The waitress left, leaving them alone.

Across the table, Patrice looked soft and cuddly with her hair down, curling gently around her shoulders. "You look beautiful," he said.

"Uh, thank you." Her eyes narrowed. "Is this part of the apology?" Her face grew red.

"No." He shook his head. "I just like the way you look."

"Oh...well, thank you. I have a date tonight."

His smile froze. She didn't want him to think she'd gone to any effort for him. "I remember—six o'clock, wasn't it?"

"Yes."

He didn't know how to respond. Thankfully, the waitress chose that moment to arrive with their drinks.

Patrice reached for hers and took a long sip. She probably wished she'd ordered something stronger. He certainly did.

"How is work going?" Patrice asked over the rim of her wine glass. "Has anything changed since you made partner?"

Mike looked into her eyes. "A lot of things have changed since last Monday."

She looked away.

"It was a really nice thing that you did. The party, I mean. All the work and expense and all, and I was such a big jerk." It wasn't how he'd meant to apologize. He was normally more eloquent than this. It was just that she'd flinched when he touched her, and now she wouldn't look at him.

Patrice narrowed her eyes. Her hand shook as she set

down her glass. "You've already apologized, and I accepted it. It was embarrassing for both of us. I'd rather not waste any more time thinking about it. Could we just move on?"

"I'm sorry," he said, taken aback by the vehemence in her tone. "I just wanted to apologize."

"And you have now—twice." She shook her head. "This wasn't a good idea." She stood, grabbing her coat.

"Don't leave." He touched her arm. "Please. There's more I need to tell you."

"About what?" Her voice sounded suspicious, but she sank back into her seat with her jacket on her lap.

"Monday night brought a lot of things to a head."

Patrice sighed and looked at the ceiling. "I know," she blurted. Her voice had that I-don't-care quality of an unrepentant teen repeating a litany of her crimes. "I've been chasing you for years, nearly throwing myself at you, and Monday night it finally got to be too much. Don't worry. I know. I finally realize that you don't want me. Now I suppose it's my turn to apologize." She finally looked at Mike.

"No." He stared dumbfounded. How could she blame herself when it was all his fault? "You don't have to apologize."

"Good." She rose once again. "'Cuz I'm not going to." She didn't look at him, but he could see the tears fill her eyes as she started toward the door.

He couldn't let her leave. Springing to his feet, he caught her before she'd taken more than a handful of steps. She tried to yank her arm free as he turned her into his embrace.

"That wasn't what I wanted to say." He held her gently but firmly until she stopped struggling. She had met him tonight. He couldn't blow this. "It wasn't until Monday night that I finally admitted to myself something I've known for years—that I love you and don't want to lose you."

"Liar." She glared at him.

Frustrated, Mike did the only thing he could under the circumstances. His lips captured hers. All the emotions he'd suppressed were in the kiss—the longing, the loneliness, the self-denial. The love.

After a moment, Patrice drew in a deep, shuddering breath and kissed him back. Their tongues mated, his hands drifted down her back to pull her close. She clung to him, melting in his arms there in the middle of the Blue Moon Lounge. Her coat slipped from her grasp and fell to the floor. He kissed her with the pent-up desire of a lifetime of denial.

Patrice pushed him away, breaking off the too-private kiss in the too-public place. Her face blazed crimson.

The kiss had been perfect. Patrice was perfect. Mike ran his hand down her arms. It wasn't too late. It was going to be okay. "I'll take you home."

She looked at him as if she hardly knew him. She touched her fingers to her lips for a fraction of a second and then stared at her fingertips as if wondering what had happened.

"You can't..." She stepped away from him. Her hand shook as she checked her watch.

He frowned. "That's right. You have a date." How had he forgotten? He looked at his watch as well. Five twenty-five. "I suppose it's too late to break it, isn't it?"

She nodded. Her eyes reflected her confusion.

He was equally confused. The kiss had been scorching, binding. It should have signaled the start of something new and wonderful between them. He wanted to expand on that start, to talk things through, to hold her, to love her, to move forward on this new level, but there she stood ready to go out with another man. He wanted to hit something.

There shouldn't be other men in her life. Wouldn't be, if he had any say. Still, he knew that one kiss didn't give him the right to demand anything. He shoved down his jealousy and forced himself to keep their encounter light.

"You'll have to go then," Mike announced, determined not to give her any reason to regret her decision to let him back into her life. Throwing her over his shoulder like a caveman would set the wrong tone.

"O...kay," she said, hesitatingly.

He could almost hear her thoughts. How can he kiss me and send me off on a date? Doesn't he care? Didn't it mean anything?

"Oh, I mind, all right." Mike hoped he was reading her furrowed brow correctly. "Tell Bubba to keep his hands off you, or I'll..." He punched his palm and grinned in mock seriousness. Was that too light?

Patrice's eyes cleared. She looked like herself again. Confident. Relaxed.

Mike relaxed. Everything was going to be fine. He knew what he was doing after all.

She laughed.

His smile froze.

"You can tell him that yourself if you want. I won't be seeing him tonight."

"You won't?" Mike's stomach turned to acid, and his smile faded. "How many guys am I up against?"

Patrice looked him in the eye. "There's only one person you need to concern yourself with—me."

Mike nodded, his courtroom mask firmly in place. "And the other guys?"

Patrice shrugged. "That's not your worry."

Mike's kept his expression neutral. This conversation was about to deteriorate again. He changed tactics. "What if I'm really good?"

"At what?" Patrice asked.

"At treating you well."

"I guess I'd have to see it to believe it." Her eyes sparkled as she issued the challenge.

"Oh, you'll believe it," Mike growled and pulled her into his arms, forcing her to look at him. He needed her like he needed his next breath.

Patrice raised a questioning brow.

He kissed her again, deeply and possessively. Her lips were firm and dry, but her mouth was hot and wet. She trembled in his arms.

After several long, blissful moments, she ended the kiss, whispering breathlessly, "We can't do this. I feel like I'm on display." Her face was flushed with desire.

"Sorry." He wasn't though. He was burning with a potent combination of desire, wonder, and worry. How did he win a heart he'd always known was his? He'd never wanted anything as much as he wanted Patrice's love. "Pet, I promise to only give you chaste kisses in public from now on."

Her eyes narrowed. "Uh, thank you."

It was a lie. He pulled her even tighter against him, slanted his mouth over hers, and kissed her with a hunger that made her shiver. She clung to him. He deepened the kiss. She moaned into his mouth and pressed every soft, luscious inch of herself against him.

"Mike," Patrice gasped, finally pulling her lips from his. The air between them nearly sizzled with electricity. "You promised." Her voice was husky and a little breathless. "That kiss wasn't chaste."

He smiled, well pleased at the results of his kisses. Patrice was flushed and flustered. Her lips were kiss-swollen, and her hair slightly mussed. He held her against him and looked into her passion-heated eyes. "It was chaste," he protested. "At least in comparison to how I'll kiss you when we're alone."

Patrice turned crimson and pushed her way out of Mike's arms. "I have to go." Her breath was ragged.

He picked her coat off the floor and helped her on with it. "Shall I walk you to your apartment and kiss you good-bye?" he asked, hoping she'd say yes.

"No!" She stared at him agape, her blush deepening. "I...I'll be late."

He watched her flee the lounge, confident that they'd each think of that kiss again and again as the night progressed. He would have felt sorry for her date if he weren't so damned jealous.

Chapter 20

Patrice arrived at her apartment with scarcely enough time to fix her lipstick and brush her hair. She was still flushed and heated, but she told herself that was due to running several blocks in the cold.

Who would have predicted the way things turned out tonight? She'd given up on Mike. Really, she had. She had the date with Alex as proof of that. And now—now the tables had turned—the hunter had become the hunted. Patrice smiled into the mirror as she went to answer Alex's buzz.

Mike as hunter...she liked it.

****

"You don't need to find a parking spot," Patrice told Alex as they neared her building. She'd had fun on their date, but she wasn't sad that it was over. "You can just drop me off out front."

"If you're sure," Alex said. "I don't mind."

"I'm sure." She needed to go, needed time to think about everything that had happened in the last few hours without any more emotional entanglements.

He double-parked in front of her building.

Their date had saved her from falling even further into Mike's arms. For that alone she was grateful. "I had fun," Patrice said, looking at him. "Thank you."

He leaned across the console, pulling her gently into his arms for a kiss.

It was a nice kiss from a nice guy. Part of her wished that she felt more at home in his arms, that she wanted more from him than the brief kiss if only to spite Mike. But she didn't.

"Can I see you again?" he asked when she'd pulled away.

"I..." she hesitated. It would serve Mike right if she said yes to Alex, but that wouldn't be fair to Alex. She simply wasn't the type of girl who led guys on.

"I know about Bubba, and I know that Mike is going to try to get you back," he said as if reading her mind. "I don't mind starting out in third place. Competition is good, especially where a professional football player and a childhood crush are concerned. What I lack in job prestige and history, I make up in fun. I like you, Patrice. I really like you. And I think you like me. We have fun together, and if that's all our dates ever are is fun—that will be okay. Say you'll see me again if only to give the others competition."

Patrice smiled. What he'd said had merit. Mike deserved to have competition. He deserved to work for her. "Alex, I do like you."

"No buts," he pleaded. "Please, no buts."

She laughed, grateful that he'd made the decision so easy. He had no illusions about how things stood. Dating him wouldn't be leading him on; it would be giving her the space and freedom to let her decide what she wanted.

"Okay. No buts. I like you, and I had a good time with you, so...yes, I'd like to go out with you again."

"Thank you," he said, kissing her hand. "You won't be sorry."

Chapter 21

Mike finished his paperwork and joined Randy in the living room to watch a sitcom. Restless, he tried to figure out how to make it through the evening without obsessing about Patrice.

"He's out with her, you know," Randy blurted out, watching carefully for Mike's reaction.

Mike looked at Randy, too shocked by the abruptness of his roommate's comment to do anything else.

"Alex and Patrice," Randy clarified, unnecessarily.

"How do you know?"

"He came home early to shower and shave before picking her up. You should have seen the smile on his face as he went out the door."

Randy stood, turning his back on Mike, and walked through the swinging door in to the kitchen. "You want a beer?" he asked over his shoulder.

"Okay." Mike stared blindly at the television until Randy returned. Patrice was out with Alex.

Randy tossed Mike a cold beer and then, resuming his seat in the recliner, popped the top on his own. "So, did you apologize to her?"

"Yes." Mike tapped the top of his beer can several times before opening it.

"Everything settled between the two of you then?"

"Between Patrice and me, or between Alex and me?"

"Either. Both."

"Why are you so interested?" Mike took a swig.

Randy shrugged. "Why wouldn't I be? She's my sister. You and Alex are my housemates. Somehow I figured it might be rough watching you come to grips with Alex dating her."

"It's more complicated than that," Mike said. "Both he and I want to see her, but I'm hoping she won't want to see him." He was fairly certain she wouldn't—at least not for long, not if her kisses this afternoon meant anything. With any luck, this would be Alex's one and only date with her.

Randy looked at Mike in disgust. "God, Mike. You're not still thinking of dating Patrice, are you? What happened to thinking of her as 'The Pest'?"

Mike cringed. "Don't call her that. That's ancient history."

Randy snorted. "Ancient history. Try last week."

"What would you know? Besides, I haven't called her that in—"

"Nearly two weeks," Randy finished for him.

Mike frowned. Randy was exaggerating. It had been a lot longer than that.

"I just think it's odd that you went from decades of alternately ignoring Patrice and making snide comments to declarations of love in minutes."

"It wasn't a matter of minutes."

"That's right. You've loved her forever. You were just in denial."

Mike narrowed his eyes at Randy.

Nearly ten minutes passed before Randy spoke again. "So, did she really forgive you?"

Suppressing a smile, Mike thought of that afternoon. "It seemed like it."

"You're just yanking my chain, aren't you? You aren't going to date her. You really cut her loose, didn't you? That's why it's okay that Alex is out with her." Randy smiled. "I have to say, I'm glad you decided to listen to me and do the right thing for Patrice."

"I didn't cut her loose. I said I loved her, and I meant it. I am going to date your sister, Randy. It's the right thing for both Patrice and me."

"For you maybe."

Mike chose to ignore Randy's comment, drinking his beer in silence.

Randy didn't allow the silence to last long. "Now that you and Alex are both going to be dating my sister, should I be placing bets or something?"

"I thought we went through this." Mike tented his fingers as he explained it again with growing frustration. "Alex and I have an understanding. He's welcome to date Patrice for as long as she wants to date him."

"And Bubba Scott? Is he welcome to date her too?" Randy asked.

"Patrice is free to date whoever she wants—Alex, Bubba, David Welch, Mahatma Gandhi..."

"He's dead."

"Whatever. You get the idea. Patrice can date whomever she wants."

"You're that confident that she won't want to date anyone but you?"

Mike shrugged, turning back to the program. "This isn't about you, Randy, so back off."

Randy wouldn't let it drop. "How much you want to bet that she goes out with Bubba again or that Alex gets another date?"

Mike glared at him.

"Oh, yes," Randy snickered. "You've bet your heart— you don't need to bet money as well."

It took all of Mike's will not to punch Randy in the face.

"What is with you tonight? When did you get to be such an asshole?" Mike finished his beer.

Randy laughed. "Just looking out for the poor and downtrodden."

"Since when?" Mike asked, crushing his can.

"Since a week ago Monday. Patrice is my sister and a nice girl besides."

Mike groaned. "She's been both for a long time. Why the sudden interest?"

Randy shrugged. "I could ask you the same question, Tucker. I just want to see her happy." He finished his beer and headed into the kitchen.

Mike turned back to the program.

"Just don't hurt her again," Randy said, returning to the living room with bag of chips. "If you do, I'll have to..."

"You'll have to take a number," Mike grumbled. "Why won't anybody believe that I just want to make her happy?"

"History is against you, Mike. Those who shit on those that love them are apt to do it again and again. You're going to have to prove it before anyone will believe you, and that includes Patrice."

Mike was pacing when Alex finally walked in. He stopped mid-stride, crossing his arms as he faced Alex. "Do you know what time it is?" he asked, unable to stop himself.

Alex glanced at the clock on the wall. "It's ten-twenty-six, Dad." He looked quizzically at Mike. "What's up? I didn't know I had a curfew."

"He's been like this since eight," Randy said, looking up from the television. "You picked up Patrice for dinner at six."

"So, what took you so long?" Mike asked.

Alex removed his coat. "Nothing. We had a nice time at dinner. The service was a little slow, but we didn't really mind—we were busy talking. Did you want to know what we ordered?" he asked Mike, amused.

"No," Randy said. "What he really wants to know is did you kiss her?"

Alex frowned at Randy before hanging his coat in the closet. "A gentleman does not kiss and tell."

"So, did you kiss her or what?" Randy laughed.

Despite all his talk about letting Patrice date whomever she wished, Mike found that now that he was faced with one of her dates, he wanted to hit something or someone—namely Alex.

"I guess it's or what," Randy continued. "Did you ask her out again?"

Alex gave Randy a warning glance.

"Did you?" Mike asked when Alex remained silent.

"Actually, I did." Alex crossed his arms.

"Oh." Mike's response was so cold it hung in the air like breath on a frozen winter's day.

"Did she accept?" Randy asked.

"Would you just shut up?" Alex shot at Randy.

"He's enjoying this," Mike commented.

"Why?" Alex asked.

"I don't know." Mike shrugged. "To punish me, I guess. I haven't been able to figure it out."

Alex turned to Randy. "Knock it off, Randy. It isn't helping." He turned to Mike. "Patrice and I had a good time. I dropped her off around nine. I asked her if I could call her again, and she said yes. That's it. I treated her like the lady she is."

"I know." Mike sank into a nearby chair. "I didn't mean to pry."

"You didn't," Alex said. "It was this asshole." He glared at Randy.

"Watch out, Big Brother is watching," Randy laughed, heading off to bed.

Chapter 22

Patrice woke up to the telephone ringing.

"Hello, beautiful." Mike's voice filled her ear.

"If you could see me right now, you wouldn't say that," Patrice said, stifling a yawn.

"Did I wake you?"

"What time is it?" Patrice squinted against the glare of morning light streaming through her window.

"Seven-fifteen. I'm about to head to work and thought I'd call and see if you were available for dinner tonight."

"It's Tuesday, right?"

"I did wake you. Sorry."

"It's okay. As my dad would say, 'I had to get up to answer the phone anyway.' That is so stupid. I never did get why he'd say that. It's not even funny. Do you think that it's funny?"

"No. Not really. Anyway, I am sorry I woke you."

"Thanks," she said. "Hey, Mike, can you hold. I'm getting beeped—call waiting. What time did you say it was?"

"Seven-fifteen."

"Seven-fifteen," she repeated. "Hold on a second." She fumbled for the button that allowed her to switch lines.

"Hello?"

"Patrice? Good you're up." Alex's voice filled the line.

105

"Barely," Patrice admitted. "Oddly enough I've got someone on the other line. Could you call back in five minutes or so?"

"Sure, but are you available for dinner tonight?"

Patrice thought a moment about Mike's invitation. Did she want to say yes to him on such short notice or did she want him to cool his heels? Did she want to go out with Alex tonight when she could be with Mike? She should, but she didn't. "Alex, I'll check my calendar and get back to you."

She clicked back over to Mike. "Sorry about that. The only one who ever calls me this early is my mother, and she doesn't call this early."

"Are you sure you're awake?" he asked.

"Positive. And getting more alert by the second. What can I do for you this very sunny morning?"

"You can tell me that you are free for dinner tonight."

"It just so happens that I am." Her voice carried with it a smile.

"Great. Would you like to have dinner with me?"

"I'd like that," Patrice admitted.

"Great." His voice sounded pleased and relieved. "I'll pick you up at five-thirty. Do you like Thai food?"

"I love it. Where are we going?"

"I've heard the Willow Tree is good."

"It's fabulous. I know the owner, Leanne. We exchanged letters when I lived in France."

"Speaking of mail. I missed your letter Friday. For years I've planned Friday around receiving your letter. It's just not the same without it."

"Really?" She wasn't sure how she felt about his confession.

"Really. No matter where I lived, I made sure I went home for lunch so that I could pick up your letter and read it as I ate. I had withdrawal symptoms when I didn't get one last week."

"Then why didn't you ever write back?" she asked.

"I wrote back sometimes."

His stupid protestation rubbed her wrong.

"Who are you trying to fool? I kept all your letters, and there weren't that many to keep."

Mike was silent for a moment. "I know. I'm sorry. I

106

haven't been very good to you in the past, but I promise that it will be different from now on. What I was trying to say is that I always looked forward to Fridays because of you. Reading your letters was like having lunch with you. I'd like to do that—have lunch with you on Friday. Can I meet you somewhere?"

"No. I can't. Fridays are bad, especially this week. Victor scheduled a meeting about the upcoming holiday season that I can't miss. Anyway, aren't you in New York with your family?"

"No. I have a full day scheduled this Friday."

"Oh." That meant he'd be alone for Thanksgiving. She hesitated, knowing that she should invite him to her parents' house, but she wasn't quite ready for that.

The phone beeped again, saving her from issuing an invitation she was sure to regret.

"Mike, I've got to answer the other line, and you have to get to work. I'll see you tonight at five-thirty."

She answered the other line, prepared to tell Alex that she was busy tonight.

"You sound awake," Randy said.

"I am. Why are you calling so early?"

"I should ask why you're up so early, but I won't. I just have a minute before the train gets here, and I wanted to check on you."

"I'm fine."

"Have you talked to Mom? She's called me twice fishing for information. She's dying to know what's going on between you and Mike."

"What have you told her?"

"To call you herself. But she won't. She claims she promised you she wouldn't nag or pry about Mike even though she found out that he wasn't going to New York for Thanksgiving."

Patrice felt frozen. "So she's having you call to tell me she asked him for dinner? Isn't that just like her?"

"Actually, I told her that neither of us would go home if she did. She promised you that you'd have until Christmas and, even though Mike said you accepted his apology last night, I'm going to help her stick to it."

"Uh, thanks."

"The thing is, I don't think she realizes that I'm on

your side about this."

"Oh?" She hadn't known she had a side.

"Yes. Mike may be my best friend, but when it comes to you, he's a jerk—an 'A' number one, dyed-in-the-wool asshole. He's been better with other girls, but not by much. Although, come to think of it, he never remained interested in any one girl all that long. Anyway, what I'm trying to say is that I'm glad you forgave him for the brûlée, but I don't think you need to see him again. You did what Mom asked, and that's enough. I don't think you should have to continue to see him just because she's bent on merging the families."

"She's what?" Patrice was so stunned she didn't notice the call waiting beep.

"Oh, come on, Pet. Surely you know. She encouraged you where Mike was concerned all the while you were growing up. Not that you didn't have it badly enough all by yourself. I thought she'd have finally gotten over it when you did after the damned brûlée incident. You realized there is no future with Mike, so why can't she? But no—she made you promise to see him, and she got Melanie to make Mike do the same."

"She did?" Had Mike insisted on meeting her for drinks because he'd wanted to or because he'd promised his mother he would? "Are you sure?"

"That's what Mom told me."

Patrice said nothing in response. Mike may have insisted on meeting her at the Blue Moon because of his mom, but the kisses and second date were his idea.

"Pet? You okay?" He paused, listening. "I'll let you go. You're getting another call. I'll see you on Turkey Day."

Patrice answered the phone for the fourth time in six minutes.

"Did you check your calendar?" Alex asked.

"Yes, I did. I've got something going on tonight, so I can't. I'm sorry."

"Don't worry. It was short notice. I'd ask you for later in the week, but I'm leaving tomorrow after work for my sister's in Michigan. The entire family will be there for Thanksgiving. I won't be back until Sunday night. How about I call you when I get back?"

"Sounds good." She hung up with a smile. She could

hardly wait to see what the week would hold. Would it end with Mike holding her?

Less than an hour later, Patrice was showered, dressed and sipping tea when the phone rang again.

"I'm in my car two blocks away. I'll be there in less than five minutes. Hurry, get dressed so you can buzz me in."

"Hi, David," Patrice said. "Good morning to you too."

"Hang up and get busy," he ordered. "I think I've found a parking spot." He disconnected.

Minutes later, Patrice opened the door.

"You're dressed and dry and looking good," he said, kissing her cheek. "How come you're up so early?"

"Do you want coffee or tea?" she asked, going back to the kitchen.

"What are you having?"

"English Breakfast tea."

"Give me a cup of that too." He sat at the table.

She took another cup and saucer from the cupboard and poured him some tea before returning to her chair.

"So why are you up so early?" he repeated.

"It's not so early. I usually get up at eight, and it's nearly that now."

"And look at you. You're showered and dressed with perfect hair and make-up. Who are you expecting?"

Patrice shrugged. "Nobody. But the way this day is going, who knows. Did you know I got four phone calls before seven-twenty?"

"Tell." David propped an elbow on the table and rested his chin in his palm.

Beaming, she filled him in on the events of the previous evening and the morning's phone calls.

"So you're seeing Tucker tonight. Are you sure you know what you're doing?"

Her smile wavered and faded. "I don't know. I thought I did until Randy called."

"Don't worry about Randy. It's not him you have to please. It's me." He smiled at his own joke. "And, of course, yourself."

"But why is Mike suddenly so interested in me?"

David shrugged. "Maybe it's like he said. Maybe he loves you. But I'd keep seeing Bubba and Alex until you're sure. From what you said, Alex doesn't mind, and as long as you show up at the team Thanksgiving bash and hang all over Bubba, he won't care what you do."

"What Thanksgiving bash? I thought everyone went home for Thanksgiving."

"Not this year. They're getting together to watch the game and eat turkey legs like the commentators."

"That's gross. And they expect their wives and girlfriends to go along with this?"

"Apparently."

"I'm expected at my mother's for dinner at four. Tell Bubba I can come for the early game. You can also tell him he's supposed to do the asking, not you."

"I told him, but you know how guys are..."

Patrice laughed.

"Now about your date tonight," David continued. "You have got to avoid those kisses. They mess with your ability to think straight."

"Why should I take dating advice from you?" Patrice asked, grinning wildly.

"Because I've more experience with men than you have."

Patrice suppressed a laugh. "Oh, speak on, oh wise one."

David drew himself up straight in the chair and adopted a priggish, intellectual face. "The first rule of dating is—stay out of his bed if you want a clear head."

Patrice barked out a laugh, and then took a sip of tea and swallowed, trying to regain a straight face. "All right, professor, please continue."

"Thank you," David said in a lofty voice, looking down his nose at her.

Patrice bit her lip to keep from laughing.

"The second rule of dating is—staying out of the sack is the best aphrodisiac."

Patrice giggled. "Professor? Are all your rules about sex?"

"Yes, of course," David continued in his affected tone. "Dating is a mating dance—a trial run of wedded life where each partner shows his best side in hope of distracting his partner from his worst side long enough to get him to the altar or—in my case—bed."

"Oh?" Patrice stopped laughing, thinking about what he had said. "I guess that's true—if a bit cruder and a lot less romantic than I'd have put it." Eyes twinkling as she rejoined the game, Patrice smiled. "But, professor—it doesn't rhyme."

"That's because it's not a rule; it's a fact of life," David continued in his own voice. "Mike wants you in bed. He's as good as said that. And you love him, so you are probably tempted to go there. Just make certain it's what you really want before you do it."

Patrice's smile vanished. "You're telling me to save it for the wedding night?" she asked, incredulous.

David blushed. "Well, I'd be the worst sort of hypocrite if I did, but... I guess in this case it wouldn't be a bad idea." He reached over the table to cover Patrice's hand with his.

She yanked her hand back and stared at David.

"Don't glare at me, Pet. I know you love him. I just don't trust him. He's taken you for granted for too long. If he really wants you, make him work for it."

"What kind of a girl do you think I am?" Patrice crossed her arms and managed to keep her voice this side of yelling.

"The best kind," David rushed to assure her. "Much better than Tucker-the-fucker deserves. That's why I said what I did. His ego was bruised by your defection, and now he wants you back. What better way to prove to himself that you belong to him than by getting in your pants?"

She shook her head. "It's not that way. Mike's not that way."

"Good." David nodded, trying to pacify her. "I hope you're right. Just don't go to bed with him until you're sure, though. That's all I'm saying."

Patrice stood abruptly. "And all I'm saying, David Welch, is that I have no intention of going to bed with anyone until I'm *sure*. And sure for me means married. So quit advising values you don't live up to in your own life." She rushed on before he could protest. "I'm not talking Bubba. You and Bubba are as married as you get. I'm talking Lance and Jason and all the others you tried out while you were finding yourself."

111

David winced.

Patrice noticed and bit her tongue. Her eyes softened as she looked at her friend with regret. "I'm sorry, David. I've been so weird lately—snippy, weepy—not at all like myself. And I know our situations aren't the same at all. Truce?"

David came around the table to hug her. "Pet, you've been through a lot lately. It's going to take a while for you to find your feet again. That's all I was trying to say—take it slow."

Chapter 23

That evening, when Mike buzzed up to say that he was there, Patrice went down to meet him instead of inviting him up. As angry as she'd been with David, she knew he was right—in Mike's arms she couldn't think straight. And she needed to think straight.

The Willow Tree was doing a good business when they got there. A third of the restaurant's dozen tables were filled, but that didn't stop the uproar that greeted Patrice's arrival. She was treated like a long-lost member of the family. Lin, a handsome sixteen-year-old, the youngest of Leanne's sons, left the table he was waiting on to give her a hug and call his mother.

Leanne, her gray-streaked black hair pulled into a tight bun on the top of her head, bustled out of the kitchen to give Patrice a hug. "It's so good to see you. I thought maybe all the press would go to your head, and you would no longer find time to visit your old friends."

"Are you kidding?" Patrice laughed. "And miss all this?" She spread her arms to take in the entire restaurant—a hole-in-the-wall affair with framed posters of a Buddhist temple, Thailand's floating market, and snapshots of family interspersed amongst batik silk shawls and stands of potted bamboo. "And where else would I get your world famous Coconut Custard in a

Pumpkin Shell?"

"World famous custard," Leanne snorted, obviously pleased. "Will you be needing a menu?"

"I never do, but Mike will. Mike Tucker, this is Leanne Chow and her son Lin. Lin, Leanne, this is Mike—"

"Tucker," Leanne finished for her, raising her eyebrows. "Oh..." Her tone changed as she remembered the name. "Oh..." She exchanged a knowing look with Patrice and then gave Mike an appraising stare. "Lin, you lazy dog, show Patrice and her Mike to our best table."

Lin scrambled to action, giving his mother a questioning look. There was no best table. There were only eight unoccupied tables in the place, and they all looked the same—red paper placemats and napkins framed by chopsticks and silverware, decorated with a vase of fake orchids and the normal array of condiment bottles. Lin looked to Patrice for help. She smiled and shrugged. Lin echoed her reaction, leading them to a table near the far wall.

"No, you fool," Leanne scolded, "the best table." She pointed to a table near the opposite wall, a table easily viewable from the kitchen.

"Oh," Lin said, finally understanding. "The best table." He exchanged a look with Patrice, rolling his eyes. "Why didn't you say the best table?" he said loudly to his mother as she returned to the kitchen, and then whispered to Patrice and Mike. "The best table for spying on you, that is."

He led them to the table and handed Mike a menu. "Crab, Shrimp, Bean-Thread Noodle Clay Pot is on special. It is a traditional dish served straight from the stove in a clay pot. It is very popular," he told Mike before turning to Patrice. "Are you coming to our day-after-New-Year's-party?"

"I wouldn't miss it." She smiled at him. "Are you still working here after school every day?"

"Most every." He spotted Leanne calling him with the crook of her finger. "I'd better go. I'm blocking my mother's view. I'll be back in a minute to take your order."

Mike smiled as he picked up the menu. "When you said you knew the owners, I didn't know you were their long-lost cousin."

"My blond hair threw you, didn't it? It happens a lot."

Mike laughed. "I don't know why I'm looking at this," he said, setting down the menu. "I'm sitting with a native. Why don't you order for the both of us? Get two kinds of appetizers, two different entrees with wine to go with them, and two different desserts as well."

"Do you want iced coffee?"

"Naturally. Order us the works."

Patrice caught Leanne's attention, which wasn't hard since Leanne had been peeking around the door.

Leanne raised her eyebrows in question, and Patrice smiled, holding up two fingers. Leanne nodded and disappeared into the kitchen.

"There," Patrice said. "All done."

"Mental telepathy?"

"Eavesdropping and personal history."

"So, what are we getting?" Mike whispered, amused.

"Why are we whispering?" Patrice asked, leaning across the table.

"So that I can test her telepathy."

Patrice nodded, grinning. "Wise, very wise. All I'll say is be careful of the Meatballs with Spicy Peanut Sauce. It'll be one of the hors d'oeuvres. It's Leanne's favorite and a test of your masculinity. If you use the sauce more than twice, she'll think you're a real man."

Chapter 24

The phone rang as Patrice walked into her apartment.

"Is he there?" David asked.

"No. I just got in."

"I know."

"Are you spying on me?"

"No. Well, maybe," he admitted. "I had Leanne call me when you left."

"I live in a fishbowl," Patrice lamented.

"Such is the life of a guppy."

"Guppy?"

"Would you prefer angel fish?"

"I'd prefer a little privacy," she said pointedly.

"Then don't eat at the Willow Tree."

"As if it weren't your fault that you called Leanne."

"It wasn't. Either I called her or she'd have called me. Do you think she could keep it to herself? The woman was about ready to bust, going on and on about how many of those damned meatballs he ate and how much sauce, as if it was some test of manliness."

"You're just pissed because you couldn't finish one," Patrice teased.

"Like that matters."

"Bubba thinks you're plenty manly," Patrice soothed.

"And he should know."

Patrice laughed.

"So, girlfriend, tell. I know all about dinner—what you ate, how he devoured you with his eyes, but only held your hand, how handsome and manly he is. Puke!"

"What's left?" she asked.

"You didn't ask him up?"

"No. I didn't."

"Oh, give, girl," David pleaded. "How did he take it? Did you kiss? Tell the doctor everything."

"That doctor crap has gone to your head."

"Patrice..."

"All right. Fine. He asked to come up, and I said I didn't think it was a good idea, especially on the first date."

David laughed. "What did he say to that?"

"I'd tell you faster if you'd quit interrupting."

"I'm silent."

"That'll be the day."

"Patrice..."

"All right, all right. He said it wasn't really a first date since we've known each other forever, but that he would respect my decision. He wants to see me again—soon."

"Did you kiss?"

"Do I ask you that kind of stuff?"

"No," David admitted. "But you don't want to know that sort of thing anyway."

"True."

"So..." he urged.

"Yes, we kissed. Several times. And wow! Can that man kiss!"

"Better than me?"

"No comparison. You're a good kisser, but kissing you is like kissing a... a..."

"A fag?"

"I was going to say brother, but I would never kiss Randy that way, so that wasn't right either."

"Anyway..." David called her back to the subject he was interested in. "There was chemistry?"

"I thought we'd established that," Patrice sniped. "Are you looking for pointers?"

117

"No, but I think Bubba is. You're still on for Thanksgiving, aren't you?"

"Yes. Why is this so important to you?"

"Three of Bubba's sisters will be in town."

"And going to the bash?" she asked.

"Yes. And, of course, they don't know he's gay. So they want to see this woman he's so hung up on. And Bubba wants the two of you to look totally besotted."

"Besotted? Come on, David."

"All right, totally hot for each other."

"Fine, but if Bubba tries to grope me, I'll deck him," Patrice warned.

"So Mike groped you, huh?"

"None of your business!"

David laughed.

"I'm hanging up now," she said.

And she did.

Chapter 25

Bubba picked up Patrice shortly after nine Thanksgiving morning.

"You're late," Patrice teased, opening the door. "I thought you said nine."

"I did," Bubba sighed.

Patrice finished buttoning her coat and looked up at her friend.

He gave her a weak smile.

"What's wrong?" She watched him as she pulled the gloves out of her coat pockets. "Did you have trouble finding a parking spot? I told you I'd come down."

"No. I had trouble making them stay in the limo."

"Limo, huh?" She smiled, knowingly. What good was being a big-shot football player if you couldn't ferry your family around in a limo? "Your sisters could have come up. I'm going to meet them in a couple of minutes anyway."

"I needed to talk to you alone first."

"Sounds serious. Maybe you should come in." She stepped aside to let him into the apartment. In the comparatively bright light of her apartment, Patrice could see the sheen of sweat on Bubba's brow.

"You don't look so good. Are you feeling all right?" She reached up to feel his forehead, but he brushed away her hand before it got there.

"I'm fine," he said, looking anything but fine.

Waiting in silence, watching him look anywhere but at her, she began to worry.

"What is it, Bubba?" she asked, when it didn't seem as if he was going to say anything on his own. "Is it David? Is he sick?"

"No." He looked at her briefly before staring at his feet.

Her stomach clenched as she struggled to figure out what else could be upsetting Bubba this much.

"Were you outed?"

"No."

"Is it your family?" Her eyes grew wide. "Or mine?"

"No."

She lost her patience, snapping at Bubba in frustration. "Will you just tell me what the problem is?"

He looked at her apologetically. "Patrice, I really blew it."

"What did you do?"

Bubba continued to examine his shoes.

The picture of a two-hundred and eighty pound defensive end staring at his feet like a penitent child was enough to make Patrice grind her teeth.

"Spit it out," she demanded, crossing her arms.

He looked up at her with puppy-dog eyes. "Can we go to your parents' for dinner instead?" he begged.

Patrice smiled, despite herself. "It can't be that bad. No one is sick or hurt or dead, and you and David haven't been outed, right?"

"Right." Bubba nodded.

"Then there is nothing bad enough to require that kind of punishment."

"You might change your mind once you know."

"Not possible," Patrice insisted. "My mother has that little race problem, remember? Worse yet, our cook went to visit some relatives in Vermont, and Mom has insisted on cooking dinner alone. I'm not to bring anything. Thanksgiving dinner cooked by my mother—" She shivered in revulsion. "What could be bad enough to inflict that on anyone?"

"Being engaged."

Patrice froze. "Who's engaged?"

Bubba looked up at her with sheepish hopefulness. "We are?"

Patrice was stunned. "We're not engaged. What are you talking about?"

Bubba rushed to explain. "My sisters were all over me about you, and it just slipped out."

"How could it just slip out?" she demanded, unsure if she should yell or laugh. "A secret slips out. Something that doesn't exist can't slip out."

"My sisters and David and I were sitting there over dinner last night, and David mentioned that you had made it, and one thing led to another and...Did I mention my sisters love your jambalaya?"

"Don't try to change the subject. And what?"

"And David says, 'Bubba, shouldn't you tell your sisters about you and Patrice?' And my sister Ruth started in with, 'Girls only cook for men they're trying to catch,' and 'She must be after your money.'"

Patrice raised her brows as Bubba dug himself in a hole.

"So, I defended you, saying, 'Patrice isn't that kind of girl,' and stuff. Then everybody started talking at once, and before I knew what had happened, you and I were engaged."

"You told your sisters we were engaged?"

"Well, actually, Rochelle said, 'I suppose you're going to tell us you've married the girl.' And I said, 'No. Not yet.' Which made us engaged."

"I see." Patrice stared at Bubba in disbelief. "And you couldn't tell them we weren't?"

"I had a hard time keeping them from calling Mama," he moaned.

She turned away from him and began pacing the room.

He watched her in tense silence.

After two circuits, she stopped abruptly and turned to him. "I've changed my mind. This is bad enough for my mother's Thanksgiving."

Bubba hung his head contritely.

"You're just going to have to tell your sisters that we aren't engaged."

"I can't."

"Yes, you can," Patrice insisted. "You say, Ruth, Rochelle, and Raspberry—"

"It's Ruby," he corrected.

"Whatever. You tell them that you lied."

"I can't," Bubba insisted. "They're so happy that I'm finally serious about a girl that it would break their hearts." He looked at Patrice with pleading eyes. "You wouldn't make me break their hearts like that, would you? Not on Thanksgiving."

"Yes, I would." She stared at Bubba. "You do know that we aren't engaged, don't you?"

"We could change that," he said, lowering himself to one knee and gazing up at her with a basset-hound face.

"No," she said, shoving him off balance. "Have you forgotten? I'm in love with Mike. You're in love with David."

"Please," he begged, getting back on the one knee. "Just for the weekend. They leave Sunday afternoon."

"Can't," Patrice insisted, throwing her hands in the air. "No ring." As if that were the only obstacle.

He pulled a ring box from his coat pocket and flipped the lid.

"You bought a ring?" She stared at him anew.

"David picked it out," Bubba said. "I couldn't get away from my sisters."

From five feet away, she looked from his face to the ring. "You're nuts. This thing has to be two carats."

"Two-and-a-half."

"You're serious about this." Now that he wasn't purposely trying to win her over with bad acting, she came close to him.

"Try it on," he suggested, pulling the ring from the box.

She shook her head. "Bubba, this isn't right. It's one thing to pretend to date you, but pretending an engagement..." She looked into his eyes. "I can't."

The hope fled Bubba's eyes, and his shoulders drooped.

"This would do it, Patrice," he said. "If I went to the team dinner engaged to you, all question of my sexual orientation would evaporate."

"But it's a lie, Bubba."

"I've never seen my sisters this happy," Bubba continued, almost to himself. "I just wanted to give them this..."

"But it's a lie, Bubba," Patrice repeated. "And how far would this lie go? Until we are married and have three kids? And what about David, and Mike, and me? What about me, Bubba? Don't I deserve a real romance? A real engagement? Real love?"

"It would have only been for the weekend," he said in apology, putting the ring back into the box.

"I'll still be your date," she said as he got to his feet.

"And still pretend to love me?" he asked, sadly.

"I do love you," Patrice said, laying her hand on his arm. "Just not that way."

Bubba smiled. "I never thought it would hurt to hear a girl say that to me."

Patrice hugged him. "I'm flattered."

Bubba chuckled and kissed the top of her head. "Do you suppose I could tell the guys that you broke my heart so badly when you rejected this ring that I've sworn off women for a while?"

"I was counting on it." She squeezed him tightly. "So..." Patrice said, stepping out of his embrace. "Now that we both know I'm not accepting it, can I see that ring?"

Laurel Bradley

Chapter 26

Patrice slid next to Ruby on the limo's long bench seat. Bubba's sisters were as slim and beautiful as he was big and handsome. Each wore her hair in a different, intricately braided hairdo that must have taken hours to create. None of them resembled the type of woman capable of bullying a grown man into making up a phony engagement.

Rochelle, the oldest of the three, introduced herself and her sisters as Bubba got into the car.

"We are all so glad to finally meet you," she said, giving Patrice's gloved hand a brief squeeze of welcome. "Bubba has always been a bit...shy around women. I think it's from growing up as the only boy with six big sisters. We're a scary bunch."

Patrice laughed. "Oh, I can see that," she said as Bubba slid next to her and covered her left hand with his right. "I'll bet he grew up in terror of playing house."

Rochelle exchanged a glance with Ruby and laughed. "Maybe so. All of us sisters are married, and we've always hoped that Bubba would someday find someone he could be happy with as well. Ruth here is married to a doctor and the mother of three boys. All of whom want to play football like their uncle."

"Bubba is a favorite with all the nieces and nephews.

124

He's so good with kids," Ruth said.

"Which is why it's so good that he has so many nieces and nephews," Ruby said, giving Ruth a pointed look.

Ruby, the youngest sister, was dressed in an exquisitely tailored muted-red pants suit. She greeted Patrice with a hug and a kiss, whispering in her ear. "We have to talk."

As soon as Ruby released her, Bubba pulled Patrice close, draping his right arm around her shoulders and holding her left hand in his.

"So let's see the ring," Ruth said, looking pointedly at the joined hands.

Patrice felt Bubba tense and took pity on him.

"Bubba was a bit premature with his announcement," Patrice said, looking at Bubba.

Bubba looked as if he wanted to kiss Patrice in relief.

"You aren't engaged?" Rochelle asked. There was an emotion in her voice that Patrice was sure wasn't disappointment. It sounded a lot like relief, and, regardless of the reality of the situation, it stung.

"No," Bubba said, squeezing Patrice's hand. "Patrice and I are very close, but she isn't quite ready for that kind of commitment yet."

"Why not?" Ruth asked, pointedly.

"It's none of our business, Ruth," Ruby scolded. "Besides, it's always best to be sure about these things."

Patrice was stunned. Bubba's sisters, or two of them at least, didn't want her marrying Bubba.

"I just think the love of a good woman is good for a man," Ruth said, glaring at Ruby. "I think Patrice is a fine woman. Don't you?"

"We're here," Bubba interrupted, as the limo pulled into quarterback Jake Schaefer's driveway.

Patrice wanted to bolt. No wonder Bubba had embroidered a story to appease these women. They were dangerous.

She should have taken Bubba home with her. Braving her mom's turkey had to be better than this.

Once inside, Patrice stayed by Bubba's side, clinging to his arm more for safety from his sisters than any play-acting on her part. She planned to stay glued to his side until it was time to leave. Unfortunately, even the most devoted lovers must separate if only to wash the turkey grease off their hands.

Patrice opened the bathroom door and walked into the hall. She saw Ruby headed her way and wished she could have ducked back into the restroom, but the door had already closed behind the next person in line.

The best course of action, Patrice decided, was to keep walking. She'd nod her greeting to Ruby, kiss Bubba good-bye, and head to her mother's a little early. If God were listening to her prayers, she'd get out without having to talk with the Scott girls. Maybe there would even be something she could do to save her mother's turkey.

Ruby touched her arm as she tried to hurry past.

"We need to talk."

It was the turkey, wasn't it? Patrice silently asked God. Too much of a miracle, right?

Patrice looked longingly at Bubba as they passed the family room. He was right where she'd left him, sitting on the couch, watching the game along with his teammates. He didn't see her as Ruby led her to a quiet corner.

"You really love him, don't you?" Ruby said when they'd reached the back bedroom where the coats were piled.

Patrice said nothing.

"I was afraid of that," Ruby continued, more to herself than Patrice. "How do I say this?" She looked at Patrice as if for help. "You can't marry my brother."

Patrice narrowed her eyes at Ruby, thinking all kinds of uncomplimentary things about the nosy, meddlesome bitch.

"It's not you," Ruby rushed on. "I think you're nice— just what I'd want for him in a woman. You'd fit in great with the family. It's just that..." Ruby lowered her voice to the smallest whisper and said, "He's gay."

Patrice laughed.

"No, really," Ruby said, trying to convince Patrice.

Patrice laughed louder, tears filling her eyes. She sat down on the edge of the bed, sliding on the coats to the floor.

Finally, wiping tears from her eyes, she was able to look up at Bubba's stunned sister. "I know," she admitted.

"You know?" Ruby picked up a coat and tossed it onto the bed.

Patrice laughed, struggling to her feet with her arms full of coats. "I didn't think you knew. Bubba doesn't think you know. That's why I'm here," Patrice said.

"I don't get it."

Patrice looked around making certain they were alone.

"I'm Bubba's cover," she whispered. "I'm here to make him look straight for his teammates and his sisters."

"Well, it's working," Ruby said with a smile. "My sisters and I were afraid that you'd fallen in love with him, and he was leading you on—pretending to love you for the sake of show. Ruth wanted you to get married and reform him."

Patrice shook her head. "Not possible."

"I know. We just never imagined you were in on it. Are you an actress?"

"No. Chef."

"Good, cuz if you tried to out him or blackmail him, we'd have to hunt you down."

"Don't worry. I'm trying to prevent an outing, not cause one. I'm really just good friends of his and David's. I love them both and wanted to help."

"I knew I liked you," Ruby said, giving Patrice a hug. "My sisters and Mama will be so relieved."

"They know about me?"

"Your pictures have been in the paper and gossip columns, and we all got to wondering."

"Well, now you know." Patrice motioned to the door. "I'm going to go spend a couple of minutes with Bubba before I have to go. I've got Thanksgiving with my family to brave yet."

"I'm glad Bubba has a friend like you," Ruby said as they picked up the last of the fallen coats. "It almost makes me wish..." She shook her head. "We stopped wishing for the impossible years ago. It's best to love things and people the way they are instead of trying to change them."

"I can't believe you know," Patrice laughed. "Bubba thinks he has you fooled."

Ruby smiled. "Of course. But don't worry about it. He'll tell us when he's ready."

Stepping over and around various football players and their wives, Patrice and Bubba wove their way out of the family room to retrieve Patrice's coat.

They went as a couple to thank their hosts, Jake and Lindsey.

"You aren't leaving yet, are you, Bubba?" asked Jake.

"I'm afraid not, Jake. My sisters and I are here for the duration. Patrice was able to juggle her schedule to be with me for a while, but..."

"Now I have to go," Patrice finished for him. "Thank you so much for having me. You have a lovely home."

"I'm still so embarrassed to serve a famous chef turkey drumsticks," Lindsey admitted.

"It was delicious!" Patrice leaned closer to her hostess and lowered her voice in confession. "Honestly, Lindsey, I get so tired of gourmet food."

"She's not kidding," Bubba joined in. "She's always making pot roast or jambalaya for me. She makes a killer meatloaf."

While it was true that she often cooked for Bubba and David, Patrice blushed at the implication that she was living with Bubba.

Jake and Lindsey exchanged looks and smiled.

Bubba walked Patrice to the door.

"I've instructed the driver to take you home." He lowered his voice. "Are they still watching?" he asked, referring to Jake and Lindsey and a couple of other players and their wives who'd migrated near the entryway and were pretending not to watch Bubba and Patrice.

"Yes." She smiled. "Let's make it look good."

They kissed—long and slow. It was weird kissing Bubba like that. He was as proficient as Mike was—firm tongue, good technique, no extra moisture—but there was no spark, no fireworks. It was amazing how one had time to think and evaluate a kiss when emotions didn't come to play. With Mike there was no thinking, just feeling—Roman candles with the smallest peck. With Bubba...well, she wasn't disappointed when it was over.

Chapter 27

Mike was sitting on the couch drinking beer and watching football when Randy walked into the living room. "Have fun at your folks'."

"Thanks." Randy pulled his coat from the closet. "What are you doing for turkey dinner?"

"TV dinner."

"You're lucky. Mom is deep-frying the turkey. I'd invite you over, but I like you too much."

"Thanks. What did Patrice say when she heard?" Mike asked, taking a sip.

"No one told her. She probably won't be hungry anyway. She's at Jake Schaefer's mansion gnawing on a drumstick with Bubba and the Bears. I'm going to have to get on that girl," he joked. "You'd think she could have taken me, her only brother. Imagine watching football with the team?" he said, his voice full of longing. "If she's smart, she'll forget to go to Mom's and won't know about the fire engines until she watches the news."

"You're afraid your mother will burn the house down?"

"Let's just say that when I asked Dad what I could bring, he suggested a fire extinguisher."

"Why doesn't she just let your cook take care of it? Isn't that why you have her?"

"Beats me. I don't get into it."

"Probably for the best." Mike tried to figure out a way to reintroduce the topic of Patrice without sounding obsessed. "How's your mom handling Patrice dating Bubba?"

"Patrice claims they aren't."

"Does your mom believe that? They were at that charity thing together."

"Yeah, Mom had a fit that night, and when their pictures were all over the society section, she had another one. Patrice swears that they're just friends."

"Do you believe it?" Mike tried to sound casual, even though he was being eaten up inside. He'd thought he and Patrice were off to a good start. But what was she doing with Bubba? He told himself that it must be a standing engagement. Damn. What did she really feel for him? Did he stand a chance against Bubba? Did she kiss Bubba? Mike thought of their kisses. Did she kiss Bubba like that?

"Who knows? He's a rich, handsome guy, and he seems real nice. She could do worse."

"You mean me."

"Man, are you touchy," Randy said. The animosity that had been between them the other night seemed to have burned out. "No. I didn't mean you."

"Sorry, Randy. I guess I'm not used to being on the outs with your family."

"Just give it time, Mike. By Christmas you'll be calling Patrice 'The Pest,' and she'll be wearing Bubba Scott's ring and laughing. Just kidding," he rushed to say. "Seriously, though, you really don't want Mom's deep fried bird. Hell, I really don't want Mom's deep fried bird. If I could get out of it, I'd go eat Lean Cuisine with you."

"Thanks," Mike said.

Chapter 28

Friday, Mike stopped at a florist on the way back from court and picked a perfect, long-stemmed yellow rose from the bucket of roses on the floor. Patrice loved yellow roses.

"Do you want this in a vase?" the woman behind the counter asked, taking it from him.

"No, just the rose."

He arrived at the door of Patrice's apartment building just as a man with a dozen roses covered in plastic was buzzed in.

"Here, let me get that for you." Mike reached around to get the door.

"Thanks," the man said, heading straight for the elevator.

Mike took the stairs as usual, pausing outside the fire door to remove the protective plastic from the bud. He folded the bag and tucked it into the pocket of his overcoat before tugging open the door. On the way down the hall, he saw the floral deliveryman walk back to the elevator, tucking his tip in his front pocket.

Mike knocked on Patrice's door.

She was dressed for work in white blouse and slacks. Her hair was French braided, but not yet coiled into the bun that she wore when cooking.

"Hi, Mike." She sounded happy to see him, but surprised. "I thought you were in court today."

"We settled. Then, walking to my car, I passed a little flower shop and remembered how much you like yellow roses. So I bought you one." He took the flower from behind his back and presented her with it.

"Thank you. It's beautiful." She beamed at him a moment before giving him a thank you kiss. He would have given her the world for another kiss, but she stepped out of his arms to smell the rose.

She was so beautiful standing there inhaling the rose's perfume, all in white with the white wall as backdrop—white on white. It brought out the soft colors of her skin and the yellow of the rose and the riot of red flowers on the coffee table. His eyes focused on the red flowers. Roses. They were roses. The man had delivered a dozen blood-red roses to Patrice moments ago, yet she stood sniffing the single bud he'd given her as if it were the most wonderful of gifts.

He felt small and unworthy—and angry. He left Patrice sniffing her flower and strode to the bouquet on the table.

Patrice looked up from the yellow rose and cursed the timing. Mike had brought her a wonderfully fragrant rose, her favorite flower, in an unexpected, perfectly romantic gesture inspired by affection and whimsy. Bubba had sent a dozen red roses as a thank you. Looking at Mike, she knew he wouldn't see the difference. He wouldn't know what each meant. He'd read Bubba's card, and it would ruin everything.

"What does this mean?" Mike asked, holding up the card he'd taken from the vase. "'You were perfect. Thank you, Bubba.' Now what the hell does that mean?" he demanded.

Patrice took one last breath of rose-scented air before letting the dream of romance fade into the reality of confrontation. Mike had no right to read the card much less question her about it.

"Just what it says. I did a favor for Bubba and he's thanking me."

"What kind of favor?" Mike asked, unreasonably.

"A little one," Patrice assured him. "I went to a

132

Thanksgiving dinner with him."

"And that deserves flowers?"

Patrice shrugged, determined not to be offended. "It was a team dinner, and his sisters were there."

"And that's all?" Mike's voice was laced with sarcasm. "That's how you were perfect?"

Patrice's kept her voice calm and friendly. "Yes. What did you think it meant?"

"I think a dozen roses is thank you for a bit more than dinner." Mike winced as if he'd realized his mistake as soon as he'd made it.

Patrice's eyes narrowed, and her voice grew chill. "I see." She pointed the yellow rose at Mike. "So...what is this a thank you for?"

"Nothing." Mike rubbed the back of his neck. "It was a symbol of affection."

"Uh, huh," Patrice said skeptically, crossing her arms in front of her. "Are you sure it's not a thank you for kisses or anything more?" Patrice asked.

Mike winced. "No," he protested. "I'm sorry, Pet. I blew it again. I gave you the flower because I thought you'd like it, and I wanted to make you smile. And now I've gone and screwed everything up again."

Patrice just stared at him, waiting.

"And Bubba was just thanking you for doing him a favor. Hey," Mike said with forced enthusiasm, "what a nice guy."

Patrice looked at her watch. "It's time for you to go. I have to get to work."

"Damn it, Patrice," Mike said, grabbing her arms. "I blew it. I'm sorry. Don't send me away mad."

"Are you mad?" Patrice asked, purposely misunderstanding him.

"Mad for you."

Patrice rolled her eyes. Yeah, right.

"But I meant you. Don't send me away when you're angry."

She shook Mike's hands from her arms. "I don't have time for this. I have to get ready for work."

"Patrice," Mike begged, "don't do this again."

She turned on him. "Don't do what, Mike? Cook? Have friends? I'm not the one who insinuated that Bubba sent me flowers because I went to bed with him."

Mike's face turned the color of Bubba's roses. "I didn't..."

"Didn't you?" Patrice demanded.

Mike cringed.

"I think it's time you left." She turned her back on him.

"I'm sorry, Patrice. I was stupid. I was jealous. Forgive me. Please, Patrice."

"Don't beg," she said sadly.

"Please, Pet." He put his hand on her shoulder.

She shrugged it off. "Just go." Her voice was full of tears.

He put his arms around her, turning her resistant body to face him.

"I love you," he said, lowering his lips to hers.

She bit him, drawing blood.

"Ouch."

"Go," she directed, pointing at the door.

His eyes opened wide. "You bit me."

She crossed her arms over her chest. "You lied to me."

"I did not. I do love you."

"If this is your love—thinking I'm easy and doubting my word—then..." she stumbled, searching for words, "...then...keep it to yourself."

"You don't mean that," Mike insisted. "You're just angry."

"And you are so clueless. Leave and take your 'thanks-for-letting-me-feel-you-up' flower with you."

"Damn! Damn! Damn it to hell!" Mike shouted. "I will not leave until we work things out."

"Then stay here," Patrice said, grabbing her purse, coat and a thick file folder. "I'll be back at ten-thirty." She stormed out of her apartment, firmly closing the door behind her.

Mike stood in the silence of her entryway, wondering how he could have made things go so wrong. Again. He went into her living room and sat on the couch.

He was good with words, good with bringing two sides together and solving problems, but he didn't seem able to do it with Patrice. Why?

He paced her living room, but stopped mid-stride to pick up a framed snapshot of them dancing at her sweet-sixteen party. She was radiant—a young beauty, leaning toward him with rapt attention as if hanging on his every word. She gazed at him with love and adoration written in her eyes.

He looked at himself in the photo. He was the picture of calm reserve—a bored man-of-the-world doing his duty dancing with the younger sister of a friend—in everything but the eyes. His eyes reflected the feelings held in hers.

He remembered the moment that photo had been taken. He remembered what he'd been thinking. It was there, clearly captured in his eyes in case he'd forgotten. He'd been wishing she were five years older and not the sister of his best friend. He'd been wishing he could make her his. And he could have that night. A few moments after the photo was snapped, he'd pulled her closer, and she'd leaned into his erection and looked at him as if she were about to suggest something. He'd passed her off to her brother, changing partners mid-dance to avoid the possibility of the question. He remembered he'd gotten laid that night. Some girl whose name he couldn't remember took Patrice's place in the back seat of his car.

Damn. He's been blowing it with Patrice for years. He needed to break the pattern. He needed to win her back and quit screwing up. But how? Flowers obviously weren't the answer. He didn't know what he was going to do to convince her that he loved her, but he needed to be here when she got home to do it. Unfortunately, he also needed to return to work.

Making a brief and fruitless search for a spare apartment key, he grabbed a roll of packaging tape from a drawer and used it to tape the latch inside the door. He opened and closed the door several times to make certain that it didn't lock.

He closed the door and left the building to plan his next move.

Chapter 29

It took Patrice nearly the entire walk to Victor's to calm down and look at the situation from Mike's point of view. She was fairly certain that he'd bought the flower for the right reasons. And she'd known, as soon as she saw him outside her door, that the timing of Bubba's flowers couldn't have been worse. She hadn't had time to toss the card—something she knew would be taken the wrong way by anyone who saw it. She couldn't really blame Mike for the assumptions he'd drawn, but she did. Shouldn't he know her well enough to know that she wouldn't crawl in bed with any man without love and commitment? Didn't he know she loved him? Couldn't he figure out that Bubba was just a friend?

Okay. Maybe not. Maybe she was being the unreasonable one. Maybe biting his lip to keep from melting into his arms had been a bit excessive. Maybe she'd been the one who'd blown it this time. Maybe she'd have to apologize.

She paused outside the service door to Victor's. No, she smiled. She wouldn't apologize. She'd just accept his apology. And maybe, after she'd accepted it, she'd explain about Bubba.

Maybe.

****

At ten-fifteen, Victor insisted on driving Patrice home.

"Thanks for the ride," she said, barely managing to give him a tired smile as they drove the four blocks to her apartment building. "I could have walked."

"You put in a long day. I couldn't let you walk home in this." He gestured at the rain that was coating everything with ice. "You'd fall, break something, and end up spending months in traction. I'd have to cancel the holiday parties. I'd go broke." He smiled at her.

"I don't know. We've a good crew. I think they'd manage just fine." She yawned as the car slid to a stop outside her building. "Spending a month in bed sounds good about now. I could skip the traction, though."

She got out of the car and walked gingerly up the sidewalk to her building, arms spread wide for balance. When she reached the door, she smiled with relief and waved Victor off.

She'd meant to look at her window before entering the building, but had forgotten in her quest to reach the front door on her feet rather than her butt.

He won't be there. You know he won't be there, she told herself as she trudged up the stairs. She never took the elevator if she could help it. Walking to work and taking the stairs was her nod at aerobic exercise. She convinced herself that it was okay that he wasn't there as she left the stairwell and walked down the hall to her door. More than okay. It was good. She was too tired to deal with him tonight anyway. She'd do yoga and go to bed.

She slid the key into the lock and opened the door to a candlelit apartment. Cream colored tapers and pillar candles glowed from every table filling the room with flickering light and the homey smell of vanilla. The roses were nowhere to be seen.

"You're early," Mike said from across the room. He slipped a CD into the stereo and walked toward Patrice as Natalie Cole's sultry tones filled the air with her father's old standards.

"I got a ride," Patrice said, trying to hide her relief at his presence by sliding off her coat.

"It must be raining." He drew his finger across her

cheek, wiping off a droplet. He took her coat and hung it in the closet.

Blood surged through Patrice's veins, banishing the chill, but making her shiver involuntarily.

"Cold?" His hazel eyes seemed to look into her soul.

"A little," she lied. The look in his eyes had made her warm. "You didn't stay here all day," she said. He had changed from his suit into faded jeans and a smoky blue chamois shirt, and she didn't own this many candles. "How did you get back in?"

"I'm resourceful." He turned from her to pour a bottle of Pinot Grigio that had been breathing in an ice bucket on the sofa table.

"I can see that." She took the glass of wine he offered. Their fingers met momentarily—a planned accident on Mike's part—and desire flared between them. "Thank you." She brought the glass to her lips. The chilled liquid danced around her tongue. "It's very nice."

"Thank you." He gently guided her to the living room with a hand at the small of her back. They sat on the sofa—a bit closer than Patrice was comfortable with.

"I'm still angry with you," she said, though it was an effort to remember why at the moment.

"I know." He draped his arm around her shoulder and started raining little kisses along the side of her neck. "I'm trying to make you forget."

"It's working," she admitted. "But it will be worse when I remember if we don't talk about it first."

"Damn," he sighed, giving her neck one last nibble before sitting up straight. "You taste so good."

She gave him a disbelieving look. "I smell like a greasy kitchen, and I a need a shower."

"I'll help," he offered, playfully.

She snorted a laugh. "Sorry."

"Then I'll wait. It'll give me a chance to gather my thoughts together for our talk."

Patrice eyed Mike disbelievingly, but then got up from the couch and, taking her wine with her, mounted the stairs to the loft.

Patrice locked the bathroom door, turned on the faucet, and undressed while she waited for the water to get hot. Mike was there. He hadn't waited for her, but he'd come back. What did he want?

She stepped into the shower, letting the hot water pound away the tension. Washing her hair, she asked herself again—what did Mike want? Were his declarations of love to be believed?

She rinsed her hair and soaped her body, her hands lingering on her breasts. What did she want—other than Mike's hands to replace hers? She was almost afraid to give words to the desire she'd held in her heart for so long.

She wanted to be Mike's wife.

Fifteen minutes later, with her hair newly dry and her face still rosy from the shower, Patrice descended the stairs in a navy sweater and well-worn jeans, her empty wine glass in hand.

"You look much more comfortable." Mike took the wine glass from her. "Here, let me fill that for you."

Patrice sat on the couch, tucking her bare feet beneath her.

Mike returned with the wine and sat next to her.

"I'm sorry," Mike said, before things could get any more awkward. "I seem to be saying that to you all the time now. I want things to be good between us. I know they will be, but we've got to get through this awkward stage first."

"We're in a stage?" Patrice asked. "You have enough experience to call this a stage?"

"No," Mike hurried to say. "I didn't say that right. I don't have any experience with this." He shook his head, staring at the table. "What is wrong with me?" he berated himself aloud. He looked at Patrice, pleading for understanding. "What I wanted to say is that I know we are new as a couple."

"Are we a couple?" she asked.

His heart clenched. "I hope so. I know you aren't sure of me yet. I don't blame you. I know I can't expect you to drop every other guy in your life just because I've finally decided to admit the truth. All I ask is that you give me a chance to prove myself. Could you please hold off making any commitments to Bubba or anyone else for a while?"

"For how long?" she asked. How long did he think it would take him to win the heart he already held?

"Until after New Years."

"Okay." She wanted to throw herself at him now, not wait until after Christmas.

"Oh, God," he moaned, grabbing her.

Their lips met.

Patrice put all of her love into the kiss. Stupid, idiot—how could he not know what she was feeling? How many times and in how many ways must she show him before he understood that it had always been him, would always be him?

She felt his hands cup her breasts and fought for control of her raging hormones. Could she give him the time he needed to prove to himself that his love was real? Could she control her desire for him until after the wedding? Would she even make it to the engagement?

She forced herself to push on his shoulders and break the kiss.

Mike sat back, panting. "Wow. I hope you never kiss Bubba like that."

Patrice punched him.

"That isn't what I meant," Mike protested. "What I meant was—"

She cut him off. "Time to go home, Mike."

Mike groaned. "Not again." He followed her to the entryway, talking the entire time. "I didn't mean it about Bubba. Well, I did, but—damn it, Patrice, why do I do this with you?"

"Because you love me?" she asked lightly as she got his coat.

He stared at her. "Yes."

She opened the door.

"Can we talk about this?" he asked as she pushed him through the door.

"No."

Reluctantly, he stepped into the hallway.

"Oh, and Mike?"

He looked at her, his eyes full of hope and fear.

"I only kiss you like that." She closed the door and flipped the dead bolt, leaning against it to keep herself from opening the door and dragging the fool up to bed.

Chapter 30

The next morning Patrice awakened to the telephone. "Buzz me in," Mike's voice demanded.

She hung up the phone and stumbled down the stairs. She buzzed him in, unlocked her door, and went to the bathroom. She had time to run upstairs to brush her teeth before Mike knocked.

"It's open," she called. Apparently unable to hear her voice, Mike knocked again. She raced downstairs in her flannel jammies to answer the door.

"Man, are you cute," Mike commented, giving her the once over before pulling her into his arms. "Do you always wear flannel to bed?"

"Only when it's cold." She gave him a quick peck before sliding from his arms to close the door. "Sorry, I'm not dressed. I was sleeping when you called."

"I figured as much. I rang your bell for five straight minutes before I called."

Patrice shrugged. "It's Saturday. I don't get up at," she looked at the clock. "...eight? You're at my apartment at eight? You didn't leave here until midnight. Don't you sleep?"

He ran his hand down her arm. Flannel had never been an aphrodisiac before, but it was certainly turning him on. "Not when it's one of the few times we both don't have to work."

"I have a lot of time off," Patrice protested. "I only have to work Friday and Saturday nights and those parties I want to."

"That might be what your contract says, but you work a lot more than that—every night except Sunday, Monday, and Tuesday from what I can tell."

Patrice shrugged. "I don't mind. I have my days free most of the time, and I really like my job. Did I tell you that Victor has given me free rein to change the menus?"

"He'd be a fool not to. You've done wonders for his business."

"It's a symbiotic relationship—we do wonders for each other."

"Is he another one of your conquests? Do I have to worry about him too?"

Patrice laughed. "Victor is the most happily married man I know, and he's about to become a grandpa sometime after the New Year. He's so excited it's cute."

"Victor, cute? I can't imagine. He strikes me as a shoot first, ask questions later kind of guy."

"You don't know Victor," Patrice laughed.

No, Mike thought, remembering the little welcome scene Victor had arranged for him, you don't know Victor. "Let's go out to breakfast, and then I'll take you wherever you'd like to go."

"Sounds good, but let me make breakfast." Patrice walked into the kitchen. "I'll start the coffee and get dressed while it's brewing."

"I can make the coffee," he suggested.

"Okay." She smiled. "The coffee maker and grinder are in the appliance garage, and the coffee is in the freezer."

He watched her leave the kitchen, thinking how homey it was to make coffee for her. He was turning into a sap. He poked his head out of the kitchen and watched her ascend the stairs. He called out to her, "Think about what you'd like to do today."

"Oh, no problem there. I already know what I want to do," she said before disappearing into her bedroom.

She liked to do that, he realized. Say something that had an impact on him and then leave. She'd always done that, he remembered. She always left him thinking about her. Did she have that effect on everyone?

Over blueberry pancakes, Mike brought up the subject again. "So what is it you want to do?"

Patrice looked up from her plate. "I want to get a Christmas tree."

"That won't take long. They've got some nice ones at the gas station."

"No. I want to drive somewhere out of the city and cut one down. I have the address of a place right here." She handed him an ad she'd torn out of the newspaper.

"Sleigh rides, hot cocoa, and Christmas trees. Sounds like fun. Too bad the rain last night wasn't snow. It would have been fun to tromp through the snow to get it."

"It snowed there. I called while I was upstairs."

"Where is this place? Outside of Rockford—that's what—an hour-and-a-half out? That'll be a nice drive."

After stopping at Mike's house long enough to pick up work gloves, padding for the roof, twine, and a saw, they drove into winter, listening to Christmas carols.

"Maybe I'll get one for the house as well," Mike said.

"I didn't know you guys did a tree."

"Oh, yes. We do a tree every year. I'm lights, Randy is garland, and Alex is ornaments."

"You don't do it all together?"

"We want to remain friends."

Patrice laughed. "Tell me about your tree—what does it look like?"

"Remember the snowflake tree my mom used to have?"

"The one with silver snowflake garland and blue and white lights?"

"That's the one."

"Yeah, I remember it. She had those crocheted snowflakes all over it."

"Yeah, that's the one."

"Oh." She bit her lip.

"I'm not all that fond of it myself," Mike admitted. "But we have to have a tree, and I'm not shopping for ornaments."

"Oh. I guess that means stopping at the Christmas Store is out," Patrice teased.

"Not necessarily. I don't mind it if you shop for ornaments; I just don't want to do it. That kind of shopping is a couple thing, not a guy-by-himself kind of thing."

Patrice chuckled. "I understand."

"So, did you want to go to the Christmas Store before or after we get the trees?"

"Neither, I was just yanking your chain," she said. "I know you hate that kind of thing."

"And I know that you and your mom exchange special ornaments every year. So, we'll go to the Christmas Store first so that you won't feign exhaustion afterwards to spare me. Besides, I told you I'd take you anywhere you wanted to go today, and I meant it."

He'd take her to the moon if she'd let him.

The Christmas Store, an indoor forest of decorated trees, was crowded with shoppers. Had Mike been alone, he would have never gone in, but for Patrice...

She disappeared almost immediately, losing him in the glittering grove. Shrugging, he decided to look while he waited for her to reappear.

He'd never shopped for ornaments before—never even considered it. Christmas shopping was a last-minute search-and-rescue operation for him—in and out. It was kind of nice, wandering amongst the trees while Christmas music filled the cedar-scented air. Someone handed him a cookie and a cup of cider as he browsed.

He munched, sipped, and looked at the trees. He focused on a tree trimmed with the twelve days of Christmas ornaments. Grinning, he picked up the boxed set. What better way to stay in Patrice's mind than to give her these ornaments one at a time?

He meandered his way toward the checkout counter, looking at trees as he went along. By coincidence, he found himself in front of a tree adorned in shiny Old World ornaments. Right in front of his eyes, as if it had been placed there just for him, was a pink-cheeked, blond chef carrying a pink, white, and gold cake that said, "Mine."

As he slipped it from the branch, the cookie and cider lady appeared at his elbow.

"Can you ship these?"

"Certainly." She took the ornaments from him. "Oh, dear, I thought we'd sent all of these back," she said, holding the chef ornament aloft. "You don't want this, sir. It's flawed. It was part of a Valentine collection and was supposed to say, 'Be Mine.' See," she pointed to the top of the cake. "Anyway, we have some other nice chef ornaments if that's what you're looking for."

"I want that one," he said. Mine, he thought. She's going to be mine as I've always been hers.

Chapter 31

Big snowflakes drifted gently to the ground as they pulled into the tree farm's parking lot. At the edge of the lot, two large Belgian draft horses waited patiently for the hay wagon on runners to exchange loads of passengers. Tugging on hats and mittens, Mike and Patrice raced across the lot to join the group of families waiting for their turn to embark.

Once the wagon was filled, the driver climbed into his seat and gave a word of welcome as the sleigh lurched into motion.

They passed snow-covered trees as they glided through the picture-perfect setting. The bells on the horses' harnesses rang cheerfully as the Belgians pulled, prompting a chorus of "Jingle Bells" from the occupants of the sleigh.

"It feels like we're in a Christmas special," Patrice whispered.

"Whose?" Mike asked.

"I don't know, but it must be someone big—they're using real snow."

Mike laughed, watching Patrice as she joined the singing. Her cheeks were pink, and her eyes bright. Fat snowflakes landed on her purple hat and clung to her hair and eyelashes. It couldn't have been more perfect. He looked at the families lining the wagon—moms and dads smiling as their children laughed and sang—and felt, for the first time ever, a longing for kids of his own. He looked back at Patrice. She was looking out of the wagon, watching the world go by. Someday they'd do this with their own kids. Maybe even make it a family tradition.

Mike grinned to himself. Boy, Tucker, you have it so bad.

****

"This is it," Patrice announced pointing to a Frazer tree three feet from the main path.

"You're kidding, right? You haven't even looked at any others."

"You can look if you like, but this is the one I want."

"I'll tag it, if you insist," Mike said, humoring her. "But you can change you mind after you've seen a few others."

"What kind do you want?"

"Balsam."

They trudged through the snow, carrying the saw for another fifteen minutes before Mike stopped at a tree near where they'd started. "I'll take this one," he said.

"I thought you wanted a Balsam."

"I like this one better."

Patrice laughed. "Well, too bad. You can't have it—it's mine." She showed him her tag.

"Damn. How did you do that? It was the first tree you saw. How did you know it would be the best?"

"I know what I like."

"But how can you can make your mind up without seeing what else is out there?" he demanded.

"Easy. When it's right, why not grab it if you can. If you wait long enough, someone else will notice how great it is and try to take it."

He wished he'd learned that lesson earlier.

Chapter 32

Patrice went to Doctor Delicious on Sunday as usual. She was able to park right outside the store, an oddity even for a Sunday. More than normal, the Chicago breeze was blowing, and snowflakes swirled in the eddy caused by the surrounding buildings. She opened the door, coming in from the snow. Three tables were occupied. She'd half expected to have the place to herself. A winter storm advisory interrupted the music on the radio.

"Hi, David. How was your Thanksgiving?"

"Depressing as usual. Mom was in rare form, and Dad didn't say a word. Carmen's so pregnant, she's ready to pop. She and Devon stopped by with the boys on the way to Devon's folks'. They were there all of twenty minutes before Dad shooed them out."

"Oh, David," Patrice sympathized. His father didn't want David's gayness rubbing off on his grandsons.

He sighed. "I don't know why I bother."

"Because, despite it all, you're a good son."

David snorted.

"Did you survive Bubba's sisters' visit?" she asked.

"I did fine, but not as well as you. You wowed 'em, girl."

Patrice smiled and spread her coat in a curtsy. "I'd like to thank the Academy..."

"Before you get too far into your acceptance speech, I should warn you—you have an audience." He pointed toward a table near the inside wall.

Patrice glanced over her shoulder. "Alex." She smiled, leaving the counter to meet him halfway across the dining area for a hug. "I didn't see you when I came in. You're back early," she said, stepping back from the greeting. "I thought you said you wouldn't be getting back until tonight."

"I thought I'd beat the storm to the city and see you."

"Well, I'm glad you're back and safe. Did you have a good time?"

"Great time. It's always fun when the family gets together—nieces and nephews all over the place. It makes the loop at rush hour seem quiet in comparison, but I love it. I can't wait to get back for Christmas."

"If you miss your family so much, why do you live so far away?"

"Michigan is the perfect distance. I'm close without being too close."

"I understand. There are some days I'd like to go back to Paris."

"Was Thanksgiving that bad, or was it today's pot roast?"

"Both. My mother deep-fried the turkey, and— surprisingly—it turned out edible. Now she thinks that deep-frying is her cooking niche."

"She made fondue? That can't be so bad."

"Fondue would have been fine. She deep-fried the entire roast. There was grease everywhere. I got there just in time to put the fire out. I'm afraid their cook is going to take one look at that kitchen and quit, and then my dad will move in with me." She groaned.

"Oh, Doctor," Alex shouted across the room. "Bring Patrice something soothing—like..." He dropped his voice "...I don't suppose mashed potatoes and gravy would be good as ice cream."

"Not very comforting either. My mother is dangerous with potatoes, and I don't even want to think about her gravy."

Alex nodded before raising his voice and instructing David once again. "Something soothing like French chocolate and peanut butter."

David came out from behind the counter, bowl in hand. "You have the right idea. You just need a little training to be great," he told Alex. "You are right that she needs something smooth and creamy—something that will melt in her mouth and slide down her throat without any effort. Peanut butter, though normally a comfort food, is in this case counter-indicated. She's dealt with her nutty mother all afternoon. She needs something cool and soothing to make her forget grease fires and good meat prepared poorly. She needs—" he set the bowl in front of her with a flourish "—my special smooth peppermint." He handed Patrice a spoon, but continued to direct his comments to Alex. "No candy chunks, mind, and not a grasshopper green. She needs the subtle swirls of pale pink and green in the richness of cream to calm her mind and soothe her spirit." David watched Patrice's face as she took the first spoonful and sighed. "See," he told Alex with satisfaction.

"You're an artist," Alex said in exaggerated awe.

David bowed his head in modest acknowledgement. "It's a gift."

Patrice laughed through her nose, trying to swallow her ice cream without choking.

The chimes on the door jangled. David looked up.

"Better have another spoonful," he told Patrice as he left the table. "You're going to need it."

Patrice and Alex looked up as one. Mike stood just inside the door, looking at them as he brushed snow from his coat. Patrice only saw Mike for a moment before David positioned his body to block the view.

Patrice turned to Alex with a panicked look.

"Don't worry," Alex, reassured her. "Mike knows we've been out."

"Oh, great," Patrice groaned.

"No, it's okay. He's fine with it."

Patrice raised one brow. "Really?"

"Okay. Maybe 'fine' is too strong a word, but he's committed to let you decide."

"Oh. Great." She rolled her eyes.

Alex winced.

Patrice heard Mike and David's verbal sparring from

across the room.

"I'm impressed that you're this busy in the middle of a snow storm," Mike said, obviously trying to be nice.

"It's really not ice cream weather. I'm thinking of closing early." There were too many customers for there to be any truth to David's comment.

Patrice frowned. He wasn't going to play nice. And Mike wasn't going to back down.

"I can see that," Mike said. "But I think I'll stay anyway."

Patrice closed her eyes and shook her head. What was she going to do? She opened her eyes in time to see David slip behind the counter.

It was either slide beneath the table or wave. She chose to wave.

"You want something?" David asked in the same tone a punk would use to say, "You want a piece of me?"

Mike turned to answer him and Patrice's stomach cramped around the two spoonfuls of ice cream. Please, God.

Mike ordered a small dish of ice cream and walked to their table.

"Hi, Pet. I'd hoped you'd be here." Mike kissed Patrice on the cheek. "Alex." He extended his hand in greeting. "How was your Thanksgiving?" The men shook hands and exchanged pleasantries as if nothing was wrong. Alex asked Mike to join them and he did.

There was something wrong with that, wasn't there? Patrice swallowed the bile rising in her throat.

"Did you get your tree decorated?" Mike asked Patrice, and then, before she had a chance to answer, draped his arm around the back of her chair and proceeded to tell Alex all about their trip to the tree farm.

Mike was marking his territory. Patrice looked at Alex, who didn't seem to notice.

David arrived at the table, slapping a dish of ice cream in front of Mike. "Here you go, Tucker." The dish wobbled precariously, causing Mike to grab it with both hands.

He looked into his bowl as if he expected to see something other than ice cream. "What is it?"

"Mocha," David said, leaving.

"I don't like mocha," Mike called after him.

"Good."

Alex laughed. "I don't think he likes you."

Mike frowned at his bowl.

"Here, take mine," Alex said. "I like Mocha."

"What is yours?"

"Death by Chocolate with white chocolate chips and chunks of strawberries." He raised his head and called out to David, "Yo, Doctor, what did you call mine?"

"Sweet Success. Don't give it to the loser. He's meant to have the mocha." David glared at Mike. "Don't be a baby, Tucker. Taste it. It's what you were meant to have."

While Mike looked into his bowl, the door chimed again.

"Bubba, great to see you again." David announced the new arrival as if he hadn't seen him in months instead of that morning over breakfast. "And Jake Schaefer and Larry Young. What brings you out in the snow? You looking for a sure-fire recipe for an easy win against the Vikings tomorrow night?"

Patrice cursed under her breath. What else could possibly go wrong?

Bubba laughed. "Wouldn't hurt. We're just here for the ice cream and to see my Pet." Bubba walked to the table, his teammates trailing behind.

"Bubba!" Patrice forced a smile as she sprang from the table and rushed into his arms for a wet kiss. "Your timing stinks," she whispered against his lips.

"Just this last time, please." He kissed her again.

When he finally released her, she noticed that both Mike and Alex had risen. Mike's expression was unreadable. "Bubba, you remember Mike. He's an old friend of my family," she gestured toward Mike. "And this is his roommate Alex Masterson." She turned to Jake and Larry. "Jake Schaefer and Larry Young; Mike Tucker and Alex Masterson."

Alex was clearly thrilled to be in the presence of three Bears' starters and launched a flurry of questions about past plays. Jake and Larry answered while Bubba ordered, and Mike stared daggers at Patrice.

Tables were pulled together, autographs signed, and it wasn't long before everyone was settled. Patrice found herself seated between Bubba and Jake, directly across the table from Mike. Every time she looked, Mike was staring at her.

"Aren't you late for an appointment, Tucker?" David asked, distributing heaping bowls to the table.

"Nope. I wouldn't miss this for the world," he said, staring at Patrice.

"Mike, you haven't touched your ice cream," Bubba commented. "Maybe you should get him something else," he told David.

"No," David answered. "If he's going to stay, he's going to eat mocha. It's the perfect ice cream for him tonight."

"The Doctor always serves the perfect ice cream. It's his trademark," Alex informed Jake and Larry. "In fact, all anyone ever tells him is the size of bowl they want. The Doctor selects the perfect combination of tastes and textures for each person."

"Alex is in advertising," Patrice said, involving herself in the conversation so she wouldn't have to look at Mike.

"I'm thinking of hiring him," David added. "Never know when you can use a good PR guy, right, Mike?"

"What business are you in?" Larry asked Mike.

"Law."

"You must have seen his picture in the paper," David added. "A couple of weeks ago he made partner and created quite a scene by dumping dessert on Patrice."

"David!" Patrice glared at her friend. She wanted to grab him by the neck and shake him.

Jake turned to stare at Mike. "That was you? I thought you and Patrice were old friends."

"Their families are," Alex piped in. "Or were."

Everyone but Mike and Patrice laughed.

"Stop this." Patrice elbowed Bubba.

Bubba got the hint and turned the conversation to football.

The discussion was lively and upbeat. Even Mike joined in—friends with the guys now that the teasing was done. Patrice slapped on a smile, pretended to laugh when the others laughed, and wondered how she'd explain tonight to Mike. If they were still talking, that is. Never had she wished to be somewhere else as fervently as she wished it that moment.

By the time Jake and Larry left, the snow was over an inch deep and still coming down in heavy, wet flakes. Mike left just before Bubba's teammates without saying a word to Patrice. She felt his loss like a blow to the stomach, but she was determined not to show it. The shop had emptied as the storm intensified, leaving only Alex, Patrice, Bubba, and David.

Patrice walked with Alex to the coats. As he put his on, he wished her luck. "I'll tell Mike I'm out of the running too. We'll console each other."

"What does that mean?"

Alex glanced meaningfully at Bubba. "It's so obvious, Patrice. There is something between you two. If I'd seen you with him before, I'd have known I never stood a chance. But I'm glad I didn't know if only for a short time. You're what a guy wants in a girl—you're smart, funny, beautiful, and a fabulous cook. I just wish I'd have met you sooner. That's what's going to kill Mike. He knew you before you met Bubba. He had a chance. Hell, he had more than a chance, and he blew it. He's going to spend a lot of time kicking himself—the fool." He smiled at Patrice and kissed her cheek. "You'll invite me to the wedding, won't you?"

She didn't have time to answer before Bubba joined them.

"Why is it that every time I look for you, you're with another handsome guy?" Bubba asked, holding her coat for her.

"Jealous?" she teased, sliding her arms into the sleeves.

Bubba looked from Patrice to Alex and then back again. "Should I be?"

Patrice laughed at the question in his eye, knowing that Alex would misinterpret the conversation.

"No," both Alex and Patrice answered as one.

Bubba looked Alex in the eye. "I didn't think so."

Bubba touched Patrice's arm, urging her to stay as Alex left. "Thanks for tonight. Sometime in the next few weeks, you'll break my heart and we'll be done."

"It might be tonight," Patrice cautioned, turning her

head to watch David put the chairs on the tables in preparation for cleaning the floor.

"What?" Bubba followed her glance.

"I'm going to kill David."

"Oh." Bubba looked back at Patrice. "Okay...well, I guess I'll see you at home, David." He watched Patrice take off her coat again. "Or not," he said, heading to the door.

Patrice walked up to David to stand in front of him, crossing her arms and glaring. "All right, David. Let's have it."

David moved away from her to put the last group of chairs on its table. "I tried to get Tucker to leave, but he wouldn't take a hint."

"You knew Bubba was coming?" Patrice upended a chair and placed it seat down on the table.

"He'd mentioned he might." He looked at her between chair legs before going to get the broom.

She followed him. "And you didn't think it was something I needed to know?"

"There wasn't time." He handed her a broom and took one for himself.

"How long does it take to say, 'Bubba's coming by with some friends'?"

"Longer than I had. I was busy tonight. I let Francie go early because of the storm. I didn't think I'd be so busy."

"You weren't that busy. I've seen you do hot summer days by yourself when people are using the window ledge for seats, and you've always had time to say a few words to me."

"Those words being, 'grab an apron.'"

"Okay. Fine." She attacked the floor as she spoke. "Let's just say, for the sake of argument, that you didn't have time to warn me about Bubba. How does that explain the mocha and the comments about the crème brûlée incident?"

"He'd have liked the mocha had he tried it. The purpose of the mocha was to show him that things aren't always as they seem."

"It wasn't mocha?"

"It was chocolate mocha—more chocolate than coffee.

He'd have loved it. It's what he's getting next time too."

"If there is a next time," Patrice grumbled.

"Oh, there'll be a next time. You underestimate your draw with the boy."

"Boy? He's older than you."

"He's still a boy, girlfriend."

"Whatever. I think you overestimate it. After tonight, I won't ever see him again."

"You'll see him again less than a minute after you leave here."

Patrice stopped sweeping to look at David as if he were crazy.

"He's waiting for you." David nodded at the window.

Patrice looked outside. Mike stood on the other side of the glass in the swirling snow looking at her. She threw her broom at David and grabbed her coat as she raced to the door.

"Don't think you've gotten off this easy, David. I'm not done with you," she called over her shoulder as she shoved her arms into her sleeves and opened the door.

His laughter followed her outside.

Chapter 33

Mike caught Patrice as she threw herself at him, but abruptly ended the kiss.

"Is that how you greet all your men?" He disentangled himself from her embrace, holding her at arm's length.

Patrice felt as if she'd been struck.

"No...I..."

"You greeted Bubba with a steamy kiss. Did Alex get one as well?"

Patrice shook off Mike's hands, becoming angry and defensive. "No, I just hugged Alex."

"What the hell is going on, Patrice?"

"Don't yell at me."

"I'm not yelling," he said from behind clenched teeth.

"You could have fooled me." She zipped her coat and pulled on her gloves.

"Fooled you, huh? And how do you think I felt watching you rush into Bubba's arms and give him a kiss steamy enough to make a saint stiff. You made Alex and me look like fools."

"I made you and Alex look like friends," she argued back.

"Is that what we are?" he accused. "Your friends?"

Patrice crossed her arms over her chest. "Alex is."

"And what am I?" He grabbed both her arms. "Am I a friend? Does a friend kiss you like this?" He crushed her in his embrace, kissing her savagely. He tried to force her lips apart, but she wouldn't open her mouth for him.

She shoved at his chest and shoulders until he let her go. She swung at him with her gloved hand, but he caught it easily.

"Don't..." She wrenched her hand out of his. "Don't ever kiss me like that again. I'm not a whore who owes you service. I'm..." She glared at him through narrowed eyes. "I'm..."

"You're what?" Mike asked, cruelly. "A tramp? A tease?"

Patrice's eyes grew wide at Mike's words, and he knew he'd hurt her. She spun on her heel and headed toward her car.

"Patrice." He raced after her, reaching her as she yanked open her car door. "Patrice, I didn't mean it. I was just angry and frustrated and..."

"I don't think we should see each other any more," she said, getting into her car.

"Because of Bubba?" he asked.

"Bubba is a friend I'm helping out," she said, closing the door in Mike's face and pressing the automatic lock.

He stared at her as she started the car and sped off. He didn't know what was going on, but he was determined to find out. He returned to Doctor Delicious and pounded on the locked door.

****

Despite the storm that raged both inside and outside of Patrice, she managed to get home without crashing. She felt empty—hollow and barren. Her stomach ached and her eyes burned with unshed tears. Not bothering to turn on any lights in her apartment, she fumbled through her coat closet for a hanger and kicked off her shoes.

Her Christmas tree stood in the dark, a shadow against the swirling white outside her window. Shuffling barefoot into the kitchen, she filled a large plastic cup with water for the tree. She wished Mike hadn't gone with her to get it; now the tree reminded her of him. She should have explained the situation to him. And she would have, given time. But not anymore. Now there was nothing to explain, and no one to explain it to.

Why had Mike reacted as he had? Why did he have to treat her like a whore and say the words he did? She filled the tree's reservoir to the top, taking care not to slosh water on her cream carpeting. Maybe she and Mike were never meant to be.

With that dismal thought, she crawled out from under the tree and headed for bed.

Chapter 34

David pointed to the sign on the door. "I'm closed."

"I don't want ice cream. I want to talk," Mike said through the door.

They stared at each other through the glass for nearly a minute before David shrugged his shoulders and unlocked the door.

"Stay off the floor. I just washed it."

"I'd levitate, but I'm not feeling particularly light right now."

"Well, it isn't because you ate too much ice cream." David relocked the door.

Mike shrugged. "I don't like mocha."

"You didn't try it." David led the way behind the counter to the kitchen in the back. "Appearances can be deceiving, you know."

"That's what I want to talk to you about."

"Why me?" David asked, not bothering to look at Mike as he pulled a mixer, and an ice cream maker out of a cabinet and plugged them into the wall.

"Because I think you know what's going on."

David didn't comment. He gave Mike a long look before going into the walk-in refrigerator for cream and other ingredients.

"You don't like me, do you?" Mike asked when David

returned.

"Not really. You've hurt Patrice for too long."

"Yet, you let me in to talk with you." Mike leaned against a long stainless counter. "Why?"

David shrugged, pulled out a bin of sugar, and measured heaping scoops into the mixer bowl. "What difference does it make?"

"None I guess. I just wondered why."

"I don't like seeing Patrice hurt. Maybe talking to you will keep you from hurting her again. So tell me what you want. I've got work to do."

"What's going on between her and Bubba?"

David looked at Mike. "Why don't you ask Patrice?"

"I did. She said he's a friend, and she's helping him out."

"That's the truth. So what's the problem?" He turned back to his measuring.

"I don't buy it. What kind of help requires kissing and hand holding?" When David didn't answer, Mike continued. "I want to know how seriously involved they are." David said nothing. Mike continued as if to justify his right to ask questions. "You know Patrice's mom. If she thinks her daughter is seriously involved with a black man, there'll be hell to pay."

"Isn't that Patrice's business?"

"Yes...but..."

David turned back to Mike. "But you're going to make it yours, right?"

"Well, yes. I really care for Patrice."

David took a deep breath and sighed. "Tucker, I don't like you, and you don't like me, but let me give you some advice. Not everything is as it appears to be. Take the mocha ice cream. Eat it and you'll see that something you thought you didn't like is actually perfect for you."

"How does that relate to Patrice?"

"Give it some thought, counselor. Now, if you'll excuse me, I've got a lot of ice cream to make before I leave tonight, and I don't really want to get snowed in with you. So if you'll just let yourself out, the back door will lock automatically when you leave." He dismissed Mike with a flip of a switch, the mixer drowning out the sound of Mike's departure.

Chapter 35

Patrice was making spritz cookies. The smell of baking flavored the air, and Bing Crosby was crooning "White Christmas" from the living room stereo when Randy called.

"What are you doing?" he asked, accusingly.

"Well, good morning to you too, Scrooge. I'm making Christmas cookies. What are you doing? Rationing coal?"

"Christmas cookies?" His tone lightened. "Are you making those little pecan pie ones I like?"

"They're cooling on the rack."

"Okay. I guess I won't kill you."

"How thoughtful of you." She finished the pan of spritz and put it into the oven while she talked. "Why were you going to kill me anyway?"

"First thing this morning, Alex congratulates me on your up-coming engagement to Bubba Scott."

"Alex is jumping the gun. Bubba and I are just friends."

Randy continued as if he hadn't heard her. "It's not as if I care one way or the other. Your love life is your concern, and I'm sure Bubba is a great guy. It's just that Mom is going to blow a gasket, and you promised to make up with Mike."

"Hold it a second, Randy." Patrice's good mood had

evaporated. "Bubba and I are just friends. Period. There isn't going to be an engagement. I don't know what Alex is talking about. And as far as Mike goes, I've already made up with him a couple of times, but he won't stay made up with. He is determined to see me in the worst light at all times. I'll be nice to him at Christmas, and that's it."

"What did he do now?" Randy sounded exasperated.

"It doesn't matter." Patrice's sigh belied her words.

"Liar. You're still hung up on him, aren't you? Why are women so attracted to losers?"

"I don't know," she sniped. "I'll ask your girlfriend."

"Ha, ha, very funny."

"So is that why you called? To check out rumors and act as my personal romance police?"

"Basically."

"Randy, I'm going to send all but one of those little pecan pies to a homeless shelter, and then I'll eat the last one in front of you in one satisfying bite."

"You wouldn't be that cruel."

"Call me once more about my love life or lack thereof, and I swear I'll do it," she threatened.

"Fine. I'll let Mom do her own calling."

"You sic Mom on me, and I'll never forgive you."

"It's unavoidable, Pet. She's sure to call you to check up on the Mike situation any day now."

Patrice groaned. "I know."

"You have to tell her something."

"I will."

"What?"

"I don't know," she sighed. "I'm sure I'll have thought up something by then."

At least she hoped she would.

****

Patrice's mom waited until Wednesday.

"I hear you've been making cookies," she said by way of a greeting. "Will they still be fresh on Christmas?"

"I freeze them, Mom." They had this conversation every year.

"Well, I wouldn't want to serve anything that isn't top notch on Christmas."

"They'll be fine, Mom."

"Well, you know best. You are the chef."

163

Patrice rolled her eyes and prayed for patience as her mother continued. "Speaking of preparing for Christmas, have you seen Mike yet?"

"We got Christmas trees together."

"Did you now? I knew you would get along once you got together again."

Patrice could almost see her mother's smile. Again? What again? They'd never been together in the first place. And she couldn't allow her mother to try to shove them together now, not when Mike thought so little of her. "Yes...well, he told me that we liked different kinds of trees."

"Oh?" Her mom sounded disappointed. "Well, relationships are about compromises."

"And then he changed his mind and got the same kind I did."

"See?" Her mom sounded pleased with herself. "He's flexible. That's a good thing in a man."

"I'm pretty certain he doesn't know what he wants," Patrice told her.

"Nonsense. He's flexible and willing to accommodate. Wonderful traits. Besides we're talking Christmas trees."

"Are we?"

"Of course we are, dear."

"I don't know. I'm grown up now, Mom. I think it's time I gave up certain childhood dreams and crushes." Patrice's eyes filled with tears that she angrily brushed aside. She would not cry over Mike again.

"You're grown up now, and I think certain people are just realizing it."

"And is one of those people you?" Patrice could hope.

"I meant Mike."

"I know you did. But I don't think it matters." Patrice cleared her throat. It felt constricted, and she hoped it didn't sound that way. "He didn't like me as a kid. He doesn't like me now. The crème brûlée just proved that."

"I thought you'd forgiven him that. You did accept his apology, didn't you?"

"We've kissed and made up, Mom. That isn't the point."

"You kissed?"

She wasn't about to admit that—not to her mother.

She'd never live it down. "Mother, it's a figure of speech."

"I know that. What kind of idiot do you take me for?"

Patrice groaned at the futility of it all, both the conversation and any possible future relationship with Mike. Tears filled her eyes again. She just wanted to bash her head against the wall until she was senseless. Then at least she'd have a reason for the tears, and she wouldn't care.

"Are you all right?" her mother asked.

She wanted to say, No, Mom. I'm sick of everyone interfering in my love life. I'm perfectly able to have none all by myself. Instead she answered like the good daughter she tried to be. "I'm fine. Mike and I are fine. We'll get along on Christmas."

"That's all I ask," her mother said.

Bull.

After she hung up, Patrice realized that she couldn't guarantee she and Mike would get along at Christmas.

It was time she sat down and wrote Mike a letter.

Chapter 36

As soon as Patrice hung up, her mother called Mike's mother.

"They've kissed and made up."

"Kissed? They've kissed?" Melanie didn't need to ask who Janice was talking about. "How do you know?"

"Patrice told me. And," she said, forestalling Melanie's interruption, "they went out and got Christmas trees together."

"Really? That's wonderful. I can't believe how easy that was."

"They may still need a nudge or two. Patrice said that Mike doesn't know what he wants."

"He doesn't know what he wants? How can the boy be so smart and yet so dense?" Melanie wondered aloud.

"That's the definition of men," Janice offered. "Though not all of them are smart."

Melanie laughed before continuing in a serious tone. "How can he not know what he wants? You've seen the way he looks at her—like forbidden fruit."

"He's been looking at her that way forever. You know how I worried when she was younger."

"And I didn't?" Melanie protested.

"Don't fuss. I know you did. We both did. But now I'm wondering if maybe we were wrong. Maybe that leashed lust look he has is just the way he looks at girls."

"It's not. He's my son. I know."

"Well, then," Janice continued. "I don't know what's going on. Patrice said she's forgiven him, but still he hasn't made his move. Maybe he's seen her as forbidden fruit for so long that he needs encouragement."

"As if Patrice hasn't been encouraging."

Janice's hackles rose. "She's shown interest, but she's been the picture of propriety."

"I agree," Melanie hastily interjected. "I wasn't saying anything bad about Patrice. I love the girl. I lay the blame entirely on Michael's shoulders. I need to figure out a way to push him without seeming to push." There was silence as each woman considered the possible courses of action. "Patrice isn't seeing anyone, is she?"

"Not that she's said."

"What about Bubba Scott?"

"She claims they're just friends." Janice's voice carried her doubt and concern.

"Hmmm," Melanie said, buying time as she thought. "Maybe I'll play up their relationship and your concern about it when I talk to him. Play the jealousy card as it were."

"Be discreet, Mel. Patrice said that she and Mike were fine and would get along at Christmas. You don't want to push too hard and ruin anything."

"Don't worry," Melanie assured her lightly. "I'm nothing if not discreet."

Chapter 37

Mike was in a meeting when his mother called. He managed not to groan when his secretary gave him the message. Luckily, the note didn't say he should return the call. So he didn't.

Instead he threw himself into work. His plan was to keep so busy that he didn't think about Patrice. It worked half the time, leaving him longing for her only every other minute. It also cut down on the amount of time he spent kicking himself, but not by much. His goal was to give her a week to cool off, giving himself a week to decide if he was better off without her.

It wasn't that hard, he told himself again and again. He just had to pretend she was in Paris. And it worked in a limited way until Friday morning when his mother finally got through.

"Where have you been?" Melanie demanded without even a hello.

"I work, Mother."

"You've been avoiding me," she accused.

"None of the messages said to call you back." It was a lame defense, but it was all he had.

"Is that how it goes? A mother has to ask her only child to return her calls?"

Mike cringed at the accusation in his mother's voice.

"Sorry, Mom. I've been very busy."

"Busy not keeping your promise."

"I apologized to Patrice," he protested. Then I insulted her again at least twice.

"Well, I'm glad to hear it. Did she accept it?"

"Yes." The first two times, his guilty conscience reminded him.

"Good. Then you'll be nice to each other at Christmas?"

"Sure..." If he could make it up to her by then. "I promised we would be."

"I've another small favor to ask. I told Janice that you'd check out what's going on between Patrice and Bubba Scott."

His heart clenched. Even her mother thought something was going on. He took a deep breath and told himself to calm down. Of course, Patrice's mother was concerned. Bubba was black. There could be nothing between the two, and she'd still be worried. Patrice had told him the truth—she and Bubba were just friends.

"She says they're just friends," he repeated aloud to his mother.

"You've talked to her about it? You were worried too? Oh, Janice isn't going to like this," Melanie fretted. "Could you take Patrice out and just be sure?"

"You want me to date Patrice?" A light came on in Mike's brain. He was being encouraged toward Patrice.

"Just as a favor to Janice. Just to take her away from Bubba."

His mother and Patrice's wanted them together. He could have cheered. He'd been afraid how the families would react to them as a couple, and now he knew for certain—they'd applaud. Or at least their parents would. Randy seemed honestly repulsed by the idea.

"Mom, if Patrice thinks you and her mother are trying to micro-manage her love life, she's apt to revolt and do precisely what you don't want her to do." Now that he knew they supported his suit, he wanted them to back off. They could ruin everything if they tried to meddle.

"Oh." The concept silenced Melanie.

"Tell Janice that she needs to be more discreet with Patrice. If she pushes, she's apt to end up with Bubba for a son-in-law." God forbid.

She echoed his thoughts aloud.

By the time Mike was off the phone, it was time for lunch. Out of habit, he headed home to eat it while reading the mail. There were two things of note in his mailbox—the box of ornaments he'd bought for Patrice and a letter.

He looked at the letter for a long time without opening it. Never before had there been fear attached to her correspondence. They hadn't left things very well on Sunday. He'd been angry, jealous, and cruel—and she'd been confusingly female. He'd relived their last conversation enough times to know that he'd blown it once again. He'd attacked her rather than allowed her to explain. And his conversation with David hadn't helped either. David seemed to think that Patrice had told the truth about her relationship with Bubba. How many times had David told him that things aren't always as they appear?

Did he really doubt Patrice's feelings for him? Could he ignore how he felt about her? How long could he delude himself, pretending that Patrice wasn't a few blocks away, cooking in a fancy restaurant? It was Friday. He had the letter to prove it. And there he sat—five days into a life of missing her. He had to do something. If Alex tried to commiserate with him one more time, he'd scream.

He opened the letter.

Mike,
I can't go back to the way it was before your party, and it is clear there is no "us" in the future. With luck and time we will someday individually look back on the past and smile at the memory of me as The Pest and you as my impossible dream. But until then, we need to go forward. I propose that on Christmas Day we present a façade of cordial indifference, exchanging sweaters and holiday greetings for the sake of our families.
I know we can trust each other to put our personal feelings aside for our families' sake for one day out of the year.
Cordially, Patrice

Cordially. She'd written "cordially." In all the years and in all the letters he received, she'd never written "cordially." It was always "love," or "with love," or even "as always." There may have even been an "affectionately," but never, not ever, "cordially."

Could he live in a world where Patrice thought of him cordially?

No. He had to do something. And he had until Christmas to do it.

Mike gave up calling Patrice after his ninth call in as many hours. She was either working extra hours or avoiding him. Either way, calling was obviously not going to work as a courting technique.

On Sunday, he planned his day around seeing her at Doctor Delicious, silently rehearsing what he'd say.

He sat in his Lexus watching the clock until precisely ten minutes after four. He had to force himself to wait until then to walk into the shop. He didn't want to be waiting for her in case she was avoiding him and, seeing him, decided not to go in, but he didn't want to be any later and miss her.

David nodded in greeting. "Tucker."

"Give me a medium," he said as he took off his coat and eyed the tables, looking for Patrice.

"It's going to be mocha," David reminded him, lifting a medium bowl from the rack.

"You're the Doctor." He hadn't spotted Patrice yet. Maybe she was in the restroom.

David handed Mike a spoon and the bowl over the counter and took Mike's money. "She's not here."

"What do you mean, 'she's not here?' It's Sunday. She's always here."

David shrugged. "She didn't come."

"Maybe she's late?" He knew she wasn't. She was never late. Her reliability was one of the things he'd come to...well, rely on. She did the same things over and over again. Good things. Traditions of sorts that the people around her believed would always be there. Her undying love for him, Friday letters, and Sunday dinner with the family followed by a trip to the Doctor's for something to eat. "Maybe she's still at her folks' house?"

"I don't think she's coming."

Mike looked from the bowl to David and back again twice before putting the bowl on the counter. "Maybe she's sick."

David shook his head. "She'd have called."

"Maybe she's with Bubba." Anger coursed through Mike's veins.

"He's playing." David nodded to the television mounted in the corner with the sound turned low. "I think we just did her in last weekend."

Mike frowned, looking at the bowl on the counter. "I guess it's my fault. I really blew it this time. She sent me a let's-be-friends letter."

The bells on the door announced another customer.

"I said we, not just you." David turned away, greeting the newcomers with a smile and a hello before lowering his voice and addressing Mike again. "Take your bowl and sit down. I'll join you in a minute."

Not knowing what else to do, Mike did as he was told. He even ate a couple of spoonfuls of mocha before realizing what he'd done. The ice cream, more chocolate than coffee-flavored, was good. He looked into his bowl. He'd never had mocha that tasted this good before. He might have to revise his opinion.

The thought gave him pause.

Hadn't David been saying all along that he needed to revise his opinion? Patrice and Bubba weren't what they seemed. Things that he thought he didn't like would actually be perfect for him. It seemed as if David actually knew his stuff. Maybe Patrice's absence this once would be a good thing. If he used this time as a planning session and maybe called on David for some insight, he might be able to figure out how to permanently win Patrice.

David joined him as Mike scraped the last of the ice cream from the bowl.

"So it didn't kill you." David pulled out a chair and turned it around to straddle it backwards.

"You were right. I liked it, and I got the message."

David grinned. "A break through."

"You dated her all through high school," Mike said. "Are you still in love with her?"

David looked Mike in the eye. "We dated in high school, but she was always in love with you."

"And you hate me for it?"

"Not for how she felt about you. For how you treated her."

Mike nodded. "I've been denying my feelings for her for a long time, almost as long as I've relied on hers. I thought when I finally admitted my true feelings that she would just fall into my arms."

"But it hasn't turned out that way, has it?"

Mike shook his head sadly. "No. I had to completely humiliate her and tromp on her first. I didn't mean to. I guess I needed the threat of losing her to make me admit what I've always felt for her."

"So you told her this, and she didn't run into your arms." It wasn't a question. David knew what had happened.

Mike shook his head, refusing to look into David's eyes. "She was already in someone else's arms."

David shook his head looking disgusted. "I thought you said you understood the message of the mocha."

Mike looked up. "I do. I know I'm supposed to believe that what I saw between her and Bubba isn't what it seems to be, but she has been in his arms."

"She's been in my arms and your arms—hell, she's even been in Victor's arms. She's huggable and sweet. It means nothing."

"Still," Mike protested. "There is something going on that I don't understand."

"But you're going to feel sorry for yourself instead of acting anyway, right?" David stood and turned the chair around in preparation to leave.

"No. I'm going to fight for her and win her back."

David put his hands on the back of the chair and leaned toward Mike. "How?"

Mike told him.

David demanded details and added suggestions before another group of customers arrived.

Chapter 38

Patrice told herself she was relieved that Mike hadn't called. She went shopping a lot to keep herself from waiting by the phone. She wrote her Christmas cards, even reluctantly addressing one to Mike. Still, she couldn't help thinking about the abrupt change in her popularity. Before Thanksgiving she had three guys calling for dates. Sure, one was gay and the other was being forced by his mother, but still she had dates. Now the phone didn't ring.

Sunday came with its obligatory family dinner. Patrice arrived early to go to church with her folks.

"What's wrong, Pet?" her father whispered to her during the offertory hymn.

"Nothing," she lied, staring at her hymnal, but not seeing it. Her eyes burned with unshed tears. Fighting the impulse to cry, she blinked several times. Attending Mass at the church where both she and Mike had grown up was hard. She'd always thought she and Mike would get married here. Her father would walk her down the aisle to "Trumpet Voluntary." She'd be in white with a sinfully long train, and Mike would be in a black tux with tails and pinstriped pants. And now, it finally dawned on her that it would never happen.

"You can't kid an old kidder," her father whispered.

"Something is bothering you."

Janice elbowed her husband and hissed, "Shh!"

Roy ignored his wife and leaned closer to his daughter. "Is it your mom or men? Or both?"

Patrice looked at her father in surprise.

"What? You think I don't know what a pain she can be?"

Patrice smiled, biting her lip to keep from giggling.

"She's been on you about Mike and Bubba, hasn't she?" He patted Patrice's hand. "You follow your heart. Don't let her bully you into or out of anything."

Janice glared at her husband. "We're in church."

Patrice waited until her mother turned back to the front before whispering in her father's ear. "Bubba's black."

"I've noticed," he whispered back. "She'll forget all about it after the first grandchild comes along."

Patrice smiled at the thought of her mother with black grandkids. Of course, that meant she'd have to have sex with Bubba. It wasn't something either she or Bubba could begin to imagine.

After dinner Patrice went home and got into her flannel pajamas even though it was only four in the afternoon. There would be Christmas specials to watch later over a bowl of bœuf bourguignonne. But now she turned on the tree and Christmas music, poured a glass of chilled white wine, and rifled through the newspaper for the crossword puzzle.

It was the first time since she'd move back to Chicago that she hadn't gone to Doctor Delicious on Sunday afternoon. It felt strange and sad. For the second time that day she felt like crying, but again she fought it off. She'd cried as many tears as she was going to over Mike.

Scenes from their too-few dates ran through her mind. Memories of his kiss and touch left her sighing with loss. She never should have kissed him. If they hadn't kissed, she'd be over him by now. Okay. That was a lie. Maybe not over him, but definitely not as deeply in love with him. Another lie. Their kisses highlighted their feelings, but they hadn't created them. Still, it was one thing to imagine being in his arms and another thing to experience it and re-live it over and over again. She'd have been better off without those bittersweet memories, but she couldn't in honesty wish they'd never kissed.

"It's hopeless," she said aloud. "I'm a basket case."

Chapter 39

Business at Victor's the following Thursday night was steady. By nine, the rush was done, and Patrice was nearly finished reducing beef broth for a fine demi-glace sauce.

Victor stuck his head in the kitchen. "Patrice, there's someone here to see you."

She motioned for one of her assistants to finish the sauce, wiped her hands on a towel, changed her apron for the pristine one she reserved for such occasions, and accompanied Victor into the dining room.

A handsome man stood in full armor just inside the dining room. Victor motioned him in.

"Patrice Wilson?" the knight asked, pushing the visor back from his face.

"Yes." She smiled, blushing as he offered her a rose.

"Oh, fair Patrice, I, Don Quixote, have come to confess my foolishness. Mike Tucker and I have been tilting windmills, believing them to be giants competing for your love. And now, I have come in his name to beg your forgiveness and plead that you continue to..." Pulling a tuning wheel out of his pocket, he blew a note, copied its pitch and began to sing "The Impossible Dream" from the musical *Man of La Mancha*.

Patrice's heart was in her throat as she listened to

177

the talented troubadour belt out his song. Everyone in the restaurant and bar found their way into the dining room to listen.

When the final "star" faded to silence and the thunderous applause ended, "Don Quixote" pulled a bunch of balloons that Patrice hadn't noticed away from the wall. "Dare to dream," he admonished her, handing her the bouquet—a half-dozen red heart-shaped balloons with "I love you" scrolled across in white letters and an equal number of Mylar balloons emblazoned with "Dare to Dream."

Had Mike been there, Patrice would have forgiven him on the spot, thrown herself into his arms, and kissed him until neither one of them could breathe. But he wasn't. She thanked the knight and told him to wait while she went to get a tip.

"Don't worry, Patrice, I'll get it." Victor told her. He walked "Don Quixote" to the door, gave him a generous tip, and took a pile of his cards to hand out to interested persons.

"I don't suppose you'll be seeing Mike Tucker again?" Victor asked.

"Actually, I will. He's outside waiting. I couldn't drive in this armor."

"Good. Then you tell him, he is welcome here if he treats Patrice with chivalry and respect."

An hour-and-a-half later, Patrice waved good-bye to Victor and entered her building. Setting down the balloons' anchor, she opened her mailbox. There was a small CD-sized box with Mike's return address on it among the envelopes. Wondering what he'd sent her, she barely made it to her apartment before ripping open the box.

The soundtrack for *Man of La Mancha* was wrapped in a typewritten copy of the words with the lines about continuing to dream, bearing sorrow, righting wrongs, and loving from afar underlined. And the words, *"If you will only do the first, I will do the other three. I do love you. Please forgive me. Mike."*

Patrice wiped the tears from her face and hugged the letter to her chest. Why had he promised to love chaste from afar? She'd rather he were here and their love not so chaste.

Chapter 40

Mike went to work early the next morning. This would be the toughest part of the wooing process—the waiting. He'd told David about the "Impossible Dream" idea and David had suggested he underline the, "love pure and chaste" line.

"Nothing will get her faster than not being able to physically express her gratitude," he'd told Mike. "After she's been serenaded, she'll want to rush into your arms and kiss you."

"That's good. That's what I'm after."

David had raised an eyebrow. "A kiss? Is that all you want?"

Mike frowned. "No."

"What do you want, Mike?"

"Everything."

"Everything as in you just want to go to bed with her?" David sounded dangerously cool.

"No," Mike said. "I mean, I want to go to bed with her, but it's not just sex. I want everything—the house, the kids, the SUV. Everything."

"You want to marry her."

"Didn't I just say that?"

"Sorry, I must have misheard you," David said dryly. "Well, if you're serious about winning her completely, stay out of her bed until she agrees to marry you."

"What?" Mike stared at David. "Are you nuts? Sex brings relationships together—makes them stronger."

"Premature sex shatters relationships and makes women wonder if that is all they mean to you. Make her wait. Make yourself wait. You'll thank me."

"I doubt it. I may die of frustration. Just kissing her is enough to get me started."

"Then don't kiss her. Love her, purely and chastely from afar."

"What?"

"The song. One of the lines goes something like that. Talk to her on the phone. Talk dirty if it helps, but keep your paws and lips to yourself until you've got the ring in hand. She'll be so hot and bothered by the time you propose, there'll be no question of her answer." David paused, thinking. "Actually, if you wait until after the wedding—"

"Forget it, Welch," Mike interrupted. "I'm beginning to think that you're more interested in torturing me than in helping Patrice and me get together."

"Can't I do both?"

"Sadist."

Chapter 41

So there Mike sat, fidgeting in his chair, knowing that Patrice was almost sure to call and suggest a meeting. How could he say no and still let her know how much he truly wanted to see her? He needed to find out her work schedule, so he could ask her out for those days and times. He wished it were early enough to call Victor's.

When the phone rang, he knew it was Patrice before he even picked up the receiver.

Randy's voice surprised him. "Mike, I thought I'd catch you at breakfast, but you left the house too early."

"I've got to earn this corner office."

"You've already earned it. You're a partner, remember?"

"All the more reason to get here early. What's up?"

"It's about Patrice. The other day, Alex mentioned that the two of you saw Patrice with Bubba Scott at David's ice cream shop."

"Well, actually, Alex was with Patrice; then I came and then Bubba."

"That wasn't the way I heard it." Randy sounded suspicious.

"Alex is in advertising. 'Guess who joined Patrice and me at the ice cream store?' doesn't have the impact of, 'Guess who I saw Patrice with at the ice cream store?'"

182

"So she didn't rush into Bubba's arms and kiss him like she wished they were alone?" Randy sounded confused.

"No..." Mike hedged, "she did that."

"Okay, then. Can you tell me how serious they are?"

Jealousy and doubt reared their heads again. How serious were they? He shoved the question down. "Patrice says they're just friends."

"And what do you say?"

"I say you should keep out of Patrice's love life," Mike snapped, irritated at Randy for his questions, at himself for his doubts, and at Patrice for making all the questions and doubts possible.

"Come on, Mike. You know how my mom feels about mixed-race marriages. I need you..."

"For what?"

"I need you to talk to Patrice."

"About Bubba? Are you nuts? I made the mistake of bringing up the subject the last time I saw her, and she hasn't spoken to me since. Besides, I thought you wanted me to stay away from her."

"I've changed my mind. You chase Bubba away, and I'll give you my blessing."

Reluctantly, Mike thought. Still he took a calming breath and tried to reassure his friend. "Relax, Randy. Patrice loves your mom and is well aware of her prejudices. I don't think that she'd put herself in a position to hurt your mother that badly. Hell, she ignores the dictates of her highly trained palate and shows up to be poisoned by your mother every week without fail, doesn't she?" As he said the words, he wished he'd thought about that earlier before he'd flown off the handle. Patrice wouldn't purposely do something she knew would hurt her mother. Why couldn't he seem to think logically when it came to her? "I don't know what all is going on, but I do know that Bubba and Patrice are just friends."

"Do you know that, or are you hoping that?" Randy asked skeptically.

"I'd stake everything I own on it." He'd already risked his heart. What were material goods in comparison?

Chapter 42

Patrice hadn't called. Why hasn't she called? Mike wondered for the hundredth time that morning. Had he misjudged her feelings? Had Randy called her and said something stupid? Was their relationship too far gone to be saved? He wished he knew.

He hadn't gotten a lot done that morning in between musings, but enough so that he was ready for his lunch meeting with a client. He sorted through the pile of papers on his desk, making certain that he had just what he needed before picking them up and straightening their edges with a rap on the desk. When they were safely stowed in his briefcase, he headed out of the office.

Patrice and Mike reached the receptionist's desk at the same time.

"Patrice." The relief he felt upon seeing her was evident in his voice.

"I thought I'd bring you lunch," she said, raising the picnic basket to call attention to it. "But it looks like you're leaving."

"I've a lunch meeting." He looked at his watch. "But I have a few minutes. Come back to my office." He took the basket from her and led the way down the hall.

"I guess my timing is off," Patrice said as Mike opened his office door and ushered her in.

"What did you bring me?" he asked, putting the unopened basket on the desk.

"Roast beef on hard rolls with a creamy horseradish sauce, vinegar chips, salt-water dills, carrot sticks, and apple turnovers for dessert."

"Nothing to drink?" he teased.

She smiled at him. "Sweet tea."

The intercom on his desk buzzed. "Your meeting, Mr. Tucker."

"Damn." He looked at his watch and wished he had more time.

"Don't worry about the food. It will keep." She headed for the door. "I'll ask your secretary to stick the basket in the refrigerator, and you can have it for supper."

"I guess I'll have to. Maybe you could come back, and we could have supper together."

She shook her head. "Can't. It's Friday." She stopped at the door, feeling ill at ease. She'd planned this scene differently. "Thank you for last night. Don Quixote has a fabulous voice. I wouldn't be surprised if Victor put him on retainer."

"You forgive me then?" He reached around her for the doorknob.

"Yes." She nodded. Part of her wanted to glide into his arms and show him her thanks, but another part was hesitant. She was unsure where she stood with him. The last time she'd thrown herself into his arms, he'd thrown her back. Now she was gun shy. And then there were the underlined lyrics to consider. Maybe he preferred to love her chaste from afar. "I loved the *Man of La Mancha* soundtrack too."

"I'm glad." He turned the doorknob.

"I was wondering..." She tried to sound normal and grateful, but the tension and discomfort she was feeling permeated her voice. She cleared her throat and tried again. "I was wondering what you meant by the lyrics you underlined."

He pulled open the door. "I thought they were pretty clear."

She hesitated. "I guess."

"Patrice, I really don't have time to discuss them now. I have to get to my meeting."

"I know." She walked through the open door. "I'll tell your secretary about the food."

"I'll call you," he said over his shoulder as he left.

Patrice drove home in a haze of sadness. She understood the lyrics now. Her love for Mike was an impossible dream. She could continue to have it, but it would continue to be impossible. And it was sad—unbearably sad—because whatever was wrong between them was unrightable. Therefore the only way she and Mike could love would be from afar. Mike needed forgiveness to get on with his life, and she'd given it to him. Now she needed forgetfulness to get on with hers—forgetfulness and a life to get on with. A boyfriend would be nice, but it was clear that relationships with men were beyond her ability. Maybe she should stick with Bubba. At least a girl always knew where she stood with a gay man.

****

After the kitchen closed Friday night, Patrice made her way into the bar.

"What can I get you?" Victor asked, putting a napkin in front of her.

"How did you know Genevieve was the one for you?" Patrice asked.

"Same as you knew about you and Mike."

Patrice frowned. "I always used to know, but now I'm not so sure anymore."

"What did that boy do to you, now?"

"Nothing."

"Don't give me that. You've been chasing after him so long he's sure to think he'll see you every time he turns around."

"Well. I'm not there anymore."

"Hmmm," Victor said, pouring Patrice a glass of white wine. "That's the trouble. You've tagged the boy, and he doesn't know how to be *it*. Give him a little time, Pet. He'll come around. The trick is knowing just how long to run before you let him catch you."

"Assuming he picks up the chase."

"Oh," Victor chuckled. "He'll pick up the chase, don't you worry. Question is—how long are the two of you gonna play tag? There're a lot more interesting games a man and woman can play."

Patrice turned crimson as Victor's laughter filled the bar. "You try some of them." He winked at Patrice. "I'll bet you find them more fun."

Mike hung up the phone Saturday afternoon with an exasperated snort. Where was she? He'd been calling since nine, and now it was three. She hadn't been home all day. He knew she didn't work during the day on Saturday, and she certainly wouldn't go shopping—not when she could do it during the week when the stores weren't as crowded. So where was she? He'd told her he'd call. Couldn't she wait around for his call? Weren't girls in love supposed to do that?

Okay, he acknowledged, that was a little pathetic. Patrice had a life. And he wanted her to have a life. He just wanted to be in it. Not knowing where she was and when she was likely to be home was not being a part of her life. He didn't even know if she'd be at Doctor Delicious on Sunday. When would he see her again?

David's advice was stupid. Mike knew he should have grabbed Patrice yesterday in his office and kissed her silly instead of walking away. Loving chaste and from afar might have worked for a literary figure, but it didn't work for a flesh-and-blood man. He was physically attracted to Patrice. He needed to touch her. It was a part of his everyday thoughts. Trying to deny his physical attraction was making him act stupid. No one won a woman like Patrice by acting stupid.

He'd mailed the first two ornaments so they'd arrive today—December 13. He'd written, "Don't open until Sunday, December 14," on the turtledoves' box and planned to have the last one arrive on Christmas Eve. He didn't know if the Twelve Days of Christmas were really before or after Christmas, but it didn't matter. He was sending the gifts before Christmas.

Chapter 43

Saturday afternoon, Patrice walked into Doctor Delicious.

"No ice cream today," she told her friend across the counter. "I just came to tell you I won't be here on Sundays for a while."

"Your mom's food has improved that much?" David grinned at his own joke.

"I wish." Patrice felt her eyes fill with tears. What a basket case. She dug a tissue out of her pocket and wiped her eyes and blew her nose. "I've just gotten into a rut. I'll still come to see you, just not on Sunday."

David's eyes softened. He leaned over the counter and grabbed her hand. "I could tell Mike he's not welcome."

Patrice pulled back her hand. "It's not just him."

"Bubba works Sundays, so he's hardly ever here. Is it Alex? I knew that guy was trouble from day one—all that mooning," he said with mock severity.

Patrice managed a watery smile, but said nothing.

"I'm sorry for my part in all this," David said, looking into her eyes. "I was only trying to help."

"I know," Patrice sniffed, employing the tissue again. "It's not your fault. It's past time for me to change some things in my life—break some old habits." She tucked the tissue back into her pocket. "Anyway. I just wanted you to know that I won't be here on Sundays." She forced a smile. "I'll talk to you later." She turned on her heel and left, grateful beyond words that David didn't call her back.

During the dinnertime lull, David called Mike.

"What the hell is going on between you and Patrice?"

"I don't know," Mike confessed. "I've been trying to call her all day, but she hasn't been home."

"I thought you were going to send that guy to serenade her and then shower her with gifts."

"I did. She loved Don Quixote, and I sent the first two ornaments to arrive today. What happened?"

"You tell me," David countered. "I'm working this afternoon like usual, and here she comes all weepy-eyed and depressed to tell me she won't be coming in on Sundays anymore."

There was a moment of stunned silence on Mike's end as he replayed Friday noon. "Did she say why?"

"Not really, just something about breaking old habits. I gathered that she doesn't want to be here because people know she comes here, and she wants to avoid them."

"You mean me?" Mike was surprised and hurt. Sure, Friday hadn't gone well, but it hadn't gone that badly either.

"She said, it wasn't just you. I think she's a bit ticked off at me as well."

"So she's running?"

"More likely licking her wounds and trying to heal," David said. "So, I ask again—what the hell is going on with you two?"

"Nothing. She brought me lunch on Friday, but I had a meeting."

"What did you do to her?"

"Nothing! I didn't even touch her," Mike snarled. "I'll bet that's it. I didn't touch her, and now she thinks I don't want to touch her. That's the last time I take your advice—Doctor."

The last word, dripping with sarcasm and disdain, hung in David's ear long after Mike hung up.

Chapter 44

Patrice got home late Saturday evening and dragged her tired body to bed for a night of tossing and turning. On Sunday, the world looked no better for the few disjointed hours of sleep. With sleep impossible, she showered and dressed, and made it to the early Mass with time to spare.

Church calmed and centered Patrice. Afterward, she went to her favorite grocer—the one with the good bakery. There was something nice about starting a morning this early. She'd have time to sip coffee and linger over bakery and the newspaper before heading to her folks' house to see if her mother had found a new way to waste good beef. She selected two large, flaky croissants from the glass case before making her way to the produce department to pick up a small container of raspberries.

Standing in the checkout line behind an affectionate couple, Patrice was bombarded by feelings of loneliness. That's what she wanted—the casual caresses that spoke of tempered desire, the private jokes and ready smiles, the small public intimacies that showed the easy affection between people in love.

She contemplated going back for another container of raspberries and a few more croissants, but didn't. Who would she share them with? No one. She had no one. Even

David, the person she'd normally call for things like this, held no appeal. She didn't want to see him either. And Mike? Everyone thought there was or should be something between her and Mike, everyone except her and Mike. Well...Mike anyway. She realized the futility of the situation. Since their relationship couldn't seem to start, it was better that it ended. Two croissants were more than enough. She couldn't have what she wanted, and nothing else appealed.

It was a cold drive through downtown Chicago. She parked her car, grabbed her bag, and let herself into her building. The Sunday newspapers for the building sat in a pile on the floor. She grabbed hers and her Saturday one as well. She'd been so tired last night that she hadn't even checked her mail. Juggling newspapers and grocery bag, she managed to unlock her mailbox. It was stuffed full of catalogues, Christmas cards, and bills, all tightly wedged around two coffee-mug sized boxes. Patrice had to put down the bag and papers to wiggle the boxes out.

The boxes were from Mike.

She stood frozen with her belongings strewn at her feet. Joy and fear warred in her heart. What had he sent her? She was tempted to rip open the boxes where she stood, but they were so well sealed that they would require a knife. With a great force of will, she picked her stuff off the floor and headed toward the elevator.

Inside her apartment, she unloaded her arms at the kitchen table and reached for a knife. One of the boxes said, "Open Sunday." She opened the other first and unwrapped a partridge in a pear tree. The ornament itself had a gilded outer ring on which were painted the words, "On the First Day of Christmas, my true love gave to me..." A thin metal rod at the top and bottom of the ring suspended a three-dimensional partridge and its pear tree in the middle of the ring. Both the partridge—a large bird taking up most of the tree—and the pear tree in which it sat were made of brightly colored poly-resin.

Patrice opened the second box. The ornament had a similar design—the golden outer circle with the words, "On the second day of Christmas, my true love gave to me..." and two turtledoves suspended in the middle. Patrice stared at the two ornaments more confused than before. Did he love her or hate her? Did he want her as a friend or more than that?

The phone rang, interrupting her thoughts.

"Good," Mike's voice greeted her. "You're home."

"Yes. I'm home."

"Stay there. I'll be right over." He hung up before she had a chance to reply.

Now she wished she's gotten more fruit and croissants. Leaving her mess on the table, she ground espresso beans. She had just put the grounds and water in the machine and pushed the start button when the doorbell rang. Already? She buzzed him in. There was barely a chance for her to hang up her coat before Mike knocked on the door.

She opened the door and looked at him standing in the hallway. His overcoat was dusted with snow.

"Are we going to kiss?" she asked, shocking herself with her words. It was what she wanted to know, but she hadn't meant to vocalize it.

"Long and hard," he answered, enveloping her in his embrace and proceeding to do just that.

She melted in the heat of his kiss. He pressed her backward, into the apartment, and kicked the door closed without lessening the kiss's intensity.

A soft moan escaped Patrice as the kiss deepened. Mike's arms held her tight. She needed this closeness. Her fingers tangled in his hair, holding his marauding mouth on hers.

Several minutes later Mike ended the kiss. "So much for loving you chaste from afar."

"That was stupid," Patrice said, unbuttoning Mike's overcoat. "Why would you want to love from afar anyway?"

"I thought I owed you a good courtship, and knew I couldn't keep my hands off you when we're close like this."

"You can be near me and court me. They aren't mutually exclusive things. In fact—" she slid her hands under the back of his sweater—"some people think that dating needs to be done in person."

"Oh, God," Mike moaned at the touch of her hands. He kissed Patrice again, robbing them both of breath and sense.

Chapter 45

Later, Mike watched as she hung her new ornaments. "I didn't thank you for these," she said.

Mike smiled, looking at her kiss-swollen lips. "I don't know...I feel thanked."

"That's nice, but I think I'll make it official." Patrice kissed him again, deeply. "Thank you for the ornaments."

"With a thank you like that, you can be certain there will be more," Mike said when the kiss finally ended.

"Ten more?"

"At least."

"Sit down, and I'll get you a cup of coffee and a croissant."

Mike sat on the sofa and looked at the tree. "Nice tree."

"I had help picking it out." Patrice put the tray of refreshments on the coffee table and handed Mike his mug.

"You had help cutting it down," Mike corrected.

She shrugged, sitting next to him. "And dragging it up here—very important jobs for which I am grateful. When I signed the lease, I didn't think about how I'd get a tree in here."

"You'd have managed, but I'm glad you didn't have to."

193

"Me too."

They sat silently, sipping coffee and eating berries and croissants for several minutes. Finishing first, Mike leaned back and draped his arm around Patrice. "Are we okay then?"

She smiled nervously at him. "I guess."

"Don't guess." Mike gave her shoulders a hug. "I know I've given you all kinds of mixed messages, but you must know that I love you."

"Chaste and from afar?"

"God, no. Hot and heavy at your side."

Patrice laughed. "Good."

"And some day you'll explain what's going on with you and Bubba?"

She looked him in the eyes. "Is that going to be a problem?"

"Not if you don't kiss him in front of me again."

"I don't think I'll be kissing him at all any more, but if I do I'll make certain it's not in front of you."

Mike cringed. "Let's just stick with the first part of that, okay? You won't be kissing him again."

"I think."

"Let's keep it an absolute, okay?"

Patrice opened her mouth to tell him that it wasn't an absolute, but she was interrupted by another steamy kiss. He was staking his claim. His mouth possessed hers as he filled his hands with her hair.

She gave into him, pressing herself against him, welcoming his savagely thrusting tongue with her own, and silently proclaiming her love.

When they separated to catch their breath, Mike wanted to ask if Bubba's kisses made her feel that way, but common sense kept him silent. They talked about neutral subjects like work and the holidays for a while, mixing bouts of kissing and laughing banter into the mix.

Patrice's smile faded as she looked at the clock. "I'd better get moving or I'll be late for dinner."

"What's on the menu?"

"Mangled beef, same as always."

"Are you going to David's afterwards?" He knew what she'd told David, but wondered if this morning had changed her mind.

Patrice frowned. "No. I think I'll just make myself something here."

"Can I join you?" he asked.

"At Mom's or here?"

"Here." He cringed. Mike knew exactly what to expect at her parents' house—bad food and a thorough grilling. "Definitely here."

Patrice laughed. "I wasn't planning anything special, soup and sandwich."

"Works for me. Can I bring anything?"

"Not if you like turkey and cheese."

"I like turkey and cheese."

"Then you're in. I'll be home by four."

"I'll be here by four-o-one."

Patrice laughed. "Then I'll wait for you downstairs."

"Sounds good." He kissed her. "Are you sure you don't want me to bring the soup? I've got Campbell's and Progresso."

Patrice laughed. "What kind of Progresso?"

"You name it."

"Maybe next time. I've got some beef stock that either has to become French onion soup or compost in the next few days."

"If you're sure."

Patrice's eyes sparkled with mirth. "I'm sure."

Mike shrugged. "You'd better get moving. If you're late and you use my name in your excuse, you'll never get out of there."

"Oh, I wouldn't use your name. We'd both get calls from our mothers.

They walked out together, and four hours later walked back in.

"How was dinner?"

"Deep fried."

"And the conversation?"

"Dad warned Mom that Randy and I wouldn't come home anymore if she didn't quit prying."

"Oh?" Mike was shocked. Patrice's dad hardly ever stood up to her mom. "What did your mom have to say to that?"

"Nothing. Randy and I agreed with him, and the conversation ended right there. Randy, Dad and I talked football for the rest of the time."

"Ooh." Mike cringed.

"Actually, if you ignored the icy glares and frosty huffs coming from Mom's end of the table, you could say everything went really well."

"Did she make you apologize before you left?"

"Of course, and I had to promise to see you as well." She put her arms around Mike as they rode the elevator up. "And here I am seeing you. Am I a good daughter or what?"

"Definitely good." He kissed her.

Once inside the apartment Patrice went right to work.

"Can I help?" Mike asked. "Or is that just not done?"

Patrice beamed at him. "I would love your help."

"Good. Give me a job."

"You know, you're the first to ask if they could help me cook. Once I started attending classes, people stopped wanting to be in the kitchen with me except to watch." She smiled at him and handed him a knife. "You can slice onions."

"I think I just figured out why no one wants to cook with you."

Patrice laughed. "I'll be slicing onions too. We need a lot. But first, there's a bottle of Chenin Blanc in the refrigerator."

"Wine." Mike smiled. "I like cooking with wine, and I've heard that sometimes you chefs even put it in the food."

Patrice laughed. "This will be one of those times, but we'll use dry sherry for the soup."

They laughed together and cried onion tears together.

"I thought that chefs had a trick to keep from crying while chopping onions," Mike said, sniffling.

"We do," Patrice commented, wiping her streaming face with a paper towel. "They're called prep cooks."

"And here I thought you did all the cooking."

"Chefs cook; they don't chop."

"Really?"

"Depends on the chef. I don't mind prep work or clean up, but at the Cordon Bleu the higher skilled you became, the more you delegated and specialized. In my last year there, I didn't slice an onion or scrub a pan."

He wrapped his arms around her from behind and looked over her shoulder at the onions she was sautéing. "Those look done to me."

"The perfect French onion soup is made with onions that have been slowly cooking for forty minutes."

"Do you think Mr. Campbell does that?"

"No. Nor Mr. Progresso, which is why our soup will taste better."

"I like the sound of that: 'our soup.' You're letting me have some of the credit?"

"You sliced onions."

"Then why doesn't your prep cook get pictured in *Taste*?"

"I'm more photogenic."

They ate soup and sandwiches in the kitchen, playing footsy under the table.

"Do you want to go out to dinner tomorrow night?" Mike asked.

"No."

Mike's brow furrowed. "No?"

"No. I want you to come here, and I'll make you dinner."

"Okay, but you don't have to cook."

"I know I don't have to. I want to. I want meatloaf and mashed potatoes with green beans, but I don't want to eat it all week. If I make it for dinner tomorrow, we can split the leftovers."

Mike felt his heart surge in his chest. He wanted to eat leftovers with her forever. He was about to say so, when the phone rang.

Patrice left the table to answer it.

Mike eavesdropped.

"No, I'm not mad at David," she said. Pause. "I'm not mad at you either." Pause. "I just don't feel like ice cream." Pause. "French onion soup." Pause. "No, you can't have the leftovers." Pause. "I'm giving them to someone else." Brief pause. "Yes." Longer pause. "Okay. Bye."

Mike raised his brow in question as Patrice returned to the table.

"Bubba," she said, picking up the empty bowls and

plates and carrying them to the sink.

Mike followed her with the empty wine glasses. "Have I made trouble?"

She turned to him, smiling. "No. He's bummed about the leftovers, but he'll get over it."

Mike swallowed the lump in his throat. He hated the idea of someone else sharing the kind of evening with Patrice that he'd just had. "Has he been eating your leftovers for long?"

"He and David have been mooching food since I moved back." She kissed his cheek. "It's not like that, Mike. Bubba and David are just friends."

"I keep reminding myself of that." He put the wine glasses down and ran a hand through his hair. "Am I just a friend?"

Patrice's smile faded. "Do you want to be?"

"No."

"Okay. You're not." She turned away from him, squirting soap in the soup pot and turning on the faucet. The tenor of the entire evening had changed—tightened.

"What am I then?" he asked.

Patrice looked at the suds rising in the pot. "What do you want to be?"

He stopped, stumped. What could he say? He knew what he wanted to be, but it was too soon to propose. They'd only just gotten back together again.

The silence was getting too long. He had to say something—anything.

"I want to be your boyfriend." It was lame, he knew, but it was too early to propose and he couldn't say, I want to be your lover, now could he?

He saw Patrice's shoulders lower as she let go of the tension she'd held there.

"Can I be your boyfriend?" he asked.

Nodding, she turned off the water.

He grabbed her by the shoulders and turned her. "We can take it as slowly as we need to," he said, looking into her eyes. He glanced at her breasts and back up again. "But not too slowly."

Patrice blushed.

"Nor too fast. We'll find the right pace together."

Chapter 46

After Mike had gone home, Patrice called David.

"Don't you guys ever talk for yourselves?" she asked when he picked up.

"I didn't know if you'd talk to me."

"Idiot," she said fondly. "That's why I went to see you Saturday, so you wouldn't think I was mad at you. I'm not...I'm just...I don't know—figuring things out."

"And you can't do that over ice cream?"

"Not if I want to wear the dress I bought for Christmas."

"Is it slinky? Sexy? Meant to drive a certain man wild?"

"David, I spend Christmas Day with my family."

"Oh, yeah. Speaking of which, Bubba and I want to put a little something under your tree Christmas Eve."

"I'll be here all day cooking. I'm not going anywhere until midnight Mass at nine."

"Midnight at nine, huh? Gotta love it. We'll try to make it to your place by then, but if we can't, we'll just use our key."

"What key?"

"The one you're going to give us so that we can bring your gift over while you're at church."

"Oh, that key. Why can't you just come when I'm

199

home?"

"We'll try, but we've got a couple of parties."

"Okay, you can have a key."

"You can bring it when you come see me at work next Sunday," he said.

"I'm not eating ice cream," she insisted.

"Fine. Ruin my business."

"Take it or leave it."

"Heartless wench," he said, affectionately.

"That's skinny heartless wench," she corrected him.

"Bubba said you were entertaining tonight. How is Mike? Is he being a good boy and keeping his hands to himself?"

"You put him up to that 'chaste from afar' thing, didn't you?"

"Get the ring before you let him do his thing."

"You are so sick, David, and a hypocrite. Did Bubba give you a ring?"

"Bubba gives me other things."

"Spare me."

David laughed.

"I'm hanging up now," she said, cutting off his laughter.

****

On Monday, Patrice received another ornament in the mail—three French hens. She smiled as she hung it on the tree, imagining telling her kids about the how their daddy gave her the ornaments the year before they were married.

It was amazing how good she felt today. The sun seemed brighter, the season more joyous than it had yesterday. The dream of a life spent with Mike didn't seem so impossible now.

The intercom buzzed. "Floral delivery for Patrice Wilson."

Patrice buzzed him in, dancing around the room as she waited for him to get to her door. It was wonderful to be loved and in love. She tipped the deliveryman and took the dozen red-tipped cream roses from him. The card read:

> *The red rose whispers of passion,*
> *And the white rose breathes of love;*

Oh, the red rose is a falcon,
And the white rose is a dove.

But I send you a cream-white rosebud,
With a flush on its petal tips;
For the love that is purest and sweetest
Has a kiss of desire on the lips.
—John Boyle O'Reilly

Until tonight.
Love, Mike

Patrice sighed. Could anything be this romantic? She called Mike to thank him, but his secretary said he was in court. She called David.

"I am in love with the perfect man," she sighed.

"Sorry, love, I'm already taken."

"Not you, dolt. Mike."

"Oh...Mike," David said, drawing out the words. "Mike who?"

"I'm going to hang up now."

"No, don't. I'll be serious. What did the splendid Michael Tucker do now?"

"I'm not going to call you anymore if you're going to be so sarcastic."

"Sorry," he said in a normal voice. "I didn't think I'd be jealous when he finally returned your love, but I am."

"Why?"

"She asks why."

"David, we've been best friends forever. Nothing is going to change that. Not Bubba, not Mike—nothing."

"Spoken like a woman whose lover doesn't know her best friend is gay."

"Personally, I think he'll be relieved when he finds out."

"Don't count on it, sweetheart. Men would rather see another man as a rival than an abomination."

"You're not an abomination. Have you been talking with your dad again?"

"I called my sister Carmen's house last night. He was visiting."

"And she put him on the phone? What was she

201

thinking? Poor David. Do you want me to come over? I could bring the flowers Mike sent and the wonderfully romantic card. They'd cheer you up."

"No need. It's an old wound. So tell me about the flowers. They're red roses, right?"

"Right flower, wrong color. He gave me cream-white roses with a flush on their petal tips." She sighed. "And listen to the card."

"Will I need a tissue or a bucket?"

"Quit being an ass, David."

"Well..."

"Tissue."

"Okay, read it."

She did.

"All right, you can marry him," he grumbled.

"He hasn't asked."

"He will. Just don't tell him about Bubba and me until after he's promised to have us at the wedding."

"At?" Patrice protested. "You're only going to be at it? I thought you'd be my gaytron of honor."

"Gaytron," David laughed. "I like that."

Chapter 47

Patrice pulled Mike into her apartment and gave him an enthusiastic kiss. "Thank you for the flowers and the card. I loved the poem."

"You're welcome." He smiled down at her before indulging in another kiss. This was what he wanted to come home to every night, he realized—Patrice welcoming him at the door with a kiss, the delicious smells of cooking scenting the air, and eventually kids joining her in the greeting. "Did the ornament come as well?"

"Yes, thank you," she said, stepping back so that he could take off his coat and hang it up. "I hung it on the tree."

He closed the closet door and followed Patrice into the living room. "Would you like a glass of wine before dinner?" she asked.

"What I'd really like is to hold you," he said, sitting on the couch and pulling her onto his lap. He buried his nose in her hair and groaned. "You smell so good. I've been fantasizing about this all day."

"Smelling my hair?"

"Holding you, touching you, breathing you in," he nuzzled her neck, and she shivered.

"Oh."

"Would you mind if I did this forever?" He nibbled on

her earlobe and kissed the soft skin of her neck.

Patrice arched her neck, giving him greater access. "Not if you don't mind burnt food."

"How long 'til it's done?" he asked, between kisses.

"When the timer goes off. Ten minutes. But I should mash the potatoes before then. Say five minutes."

"Five minutes should be perfect," he said, sliding his hands up her sweater.

"For what?"

He held her close, raining kisses along her jaw.

"For this." His lips covered hers in a slow, sensuous kiss. Patrice was cocooned in Mike's embrace. Touching her sparked fires of desire. Encouraged by her ragged breath, he cupped her breasts.

They drove each other mad until the timer went off, and Patrice pulled away. "Dinner."

"Let's skip dinner and go straight to bed."

Patrice frowned, pushing herself away from Mike. "No."

"No?" he repeated, puzzled. She'd seemed so ready. He certainly was.

"We aren't going to bed."

"Okay." He stood and then, offering her his hand, pulled her to her feet. "We aren't going to bed."

Patrice looked him in the eye as if judging his sincerity. "Good." The oven timer beeped again. "I've got to get dinner."

He followed her into the kitchen. "I won't push it, but I would like to know why."

"Asking why is pushing it. Why can't you just accept 'no' for the answer?" She took the meatloaf from the oven and placed it on the cool burners of the range.

"Because I need to know why."

She didn't look at him. "I'm not on the pill, and I'm allergic to latex."

"Condoms come in materials other than latex."

"You want to do it in a sheep, go to a farm."

"You're angry again," he said, touching her arm.

She shook off his hand, but said nothing.

"And those lines about latex and sheep sound well rehearsed." He grabbed hold of her arms and turned her to face him. "You've obviously used them before. But

Pet..."

"You mean 'Pest'," she interrupted in a shaky voice.

"I mean 'Pet'." He shook her gently until she looked at him. "It's me—Mike. I'm not some guy who wants to get in your pants as a lark. I love you. Making love to you would be a physical expression of the love I feel for you. Of the love I thought we shared. I don't want to pressure you or try to change your mind. Hell, I'm willing to do the 'chaste and from afar' thing again if that's what you want. I just want to know why. Is it something I did?"

Patrice shook her head. "Well... it's not something you did recently."

"But still something I did?" He dropped his hands from her arms, stricken. "What? When?"

Patrice turned away from him to drain the potatoes in the sink. He let her, knowing that sometimes it was easier to talk about things with your hands busy.

"The night of my sixteenth birthday, I wanted you to notice me. I wanted you to love me like I loved you. I thought that going to bed with you would get me in your heart like you were in mine. I planned to offer myself to you while we danced. I was opening my mouth to do it when you handed me off to Randy. I never had another chance after that. You disappeared into the bar and made love with Nelly Molson's cousin in the back seat of your car."

"Oh, God," Mike groaned, remembering the night. He didn't even remember the girl's name. "How did you...?"

Patrice shrugged. "Randy made sure I knew."

Mike shook his head. "Damn him."

"Anyway. It was then I decided that I wouldn't make love until I was married."

Patrice turned on the mixer to whip the potatoes, making conversation impossible.

When she had finished and was spooning the potatoes into a bowl, Mike said, "I remember that night. I remember the dress you wore. It was peach, so pale it was almost white, but it made your skin glow like rich cream. You were so beautiful that Randy had his work cut out for him that night, protecting your honor. I didn't want to be at that party. I didn't want to see you." He looked into her eyes and confessed. "There's been an attraction between us from the start. You gave into it, following me around when you were little and sending me food and letters when you were older, but I fought it. I couldn't give into my feelings for you. Not when I was ten and you were three and definitely not later. There was something wrong with a seventeen-year-old who likes a ten-year-old and something sick when a twenty-year-old lusts after a thirteen-year-old. You've loved and idolized me since you were a child, and I've been fighting my feelings all that time. Hell, I've been lusting after you since you started to develop breasts. I made myself sick." He turned away. "I knew what you were going to suggest the night of your sweet sixteen party. The thought of it made me hard and disgusted. I pushed you off on Randy to keep myself from you. And I climbed in the backseat of my car with the first girl I could." He closed his eyes and shook his head. "You're right. If I were you, I wouldn't even kiss me."

"Stop it," Patrice ordered. "I won't go to your pity party. You don't disgust me now any more than you did then. I'd have gone to bed with you when I was thirteen had you given the slightest hint that you were attracted to me. I've always wanted you."

"But not now."

Patrice barked out a laugh. "Are you nuts? I want you now more than ever."

"You just won't go to bed with me."

"Let's just say I'm holding out for a commitment we aren't quite ready to make."

He almost said he was ready, but he stopped himself. He was ready—very ready. But he wanted to do this right. "We'll wait."

"Good." She handed him the bowl of potatoes. "Put this on the table."

Chapter 48

Mike went to Patrice's apartment the next two days after work. One night they cooked together; the other she put dinner on the table as he hung up his coat. Both nights, he watched as she unwrapped the day's ornament and hung it on the tree. They kissed under the mistletoe. They danced in the tree-lit living room. They lingered over dessert and coffee, talking about everything. Thursday came too quickly.

Mike had never dreaded weekends before. Thursday didn't really qualify as a weekend, but for Mike the week of seeing Patrice was over. Friday night he spent at home, refusing the invitation to party with Alex and Randy. They were three successful professionals on a Friday night and not a date among them. Pathetic.

Patrice called during a lull at work.

"I miss you," he said into the phone.

"Me too. I've some bad news about my schedule. Victor has booked us solid until Christmas Eve. I'm thinking of moving in a cot."

"That bad, huh?"

"I'm working days getting ready for the parties and my nights as well."

"I thought you only had to work Fridays, Saturdays and parties."

"Derrick's got the flu."

"Derrick?" Mike asked.

"The weeknight cook."

"Oh. I guess this means I won't be able to see you," Mike complained.

"Not unless you come here."

"Are you going to your folks' on Sunday?"

"No. I'm pretty much here until Christmas Eve," Patrice said.

"I was hoping to see you before."

"Sorry."

"Me too. I've a command appearance with my mother Sunday after church. Maybe I'll stop by afterwards for a minute."

"I should have a lull in the early afternoon."

"What about Christmas Eve?" Mike asked. "Will I get to see you before church?"

"Only if you come over to my apartment. I'll be getting stuff ready for Christmas."

"Can't I help?"

"You'll have to chop onions," Patrice warned.

Mike never considered hesitating. "What time?"

****

On Sunday morning, Patrice was at Victor's by seven-thirty.

"Where are you?" David demanded at noon when Patrice grabbed the phone.

"You called, idiot. I'm at Victor's."

"And why are you at Victor's instead of here?"

"Victor pays me."

"Oh. Well, there is that," David admitted. "But does he give you fabulous ice cream?"

"Give nothing. I pay for my ice cream."

"Well, it wouldn't look good if the boss gave away the profits, now would it?"

"What do you want, David? I'm busy."

"Can't I just call you to talk?"

"Not at work. Spit it out."

"Bubba's family is coming for Christmas. Could you make an appearance?"

"I thought we'd broken up."

"Not quite yet."

Patrice sighed her resignation. "Fine. Not until the day after, though. I'm too busy." She paused to listen to a question in the kitchen. "No," she told the prep cook. "Dip them in the dark and swirl on the white."

"You're busy," David said. "I'll pick up your key at the host's stand."

"Oh, David. I'm sorry. I forgot all about that. I didn't bring the spare. Sorry."

"That's okay. I'll copy your key and bring it back before you're off work. You'll never notice it was gone."

An hour later, David stuck his head into the bustling kitchen. Patrice's assistants were carrying trays of salads and desserts into the cooler.

"Hey, Pet."

Patrice looked up from the stuffed roast she was rolling. "Oh, yeah. My keys." She motioned David over with a jerk of her head. "You'll have to get them. They're in my front pocket."

She lifted up her elbow to give him access.

David stood behind her, wrapping both arms around her. "Which pocket?" he asked, sliding his hands into both and nibbling on her neck on a spot he knew was ticklish.

Patrice squirmed and giggled, caught by David's arms. "Stop it, idiot."

Just as David bit Patrice's earlobe, Mike poked his head into the kitchen.

"Stop it," she squealed, stomping on David's foot and elbowing him out of her pockets. She turned, saw Mike's stunned expression, and froze. "Mike."

David pocketed Patrice's keys and turned toward Mike. "Well, I've got to be going. See you later Patrice. Mike."

Patrice stared at David's retreating form. The jerk was going to leave her to explain. "David," she complained.

David didn't respond as he cut a wide swath around Mike to exit the kitchen through the service door.

"Fine," she called after him. "And don't think I won't tell him either."

"Tell me what?" Mike asked.

"That David is..." She couldn't do it. She couldn't out David in the middle of Victor's kitchen. "...certifiable," she finished. "His lover is insanely jealous, yet he flirts with me in front of people. He's going to get himself into so much trouble." He already was. Just wait until she got her hands on him. Patrice imagined herself throttling David and enjoying each gasp and gurgle, but that wasn't any help at the moment. She desperately wished that David hadn't chosen today to goof around. He hardly ever did that kind of stuff anymore. Why did Mike have to witness it?

She finished tying the rolled roast and wiped her hands on a washcloth.

"I've missed you," she said, hugging his neck.

His hands rested on her hips as he looked searchingly into her eyes. "Have you?"

"Yes." She gave his lips a quick peck before stepping back to put the roast in the oven.

"I'd like to talk about this later," Mike said, glancing at the three other people bustling around the kitchen, wiping down the counters and washing large bowls and pots in huge stainless sinks.

"Sure," Patrice said, glad for a reprieve. She would tell him all about her relationship with David when they were alone.

"Until then, you can tell him from me to keep his hands to himself."

Patrice bit her tongue to keep from laughing. Mike was more at risk of David's hands than she was.

"I'll tell him, if I see him."

"So will I," Mike added irritably.

Patrice put her hand on Mike's arm. "I really have missed you," Patrice whispered, looking into Mike's eyes.

The rigidity of his expression softened.

"I have a break coming." She smiled invitingly. "We could go to the bar, and I'll buy you a drink?"

"How long of a break?" he asked.

"Fifteen, twenty minutes."

"Grab your coat." He directed. "We'll go talk in the car."

"I've a better idea," Patrice said. "Wait here a minute." She left Mike in the kitchen.

Patrice returned a moment later, dangling a key from her index finger. "Victor said we could use his office."

Mike raised a questioning brow. It hadn't been that long since he'd been banned from the restaurant, and now he was welcome to use Victor's office. He'd come up in the world.

Victor's office was a small room crammed with a large oak desk, a filing cabinet, an over-flowing bookcase, and a couch. The couch surprised Mike.

"Come on in," Patrice said, wrestling the key from the lock.

Mike sat on the couch. Patrice closed the door and joined him.

"Do you want me to explain David now or do you want to neck?" she asked, unconsciously licking her lips.

"David who?" Mike asked, capturing those lips with his.

Chapter 49

David poked his head in the kitchen when he returned with the key.

"Is she still talking to me or am I dead?" he asked Patrice's coworkers.

Patrice's assistants exchanged glances with each other and Patrice before a dark-haired girl answered, "Dead."

"Would it help if I said I'm sorry?" he asked, contritely.

"No," Patrice said.

"How about if I begged forgiveness?"

"Bended knee begging or whining from the kitchen door begging?" she asked.

"You're smiling. I've been resurrected." He sauntered into the kitchen, grinning like a fool. The others discreetly wandered into another area of the kitchen.

"Not really," Patrice informed him. "I just want to get you closer so that it's easier to carve you limb from limb."

"Big talker," he said, giving his unwilling friend a peck on the cheek. "You can't resist me."

"Yes, I can." She scowled, stepping away from him. "Easily."

"So did you out me?" he asked in hushed tones.

She shook her head. "Not yet, but you've made it so

212

that I'm going to have to." Patrice frowned. "Why?" She shook her head. "Why do you have to make things so difficult?"

"I didn't know he was coming," David said in defense.

"Would it have mattered?" she asked, seriously.

David shook his head. "I can't help it. I am who I am."

Patrice stared at her friend, trying to figure him out. "But things were fine. Mike knew you were my friend and liked you. You weren't a threat...you weren't different...you were just a guy. Now you're a threat and to explain why you're not a threat, I can tell him that you're like a brother, which he won't believe—Randy would never nibble on my neck or bite my ear—or I can tell him the truth."

"Tell him the truth," David said, turning away.

Patrice grabbed his arm, making him turn back. "Why? Why make me and Bubba go through this rigmarole and then blow it? If you're a known quantity..."

"You think Mike would say something?" he whispered.

"No. But the way you're bent on sabotaging your happiness, he wouldn't need to."

"I don't see how goofing with you sabotages anything with Bubba."

"Don't you?" she asked, looking at him through narrowed eyes. "The more people who know, the more people who know. It's like with your dad. He didn't have to know. You knew how he'd be. You could have avoided that scene altogether, but you didn't."

"It's not the same thing. He needed to know."

"Really? Why? Why can't it be a private thing?"

"Why does it have to be a private thing? Does it embarrass you?"

"Me?" Patrice covered her heart with her hand. "No. It never has and never would. You could announce it at Soldier Field, and I'd hold your hand while you did it. But I know how it affects you and those around you. How I feel and how you feel doesn't affect how society as a whole feels. And this isn't a conversation we should be having here."

"I know," he grumped. "It's dangerous." He looked at

the floor for a moment. "But damn it, Pet, sometimes I just want to say the hell with danger, to hell with denial."

"I know. You just want to be who you are and be accepted for all of it. And you can be...with select people."

"With you, but what about Mike?"

"I don't know. We've never discussed it. But it won't change you and me."

"It might."

"It won't," she insisted.

"Right. You'd choose me over Mike? Don't think so, Pet." He turned from her.

She put her hand on his arm. "It won't come to that."

David turned on her. "And if it does?"

Patrice stared at David. There was a real possibility that Mike might be too homophobic to handle her friendship with David. And if that were the case, she'd have to give Mike up. She'd seen David once after he'd been ambushed coming out of a gay bar. She knew the violence of the hate and fear some men had for homosexuals. She couldn't be with a man like that. But the question remained: if Mike were homophobic, what would he do when he knew about David and Bubba?

It was suddenly very clear to Patrice why David was troubled by her relationship with Mike. He wanted Patrice to be happy, but he was torn. Sometimes he appeared to be helping Mike, and other times he seemed to be trying to end it in a variety of subtle and more obvious ways. David stood to lose a lot if things went badly. He could lose business as well as both her and Bubba.

Tears filled Patrice's eyes at the magnitude of the problem. "What am I going to do?" she asked sadly.

"I don't know."

They stood in silence for long seconds staring at the floor before David raised his head and eyebrows. "I don't suppose you'd consider marrying either me or Bubba? We'd let you keep Mike on the side."

Patrice bit out a laugh. "It'd have to be you. The babies would be too pale to be Bubba's."

Chapter 50

Mike arrived at Patrice's apartment at a quarter to nine Christmas Eve morning, laden with presents—the "twelve lords" ornament, the "Mine" ornament, and others—and apple fritters. He hadn't seen her since Sunday.

Patrice opened the door wearing a robe. Her hair hung in dripping clumps. "You're early."

"Actually I'm late," he said, walking past her to unload his arm under the tree. "I wanted to see the way you look first thing in the morning."

"I look tired and rumpled," she informed him, following him into the living room. "What's all this?"

"Christmas is tomorrow, silly." He kissed her cheek.

"I know Christmas is tomorrow, but I thought we'd decided to get each other sweaters that we'd open up at the party."

"And that's all you got me?" Mike asked, incredulously. "A sweater?"

Patrice blushed. "Well, no." She looked at the presents he was arranging under her tree. "But I didn't get you this much. There have to be eight presents here."

"Nine. Be happy."

"I am," she said. "I just don't want you to be disappointed."

215

Mike opened his arms, and Patrice slid in.

"Couldn't happen," he said, nuzzling her neck.

"Maybe all I got you was a sweater." She shivered as he nibbled his way to her earlobe.

"You just said that wasn't all you got me."

"It wasn't," she giggled. "I bought you two sweaters. They were having a two-for-one sale." She pushed him away from her neck. "Stop that. It tickles."

He let her go, dangling a white waxed bag in front of her. "I also brought apple fritters."

"Yum," she said over her shoulder as she headed for the stairs. "Stick them in the oven on warm and make the coffee while I get dressed."

"I could help," he suggested.

"You will be."

"I meant with getting you dressed."

"So did I." She grinned at him. "This way I'll actually get dressed.

"Don't you want to open a present first?"

"You can unwrap the lords a leaping and hang them on the tree."

"I was thinking of a different one."

She started walking up the stairs. "I think I'll wait for Christmas."

"You can open one early," he coaxed, following her.

"You just want to open yours early."

"Actually, I just want to see what you have on under that robe."

She turned to see him two steps below her. "Uh, uh." She shook her finger at him. "There's a no-returns policy on this, so there are no previews and no trial runs."

"But what if I want to buy it?"

Her smile froze. "What?"

"Nothing." This wasn't the way he wanted to do it. "Go get dressed."

Patrice stared at him a minute.

"Go on," he said, turning back down the stairs. "Go get dressed. I'll make the coffee and warm the fritters."

She watched him go into the kitchen. Was he going to propose or was he making a come-on? She stared at the empty archway for several long minutes.

"Go get dressed." Mike's voice came from the kitchen.

Shocked from her reverie, Patrice turned and dashed up the stairs.

She hovered before her closet in indecision. Excitement and electricity akin to fear raced through her body. Was he going to ask her to marry him? What should she wear? If he was going to propose, shouldn't she dress up? No, that would be too obvious. And what if she were wrong? She was probably wrong. He wasn't going to propose. Not yet anyway. They had unresolved issues. She hadn't explained about David or Bubba. She hadn't even figured out what she'd say about them. They couldn't get engaged before they'd settled things between them, could they?

She couldn't think. She loved Mike. She'd always loved Mike. If he proposed, she'd say yes by pure reflex. The trick was not to jump the gun so that when he said, "Would you please pour me some more coffee," she didn't shout out, "Yes!" before he got to "pour the coffee." She had to pretend she hadn't heard whatever it was he said on the stairs. It was obviously a slip of the tongue anyway. If he proposed, she'd accept, but she couldn't spend the entire day in agony wondering if he was going to pop the question. Just like she couldn't spend the day worrying about how she'd handle the David/Bubba issue. She'd have to cross those bridges when she came to them—if she came to them.

She tugged on jeans and a long-sleeved t-shirt, pulled her hair into a ponytail, and applied mascara and lip-gloss before heading downstairs.

Mike was standing in front of the coffee maker with two mugs in hand.

"It doesn't go any faster if you watch it," Patrice said in an effort to keep things light as she entered the kitchen. "Did you get the oven figured out?"

"It was easy once I got the control knobs up. Why do they make them go flat like that?"

"So kids can't monkey with them."

"I bet a kid would have figured them out faster than I did. Why do you push them in? There aren't any kids here."

"It makes it easier to clean with them pushed in."

"All right. I'll give you that." He poured the coffee

while Patrice got the fritters out of the oven. "What are we making first?" he asked.

"Pâté, and the sausage pinwheels."

"God, I love those," he sighed.

"Which?"

"Both."

Patrice laughed. "You're easy." She put the fritters on a plate before opening the refrigerator. "You want butter on yours?"

"No. I'm saving calories for tomorrow."

Patrice chuckled, pulling out the milk. "You bring apple fritters, and you're saving calories? Do the butter if you want—we'll have salad for lunch."

"No lunch for me," he said, taking a bite of a fritter. "I'm your official taste tester."

"I've perfected these recipes. I don't need a taster," Patrice assured him.

"Still, you have one."

She smiled. "Lucky me."

"No, lucky me." He grinned, taking another bite.

Mike didn't propose while they cooked, nor did he propose in the break they took to open the leaping lords and hang them on the tree. Patrice pushed the thought of it out of her mind as they finished the last few hors d'oeuvres.

It was two o'clock when she covered the last platter with plastic wrap and crammed it into the refrigerator with the rest. "It always looks like so much food when it's in a small refrigerator like this."

"It's because you're used to those huge walk-ins you have at work. Are you sure we've made enough? I'm worried about those riblets and little quiche things," Mike said, peering over her shoulder.

Patrice smiled, closing the refrigerator. "There is more than enough of everything, even the riblets and quiches. You didn't eat all that many for lunch."

"I was too full from doing my duty."

"Which you did very well, by the way," Patrice said as they left the spotless kitchen for the living room. She plopped down on the couch. "Thanks for all your help."

"I'm indispensable as a taste tester."

"I'm sure there's someone somewhere who needs one.

You could hire yourself out to a despot. Make sure his food isn't poisoned."

"I'd rather be your taste tester."

"I'd rather you were too."

Mike leaned down to kiss her soundly. "Do you have the "Twelve Days of Christmas" on a CD? There's something I've been dying to do since I saw those ornaments in the shop."

Patrice walked to the stereo and cued up the song, wondering what he had in mind.

A moment later they were racing around the tree like children trying to touch the ornaments in order while the song played. They ended the song in a heap on the couch, laughing so hard it hurt. Then laughter turned to kissing with Mike pressing her into the couch and his hand up her shirt.

"I can't stand it," he announced, coming up for breath.

She sat up as he got off her. "What?" she asked, concerned by the tone of his voice.

He cupped her worried face in his palms and kissed her. "I thought the whys about Bubba and David and whoever the hell else you've been kissing mattered to me. I thought I needed an explanation, but I don't. I just need you." He stared into Patrice's eyes as if looking for something.

She swallowed. "Okay." She was willing to explain, but still hadn't figured out what she'd say without telling Mike that David and Bubba were gay.

"All I need is your word that you'll never kiss another man." He waved his left hand as if erasing his last comment from the air. "Actually, I don't need you to say anything about it. I just need you to say you'll be mine."

She looked into his eyes, trying to read there the meaning of his words. "Okay."

"Not, okay." He shook his head. "I'm doing this all wrong." He stood up and paced the room in front of the couch while she watched with growing anxiety. "I've given speeches that save or cost companies millions of dollars. I can find the words to convince juries that my client is innocent or that the opposition is in the wrong. I make my living knowing what to say and how to say it, so why do I

219

always find myself struggling for the right words with you?"

He stopped pacing and looked at Patrice. "Is it because I'm afraid?" He knelt before her, taking her left hand in-between his hands, caressing her palm with his thumbs while he spoke. "Is it because you hold my heart in your hand and have the power to crush it or send it soaring with a word? Patrice, I know I've spent most of my life trying to deny my feelings for you and pushing you away, but all that has changed. I've changed. I want to spend the rest of my life with you—showering you with the kind of love you deserve, and proving to you that your faith in me all these years hasn't been misplaced." He looked into her tear-filled eyes and his heart clenched. "You have my heart, Patrice. You've always had it. Will you keep it forever? Will you marry me?"

This was the moment she'd been waiting for all her life. She nodded, dislodging tears from her eyes, and croaked out, "Yes."

She was in his arms, mingling salty tears with kisses and laughter. Somewhere between kisses, he presented her with a ring box containing a two-carat diamond solitaire on a wide gold band and the matching wedding band. He slid the solitaire on her finger, and they kissed before admiring it. Mike nodded to the tree.

"There's a chain under there for you to wear the diamond on at work," Mike said.

Patrice kissed him. "You've thought of everything."

He shook his head. "Not quite everything. When I saw your tears, I was afraid you were going to say no." Mike cradled Patrice against his chest.

"How could I say no to a man who bathed my hand with his tears as he proposed?"

"I did not," Mike protested.

Patrice gently wiped below Mike's left eye with two fingers. She showed him the sheen of tears.

"It's sweat," Mike explained. "I was that nervous."

"And here I thought you weren't going to deny your feelings anymore," Patrice teased.

"God, Pet," he grinned at her affectionately. "I was right all those years ago. You are a pest."

Despite his teasing tone, she felt a moment of

panicked alarm.

He felt her stiffen. "No." He tightened his arms around her. "It was a joke—a loving inside joke. I love you. You are my Pet and my Pest and that's the way I want it—always. I meant it when I said you have my heart. Patrice, you are my heart. I don't just want you; I need you. I want us to be married so that when I fall over my tongue like that I'll have chance to make it right without the fear that you'll disappear from my life."

"I wouldn't disappear."

"That's been my greatest fear since I blew it with that crème brûlée."

"Funny thing, your mentioning that dessert. Yesterday, Victor had me make one just like it for someone's wedding. I thought of you the entire time."

"Did you?"

She nodded.

"Affectionately or angrily?" He looked her in the eye.

"With humor and love. We are past that."

"So you'll make me another crème brûlée one day?"

She breathed a laugh. "One day."

They cuddled comfortably on the couch listening to the carols, mesmerized by the Christmas lights.

"Randy is picking me up for church tonight."

"Will you tell him about the engagement?" Mike asked.

"Before I tell my mother?" She looked at him incredulously. "Are you nuts?"

Mike chuckled. "Maybe we had best wait until tomorrow and tell both of our mothers together."

Patrice nodded as Mike continued, "We'd better have some answers before we do, though."

"Like why we didn't let them know we were getting this close?"

"No," he said. "Like wedding date and time, type of dress, color and cut of tux...those things."

Patrice groaned. "I wish we could elope."

"But then we'd have to listen to them go on about how we denied them our wedding."

"I know," Patrice sighed. "I just don't know if I can stand a year of wedding plans with our mothers."

"They aren't that bad," Mike protested.

Patrice regarded him quizzically. "Have you ever planned anything with those two? I almost didn't turn sixteen."

Mike laughed. "So what's the solution?"

"We can't elope, but we could plan a simple wedding and just spring it on them."

"And keep our engagement a secret until then?" Mike shook his head. "Not possible. The only way that would work is if we got married tomorrow."

"Tomorrow?" Patrice repeated. "That would be ideal; too bad we can't pull it off."

"Why can't we? Father McDaniels usually stops in at the party at some time."

"Doesn't it take a couple of days to get a marriage license?"

"Not if you know the right people." He gave Patrice a smacking kiss on the lips as he rose from the couch. "Let me make a few calls." He stopped. "If this is really what you want."

"I want to be married to you," Patrice said. "A quiet ceremony in my parents' living room on Christmas would be perfect. We have the food."

Mike laughed, eyes twinkling. "Yes, but is there enough?"

"More than enough," Patrice assured him. "We could even invite a few friends."

"Or," Mike countered. "We could have a reception later, after the holidays."

"Perfect," Patrice beamed. "If we can get the license."

"Let me make those calls."

Patrice listened in as he did.

He nodded to her as he spoke into the phone. "You will? Thanks, Jack. I'll be right down. I owe you one."

He hung up the phone, grabbed Patrice, and swung her around. "We've got it," he said, kissing her dizzy. "Jack will meet me at the courthouse in a half-hour to do the paperwork. Could I have a plate of goodies as a thank you?"

"I'll get it," she said, kissing him again before heading to the kitchen.

"I'll give Father a quick call and give him the heads up," Mike said, picking up the phone and then putting it right down and grabbing Patrice again. "I can't believe it. Tomorrow at this time you'll be my wife."

Patrice went still in his arms. "Are you sure this is what you want?"

"It is." He kissed her. "You are." He kissed her again. "No cold feet here? How are yours?"

"Fine. It's just happening so fast."

"Too fast?" he asked, trying to read her eyes.

"My first word was, 'Mine,' Mike. I've known what I wanted all my life. I just can't believe I'm finally going to get it."

He laughed. "Believe it, girl." And he kissed her thoroughly. "Now make up that plate while I call Father. This will make his Christmas."

"Our wedding?" she asked, puzzled.

"No, the contribution he'll get from us and both of our parents."

Mike looked at Patrice when she handed him the laden plate a few minutes later. He took the plate from her and set it down before pulling her into his arms. "What's wrong, Pet?"

She bit her lip. "I don't know what to wear."

Mike laughed. "I'd prefer you slept in the nude, but I can do flannel."

Patrice lightly punched his shoulder. "I meant for the wedding."

"Oh, that? What were you going to wear tomorrow?"

"A dress I bought."

"Wear that," Mike suggested, nibbling Patrice's neck.

"I can't—it's red!" she protested.

Mike chuckled into her ear. "I kind of like that—and the bride wore red."

"I can't wear red to my own wedding," she insisted.

"Why not?"

She ignored him, mentally inventorying her closet. "I have a white suit, but its linen."

"It doesn't matter what you wear. No one will be expecting a wedding. We'll announce the engagement as Father is pulling into the driveway, and then we'll get married. My mom won't even have time to straighten her hair before we're exchanging vows."

"But the pictures," she protested.

"You'll look great. Trust me."

"All right."

"Now," he said, kissing her nose. "I've got to go meet Jack. I probably won't make it back before church. I couldn't reach Father, so I'll need to get there early to talk to him before Mass. Plan to have me drive you home."

She clung to him. "I'll miss you."

"Me too, but not for long." He gave her another quick peck and pulled away to hurry to the tree.

"What are you doing?"

He was moving presents around, searching for something.

"Here," he said, pulling a small box from the jumble. "Open this."

Patrice took it from him, realization dawning. "The necklace."

"I want you wearing my ring tonight."

Chapter 51

Patrice couldn't spot Mike in the crowded church. Was he there? Had he talked to Father?

Patrice's family arrived a few minutes earlier than usual and searched out seats in the rapidly filling church.

"I love midnight Mass," Janice told her daughter as she followed Randy and Patrice into a pew near the front of the church.

"Too bad they got rid of the midnight part of it," Roy commented, sitting next to his wife. "Nine is too early for a midnight Mass."

"I wish it had been this early when the kids were little. Remember waking them up to get them to the church?" Janice asked.

"I remember." Roy frowned. "They were cranky little brats."

"Roy!" Janice hissed. "We're in church."

"That's why I didn't say 'bastards.'"

"Roy!"

"I remember those Masses," Patrice said, trying not to laugh as she normally did when he father baited her mother. "Walking through the parking lot to church after the warmth of bed and car was always painfully cold. Everything felt brittle. I remember how the snow used to squeak under my patent leathers and that the sound

225

made me colder. Then we'd get inside and see the trees by the altar lit with lights and surrounded by poinsettias just like now. The choir would start to sing. And Christmas would arrive. I felt like a Who from Whoville. Santa and presents didn't matter. It was Christmas. Just like now."

"I wish I'd known about the present part—I could have saved a lot of money," her father said, grinning.

Melanie frowned at her husband while he and Patrice laughed.

"Shouldn't we be saving spots for the Tuckers?" Patrice asked as the usher asked them to squish together to accommodate the late arrivals.

"Melanie and I are keeping our promise to give you and Mike until tomorrow," her mother said.

Patrice said nothing. It had been two years since she and Mike had shared a Christmas Eve Mass. His family was part of her history, part of her Christmas tradition. Trust her mother to know that and use it against her. She wondered if their absence would have felt less like a hole and more like a welcome reprieve if she and Mike were still at odds. As it was, she missed the Tuckers and especially Mike even though this enforced separation would help maintain their secret until tomorrow. Maybe she could spot them in church. She scoured what she could see of the congregation. She thought of the engagement ring that hung hidden beneath her dress, but she didn't touch it for fear of calling attention to it.

"Is everything ready for tomorrow?" Janice asked her daughter.

Patrice abruptly stopped searching the assembly and turned to her mother with a momentary stab of confused panic. How had her mother found out about the wedding so fast? "Uh, what?"

"The food?" Her mother's eyes glittered as they raked Patrice. "You were going to make hors d'oeuvres for tomorrow. Did you get them done?"

"Oh, that." Patrice nearly sagged with relief. "Yes. All the food is ready."

"What did you think I meant?" Her mother's eyes were wide with forced innocence.

Damn. Her mother was up to something. "Oh,

226

nothing," Patrice lied poorly. "I was just listening to the choir, not thinking about tomorrow."

"Don't lie in church, Pet. God watches. You were thinking about Mike and your promise, weren't you?"

Even though Patrice knew her mother was referring to her promise to get along with Mike tomorrow and not the wedding, she felt another jolt of panic. It was a good thing she and Mike only had to keep their engagement a secret one night. Her mother was watching her so closely Patrice felt certain the woman was trying to read her mind. Patrice nodded once in acquiescence.

"It's not that big of a deal, Pet." Her mother said sweetly as if she knew she'd won and was being magnanimous in victory. "I asked you to be nice to him for one day. It's not like I asked you to marry him."

Patrice froze. Did her mother know something or was she just fishing?

Her mother's warm hand patted Patrice's cold one. "I just want a nice family Christmas with our friends. You said you already forgave him. Now all you need to do is get along for one day. That's not too much for your mother to ask on Christmas, is it?"

"Uh," Patrice stumbled. "No, Mom."

"And will you get along?" Janice asked. "Or will Melanie and I have to contend with cold shoulders and frosty glares between our children?"

Patrice bit her lip to keep from smiling. Her mother was just fishing. "We'll get along. No frosty glares. I promise."

"Hmmm." Janice stared at her daughter.

Chapter 52

Delayed by his talk with Father, Mike was late meeting his parents before Mass, and his family ended up seated in the back of the church. Patrice would want to know the outcome of his talk. He searched the congregation while the choir sang.

"Why didn't we sit with the Wilsons?" Mike asked his parents. The Wilsons always got to church earlier than his family and saved them spots near the front.

His mother didn't bother to hide her grin. "Janice promised Patrice she had until tomorrow."

Mike nodded.

"So, how are things between you and Patrice?"

"We'll get along tomorrow as promised."

Melanie regarded her son with wide eyes. "Just get along?"

"That's what you asked for, isn't it? That we get along?"

"The last time we talked, you implied that you'd do more than just get along."

"You asked me to make certain she didn't marry Bubba, and she won't. That and making nice tomorrow is all you asked for, and that is all I promised."

"How can you be so certain about Bubba?"

"Patrice has assured me they're just good friends."

"And is that all you and Patrice are as well...friends?"

"Isn't that what you wanted?" he asked, innocently. It wasn't and he knew it, but he knew as well that his mother wouldn't come right out and tell him.

"Well, yes...but..." she said.

The processional hymn began and the congregation rose, pre-empting whatever his mother might have said.

Mike smiled into his hymnal.

As he went up to communion, Mike saw Patrice kneeling in her pew, surreptitiously watching the communion lines. His heart caught in his throat. Mine, he thought. Thank you, God, for making her mine.

Their eyes met as he passed her—a flicker of glorious recognition before his back was to her.

Patrice watched him take communion and follow the line as it turned toward her, taking the communicants back to their pews. As soon as she saw his face, she raised her brows in question, and he nodded once in answer.

Melanie saw the question and Janice the answer. Neither had time to confer with the other, however, before the line took them out of sight.

After Mass, Mike kissed his mother goodnight and shook his father's hand. "I'm parked in the street on the other side," he lied.

"Then I can talk with Janice a moment," Melanie said brightly.

"No," Matt stated. "I'm not standing in the cold so you can talk to someone you'll see tomorrow."

Mike watched his father lead his mother into the parking lot before doubling back to the church. He caught up with the Wilsons in time to hear Janice's attempt to convince Patrice to spend the night.

"It's not possible, Mom. I've got all the food at my apartment and your presents too."

"But it doesn't make sense for Randy to drive all the way to your side of town when he's going to be spending the night at the house."

"I'll take her home," Mike interrupted.

"That would be lovely, Mike." Janice couldn't accept fast enough. "We didn't see you come up. Merry Christmas."

Patrice looked at the ground to keep her smile from

showing as she fought for composure.

"I don't mind driving Patrice," Randy said, rushing to his sister's aid.

"Don't be silly," Janice scolded. "Why drive across town and back when Mike has offered?"

"It's across town for Mike too," Randy reminded them.

Patrice and Mike exchanged amused glances as the rest of her family discussed who should take Patrice home.

"It's settled, then," Janice announced, putting an end to the discussion. "Mike will drive Patrice home." She slipped her arm into her son's arm to enforce his compliance and ushered him to the parking lot. Roy followed his wife and son with an amused grin.

"Do you think they know?" Patrice asked, watching her family cross the parking lot and get into their cars.

"Not yet."

"I'm glad we're getting married tomorrow." Patrice waited for Randy's car to pull out before taking Mike's arm. "This way the wedding is ours, not theirs."

"They'll claim it anyway," Mike predicted, squeezing her arm.

"That's fine with me. We'll be married, and it won't matter." They walked to Mike's car, one of the few left in the parking lot. Patrice closed the door and buckled her seatbelt. "Randy was right: you're going to have to drive across town to get home."

"Not if I stay the night."

Patrice stared at him. "You want to stay the night?"

"Is that so surprising?"

"I guess not. I just thought we were going to wait until we're married."

"I can spend the night just holding you."

"Can you?" she asked, looking into his eyes.

He grinned sheepishly. "I can try."

****

The clock read one-fifteen when Mike returned from his second cold shower of the night.

"I'd have taken care of you if you'd let me." Patrice's drowsy voice came from the bed.

"God, Pet." Mike spun on his heel and went back to

230

the bathroom.

He woke her up ten minutes later when he crawled into bed wearing his boxers and shivering. "Poor baby," she said, snuggling her flannel clad body next to him. Mike wasn't surprised to feel himself harden again. Chastity was going to kill him.

Chapter 53

The sound of movement and whispers downstairs woke Mike. At first he thought it was his roommates Alex and Randy, but then he remembered where he was and who was beside him. He froze, listening in the darkness. Patrice had her back to him, her rounded backside pressed against his omnipresent erection. How could he be frightened and horny at the same time? He looked at the clock radio on the bedside table. Two-thirty. Patrice was getting robbed at two-thirty Christmas morning.

"Pet," he whispered, shaking her shoulder. "Pet wake up."

"Hmm?" she mumbled.

"Wake up, Pet. There's someone downstairs."

"Santa," she said sleepily. "He hadn't come earlier."

"It is not Santa," Mike insisted. "There's someone downstairs. I want you to call nine-one-one while I go check it out." He slid silently out of bed and searched for his pants. "Do you have a gun or a baseball bat or something I could use?" He found his pants on the floor halfway under the bed and yanked them on.

That question seemed to wake Patrice up.

"No, I don't have a gun or a bat. Mike, if you really think it's a burglar, you shouldn't be going downstairs."

"Of course, it's a burglar. It sure as hell isn't Santa

232

Claus." He pawed through her closet looking for a weapon and settled on a spiked heel. "These are a podiatrist's dream," he said, showing her the strappy-backed, black spike. "Do you actually wear these?"

Patrice stared at him, but didn't answer.

Mike ran his hands over the shoe, imagining her in a skimpy dress, seamed hose, and these shoes. She looked so good in his fantasy that he decided on the spot that she'd never wear it in public. A muffled thud and the sound of hushed voices coming from downstairs refocused Mike's attention.

"Have you called nine-one-one yet?" he asked, grabbing the other shoe for the other hand and inching out into the hall.

"No," Patrice snagged her robe from its hook on the door and followed him. "It's not a robber. It's David. He's playing Santa. I gave him a key to get in, but he was supposed to come while I was at church."

"David?" Mike asked incredulously. "You gave David a key to your apartment?" He inched closer to the balcony railing and looked over. Downstairs, tree lights lit the room with a festive glow, revealing a pile of presents that hadn't been there earlier and a couple under the mistletoe.

Mike stared at the dimly lit pair in disbelief. He walked to the top stairs and flipped on the downstairs lights.

Both David and Bubba cursed, shielding their eyes from the sudden brightness.

"Holy shit," Mike said, as Patrice slipped beside him. "That's Bubba Scott and David." He looked at Patrice and then back at the couple who had sprung apart as if doused with cold water.

"They were kissing," Mike explained to Patrice.

She nodded, wishing Mike hadn't seen that. "There's mistletoe."

Mike gaped.

She lowered her voice and said in soothing tones, "It's all right. They're gay."

"No shit."

Patrice took the shoes from Mike and nudged him toward the stairs. "Let's go downstairs."

"What is he doing here?" David asked accusingly as Patrice and Mike came down the steps. "I thought you were going to wait for the ring."

Patrice held up her left hand.

"Oh, my God! You're engaged." David rushed to meet her at the foot of the stairs. "Bubba, look, she's got a ring." He grabbed her hand and oohed and aahed over the ring.

"Yeah," Bubba, disheartened, gave the ring no more than a cursory glance. "It's not as big as the one I gave her."

"You gave her a ring?" Mike stared at Bubba in disbelief before turning to Patrice. "He gave you a ring?"

"I didn't accept it."

Dazed, Mike walked into the living room and sank into the couch. "Bubba Scott proposed, you turned him down, and now..."

"It wasn't quite like that," Patrice explained, joining him on the couch. "Bubba and I are just friends."

"Like he and David are just friends?" Mike asked, feeling sick.

David sat in the recliner adjacent to the couch while Bubba paced the floor.

"No," David said. "As you saw, Bubba and I are more than just friends."

Mike's glance flicked over David and then returned to Patrice. "You turned Bubba down, and he became..."

"The word is *gay*," Patrice said. "And no. Bubba was gay when I met him."

"Let me get this straight..." Mike stared at Patrice. "You dated a gay man, and he proposed to you?"

"Yes."

"Come on, Pet," David insisted. "Tell him all of it. Tell him how you dated me all through high school because I was gay."

"You knew he was gay?" Mike asked, still unable to wrap his mind around the concept.

"Yes," Patrice answered. "I only dated him because I knew."

"I don't get it. You like to date gay men?" His face was stricken. "Pet, I'm not gay."

She laughed. "I know. I dated David because he was safe. Even in high school, I was in love with you—waiting for you. Straight guys make demands. David didn't."

"What about Bubba?" Mike asked, glancing at the big man pacing the floor.

Patrice watched Bubba, worried. "Bubba and David are a couple, but because of Bubba's work, he needs a straight cover. I dated him as a favor."

"You were just helping out a friend," Mike repeated what Patrice had told him on more than one occasion.

"That's right." She covered his clenched hands with hers.

He looked at their hands and relaxed, turning his hands over to cradle hers. He looked into her eyes. "And he proposed because...?"

"Because his sisters expected an engagement."

"It would have been a lonely marriage," Mike commented.

"I never even considered it," Patrice said, looking into his eyes. "I was waiting for you."

"Why didn't you tell me?" Mike asked. "I was so jealous of Bubba and even David."

"I couldn't out them," she explained. "If anyone finds out about Bubba, his career is ruined."

"And you didn't trust me?"

Patrice bit her lip in hesitation. How did she admit that, no, she didn't trust the man she professed to love?

"She didn't know how you felt about homosexuality," David answered for her. "She wouldn't risk Bubba's career and our life together until she did."

"They are more in love and more committed to each other than most heterosexual couples I know," Patrice explained.

"He probably thinks we should be committed." Bubba stopped pacing to confront Mike. "Don't you? You think us queers should be railroaded out of our jobs and locked up?"

"Bubba!" Patrice scolded.

"Actually." Mike rose from the couch to return Bubba's stare. "I think a person's sexual orientation is his or her own business. Granted, I'm less comfortable with homosexual displays of affection than I am with heterosexual. But that aside, I'm actually glad that you and David are gay. It puts an entirely different spin on your relationships with Patrice." He turned to look at David. "It bothered me how close you and Patrice were. I envisioned it causing potential problems with our marriage, but now..." He shrugged. "I feel better. I minded a lot that Patrice's best friend was a guy, but I don't have a problem with it as long as you're gay."

Patrice wrapped her arms around Mike's neck and gave him a resounding smack. "Can they can come to the wedding?"

Mike nodded.

"When's the wedding? Have you set a date?" David asked.

Patrice looked at the wall clock, counting. "It's in eleven-and-a-half hours."

"Today?" David exclaimed, bouncing to his feet. "Come on, Bubba. We've got to let these two get some sleep." He grabbed his coat and threw Bubba his. "Eleven-and-a-half hours?" He looked at the clock, counting. "When is that? And where is it?"

"At my parents' house at three. And it's a secret," Pet answered.

"A secret?" David furrowed his brow in thought and then smiled. "A secret from your mother? God, Pet, that's a stroke of genius. Does she even know you're engaged?"

Patrice shook her head before turning it to look fondly at her fiancé. "He proposed yesterday."

"Then you don't have a dress," David announced. "What are you wearing?"

"The red one I bought."

David grinned. "As much as I like that concept, let me get you something else."

"On Christmas?" Mike said, doubtfully.

"If I can." David turned to Patrice. "Oh, Pet. You know that Bubba's mother and all his sisters and their families came up for Christmas. We'll try to sneak out tomorrow without the entire group, but I'm sure we'll have a following."

Bubba nodded. "Mama, Rochelle, and Ruby for sure. Ruthie too, maybe, but we'll keep it to them. No in-laws, nieces and nephews, or sisters you don't know."

David smiled at Patrice. "You're going to love Bubba's mama. Whatever you thought about his sisters, his mother is five times that."

Patrice laughed, looked at Bubba, and said, "I liked your sisters."

"They liked you too. They told Mama all about you, but I'll bet the wedding they were hoping to see this Christmas didn't have Mike in it." He grinned at Mike. "No offense."

Mike nodded. "None taken." He paused as a thought occurred to him. "Your family knows that you're gay and that there was never anything serious between you and Patrice, right?"

Bubba shook his head, sadly. "Wrong."

"Oooh," Mike winced. "I wouldn't want to be you tomorrow explaining why they're going to the wedding of the girl you were nearly engaged to. Are you sure you want to come if it means bringing them?"

David looked stunned. "Of course, he wants to come. Don't you?" He stared at Bubba.

Bubba was miserable and looked it.

Patrice couldn't stand it any longer. "Bubba, your sisters know."

"Know what?" Bubba and David asked in unison.

"Everything. Ruby cornered me Thanksgiving Day to make sure I knew you were gay. She thought you were leading me on, and she didn't want me to get hurt."

"Lord have mercy," Bubba said, shaking his head. "Does my mama know?"

"She's the one who sent your sisters out at Thanksgiving," Patrice told him. "They've known for years."

"Why haven't they said anything?" Bubba asked, not expecting an answer.

"They're waiting for you to decide to tell them."

"Lord." Bubba shook his head in wonder. "They don't hate me."

"They love you, Bubba," Patrice insisted. "And they seem fairly fond of David too."

"Lord, you never have to give me another thing," Bubba prayed aloud, his grin threatening to split his face. "You neither, Pet." He wrapped her in a big hug, kissing her soundly on the lips. When he let her go, he grabbed David and gave him similar treatment. When he started to go for Mike, he paused, thinking better of it. His hands dropped to his side, but his smile only grew. "I guess this means you can count on us tomorrow. David and me, Rochelle, Ruby, Ruth, and Mama."

Chapter 54

The insistent ring of the telephone finally woke them. Mike almost answered it by reflex, but Patrice hastily crawled over him to get to it first.

"Hello," she croaked.

"Merry Christmas!" Mike heard a voice assault Patrice with cheerfulness and winced in sympathy. It had been a very disjointed night's sleep and he felt foggy. He imagined Patrice felt the same.

"Eight forty-three," Patrice said, looking at the clock radio. "I had a late night."

Mike enjoyed the way she sprawled across him, her soft weight pressing on him, flattening her breasts against his chest and bringing to mind all the things they would share starting that night. He stroked her round bottom through the flannel nightgown and tried to ignore his erection. He was getting good at trying to ignore it— not succeeding, just trying.

Erections were difficult things to ignore. It was like having a person constantly whispering, "sex, sex, sex," in your ear. You could tune it out for periods of time, but if you dropped your guard there it was: "sex, sex, sex."

Having an erection of varying degrees of firmness seemed to be a permanent state of affairs for him when he was around Patrice. He appreciated her effect on him, but

239

longed for their wedding night when he could fully utilize his reaction.

"Thanks, but I've already arranged for someone in the building to help me. I could use your help at Mom's, though." To Mike, she silently mouthed, "Randy."

He cupped one rounded buttock in his hand, squeezing gently as he inched her gown up with the other.

Patrice hung up and tugged her pajamas back down. "We have to get up."

"I've been up," he said, guiding her hand to the evidence. "For weeks now."

"Well, then a few more hours won't kill you." She gave his turgid member a gentle pat before sliding off its owner.

Mike groaned.

"Why don't you shower while I make the coffee and get the cookies out of the freezer."

"I'd be happy to thaw your frigid cookies." Mike waggled his eyebrows.

Patrice laughed, pointing to the bathroom. "Cold shower that way."

"Don't I know it," Mike groused, getting off the bed. "The idea was to warm your cookies, not freeze mine."

"I'll thaw your cookies tonight. Right now we've got to get going. We've a Christmas party and a wedding to get to."

"Our wedding." Mike beamed.

Patrice returned the grin. "Our wedding." She gave him a peck on the lips, darting back before he could pull her in for a serious kiss. "And I've got a car to pack, hors d'oeuvres to warm, cookies to arrange, and...I really have to find something to wear."

"Wear the red dress," Mike insisted.

Patrice wilted. "I don't want to get married wearing red," she whined.

Mike captured her in his arms and sang, "Lady in red, dance with me, cheek to cheek."

Patrice laughed. "I'll wear the red, but only because the only other really dressy outfit I have is black."

"Black would be bad," Mike agreed. "It would look as if you were in mourning."

"Then why do men wear black?"

"Well," he said. "Some could argue that they are mourning the death of their freedom."

Patrice batted his upper arm.

He grabbed her hand and held it in his, smoothing his thumb over her knuckles. "But I think it's because black is the dressiest color a man can eat in and still look good."

Patrice laughed while Mike kissed her hand with a flourish and let her go.

By nine-thirty they were out the door in their respective cars heading toward their respective parents' houses for their pre-party family traditions.

"We'll have to start earlier next year if we're going to visit both houses," Mike said as they kissed good-bye.

"I bet they'll just combine everything and say the heck with it."

"Won't happen," Mike countered. "My mom doesn't like your mom's tree or her cooking."

Chapter 55

Her father and Randy helped Patrice unload the car while Janice got out serving platters.

"There seems to be quite a bit more this year," Roy said, putting down the last load. "That's good. Father always likes to take a plate to the rectory, and there was never enough left over for me. Especially of those crab puffs and pâté and those chicken wings."

"Well, there may actually be fewer leftovers this year," Patrice said. "I've invited a few extra people. I hope you don't mind."

"Who?" Janice asked. Her pursed lips and raised brows were clear indication that she wasn't pleased, but she was trying to hide it.

"David..."

Janice smiled in obvious relief.

"...Bubba, his mother and three of his sisters, Rochelle, Ruby and Ruth," Patrice continued.

Janice's smile faded. "Bubba," she choked on his name. "And his family?"

"Just his mother and three of his sisters and only for an hour or so. All six sisters are up with husbands and kids, but I couldn't ask all of them. There isn't the room. Still, I had to have Bubba, and I couldn't exclude his mother or the three sisters I know, now could I? Don't worry. There's more than enough food. I had help in the kitchen this year and made full recipes instead of half. I didn't think it would be a problem, and it's only for an hour or so. It isn't, is it? A problem, I mean?"

"Well..." Janice turned red and swallowed heavily.

"Of course not," Roy answered for his wife, obviously more pleased with the prospect of spending time with Bubba Scott than she was. "It's Christmas. The more the merrier as far as I'm concerned, right, dear?" He looked at his wife. "What's the matter, dear? Something go down the wrong pipe?"

"Uh..." She shook her head. "No."

"Randy, get your mother something to drink," he directed.

Patrice watched her pale mother stumble from the room. She had no doubt her mom was about to call Mike's mother.

****

Mike knew something was up when his mother swooped into the living room and snatched the present he'd been about to open out of his hand. "Come with me. We have to talk."

Father and son exchanged puzzled looks as Mike followed his mother into the kitchen. There were just the three of them. It must be about Patrice if his mother didn't want to say it in front of his father.

"Sit," she ordered.

Mike sat.

"Is Patrice engaged?" Melanie demanded.

Mike was stunned. They'd planned to keep it a secret, but he'd planned to do it through ignorance not bold-faced lying.

"Well?" Melanie prompted.

Mike swallowed. "Yes."

"Then Janice was right," Melanie groaned. "How could this have happened? I thought you and Patrice were getting along so well. Janice called last night to say that you drove Patrice home. Was she engaged then?"

"Yes." Mike wasn't certain exactly what his and Patrice's mother thought was going on, but he wasn't going to tip his hand until he knew.

Melanie nodded sadly. "When did it happen?"

"Yesterday afternoon," Mike answered. "How did you find out? It was supposed to be a secret."

"Janice told me. She wasn't certain, but when Patrice said she'd invited Bubba Scott, complete with family, she feared the worst."

Mike bit his lips to keep from smiling. So that's what they thought.

Tears welled in Melanie's eyes. "How could you do this to us?" She hit Mike's arm. "Ever since Patrice grabbed your arm and said, 'Mine,' we hoped the two of you would get married." Her tears began to flow in earnest. Mike tried to comfort his mother, but she hit him again and continued ranting.

"But, no! You had to dump that dessert on her and insult her in public. She loved you. She's always loved you. But you chased her into another man's arms."

Melanie eventually accepted the apology she assumed Mike had made and ushered him back to the living room to open presents while she fixed her face. "Don't wait for me. Janice needs us early."

"What was that all about?" Matt asked his son.

"Mom and Janice think Patrice is engaged to Bubba Scott."

"But she isn't, is she?" Matt said, narrowing his eyes.

"No. She isn't," Mike admitted.

Matt nodded. "But she is engaged, isn't she?"

Mike hesitated. He'd promised Patrice he'd keep their engagement a secret, but he couldn't lie to his dad. He slowly met his father's eyes. "Yes, sir."

"Congratulations, Son." Roy pumped Mike's hand.

Mike stared at him, stunned with relief and amazed at how perceptive his dad was.

"You've got a good girl in Patrice," Roy said. "I'm proud of both of you. Not just for the engagement, but for keeping it a secret from your mothers. They are going to drive everyone nuts once they know. The planning and the spending," he groaned. "I don't suppose I could convince you and Patrice to elope, could I? It would kill your mothers, but Roy and I would gladly pay for the honeymoon if you did."

"Get out your checkbook, Dad. Father McDaniels is marrying us this afternoon."

Matt laughed, loud and long. "Good job, Son, good job. You're going to spring it on them, aren't you? I can hardly wait to see your mother's face."

Chapter 56

Patrice was helping her mother pick up the remnants of wrapping paper, bows, and packaging from her family gift exchange when Mike and his family arrived at noon, an hour earlier than usual.

Her mother's standard, "Merry Christmas," was replaced by a relieved, "Thank God, you're here."

Randy hung coats, and Roy poured wine.

"Patrice, honey, why don't you go warm those hors d'oeuvres now?" her mother suggested. "Mike will help you."

"Mike can sit," Randy said, entering the living room. "I can help Pet if she needs it."

"No," both mothers snapped, not subtle in the least.

"Mike is happy to help," Melanie insisted. "Aren't you, Mike?"

Patrice gave Mike a puzzled look, shrugged, and went into the kitchen.

"What is going on?" she asked as soon as the door swung shut.

"Come with me." Mike grabbed her hand and dragged her down the hall to the bathroom. Once inside, he locked the door and turned on the fan before kissing her.

"What's going on? Why are we in the bathroom?" she asked as soon as her lips were free.

"Your mother thinks you and Bubba are serious."

"What? Why?" Patrice asked, puzzled.

"You invited him and his family over to meet your family on Christmas. Your mother thinks there's an engagement in the offing. She called my mother in a panic. I'm here to convince you not to marry Bubba."

"Okay." Patrice grinned slyly at him, wrapping her arms around his neck and pressing her body close to his. "Convince me."

They nearly devoured each other in a ravenous kiss.

"Pretty good," Patrice panted, "but I may need reminders throughout the day."

"Did I tell you how much I like this dress?" He ran a finger under a spaghetti strap of the silky red dress following the edge of the material as it outlined her breast and dipped to reveal a glimpse of cleavage.

"No," she swallowed, watching his finger and hoping it would slide a bit further under the material. Her nipples perked up as if sharing that hope.

"I don't know if I'm going to be able to last until tonight," Mike groaned.

Patrice leaned her body against his. "You can and you will."

Remarkably, pressing against each other like that calmed and soothed them both. It was as if their nerve endings had been screaming for more full-scale contact. He held her close, "Thank you."

She pressed her face into his suit coat and closed her eyes, reveling in the solid strength of his body. She would have happily stayed there forever, but she knew that wasn't an option, not yet. She looked at his face to find him watching her. "Why are we in the bathroom with the fan running?"

"To keep our conversation private. I'm guessing our mother's ears are pressed against the door, trying to find out if I'm succeeding in winning you from Bubba." He grinned at her. "Can I tell them I was successful?"

"Were you? I can't remember. You'll have to remind me."

They kissed slowly and sweetly, tasting each other— their tongues caressing in a sensuous dance.

"Yes," she sighed against his lips. "You've won me.

You can go to your mother and claim victory."

"Not yet. We still have a few hours. By the way, our dads are sending us to Jamaica for our honeymoon."

"Sending us?"

"As a reward for avoiding the hassles of having our mother's plan the wedding."

She stepped out of his arms, looking at him with wide eyes. "You told them?"

"Just my dad. He had it half figured out anyway. Don't worry; he can keep a secret."

"Better than you, I hope." She sounded more irritated than she really was. "You didn't tell him about Bubba or David, did you?"

Mike crossed his arms in front of his chest. "I know the difference between a harmless secret and a major secret."

"Sorry," Patrice said. "I didn't mean it as harsh as it sounded. I must be a little nervous."

Mike smiled. "That's understandable. I'm a little edgy myself."

"Having second thoughts?" she asked.

"No. If anything, I wish we were already married. Do you think Father could get here earlier if I called and asked him?"

"No. It's Christmas. He can't skip a Mass, and he's not likely to shorten it either. This is one of two times a year he gets to see some of his parishioners. He's not going to rush through it, no matter how anxious we are."

"Guess I'll have to wait then."

"We'd better get out of here before we cause too many suspicions." She looked in the mirror to check her appearance. Her lipstick was gone, but her lips were red and her cheeks were flushed from kissing.

"You're beautiful," he said, watching her. "And I love you."

"I love you, too, and I want the whole world to know it."

He looked at his watch. "Two hours and forty-five minutes."

Chapter 57

David, Bubba, his mama, Rochelle, Ruby, and Ruth arrived at two-thirty. Bubba's mama first act upon entering the Wilson house was to hug Patrice. And she was no shrinking violet. At five-nine, two hundred fifty pounds, when she hugged someone, they were hugged.

"You're an angel, child," she said, grabbing Patrice without introduction. "Thank you for taking such good care of my Bubba."

In order to keep from being crushed, Patrice hugged back, silently cursing Bubba, who obviously hadn't explained that she was marrying Mike today. She blushed and stammered, trying to catch Bubba's eye. "Mrs. Scott, I..."

"You'll call me Glory," she insisted, releasing Patrice. "Everyone else does."

Patrice was going to kill Bubba. She watched her mother cringingly endure his mother's embrace. Saw her wince as Glory loudly announced, "Your Patrice, our darling Pet, is an angel, a guardian angel, sent from heaven to smooth Bubba's path."

Ruby caught her in a less vigorous embrace, whispering, "Don't worry, Pet, Mama knows."

"Bubba told you?" Patrice whispered back, incredulously. "About today?"

"Yes. And we couldn't be more happy for you."

Patrice narrowed her eyes. "Just what did Bubba tell you?"

Ruby laughed, passing Patrice on to Rochelle and Ruth, who exclaimed. "Where's your ring? Bubba said you had a beautiful ring."

"Ring?" Janice gasped as the color drained from her face. "What ring?"

Patrice wanted to disappear. This wasn't how she and Mike had planned to announce their engagement.

Janice nearly sobbed. "What ring?" she repeated, turning accusing eyes on her daughter.

Patrice looked at Mike who nodded to her, smiling with apparent amusement. She'd kill him when she was done with Bubba. As if on stage, everyone watched Patrice walk to the chair where she'd left her purse and retrieve her ring. Sliding it onto her finger, she returned to the group to face the excited smiles and wounded glares. She sent Mike a silent plea for help. How were they going to announce that it was Mike she was marrying, not Bubba, when everyone appeared to think it was the other way around?

Winding his way through the crowded entryway to Patrice's side, Mike passed his laughing father only to be captured by Bubba's mother. "And you must be the groom," she announced.

Janice swayed on her feet. Roy wrapped his arm around his wife in support, exchanging amused looks with Matt who held an equally shocked Melanie. The doorbell rang.

"Good Lord, now what?" Janice cried.

David answered the door.

"Ah, the wedding party and guests," the old priest laughed. "This is a bit more of a welcome than I'm used to."

Roy caught his wife, keeping her from slumping to the floor.

"Mom?" Stricken, Patrice followed her father to the couch where he laid his wife.

Mike appeared at her elbow. "She'll be fine."

"We should have told her."

"Nonsense," her father told her. "This will make a

much better story for the grandkids than the one where your mother took an entire year to plan such a huge and expensive wedding that the bride and groom and their fathers wished they'd eloped."

"I heard that," Janice said, opening her eyes.

"And you know it's true," Roy insisted, helping his wife sit. "Admit it."

"I'll admit to nothing except that in my scenario, the bride wears white."

"And she'll wear white today too," David said, pointing at the large box he'd leaned against the wall.

"Thank you, David," Janice said. "You've saved the day." She turned to Patrice. "Of course, had Melanie and I known about the wedding before the actual day, we could have helped you find the wedding dress."

Roy put his hand on his wife's arm. "Don't start, Janice. This is what they were trying to avoid."

"But you knew about it," she said, injured.

"Only since the Tuckers got here."

Janice's eyes grew wide with pain. She flattened a palm on her chest and gasped. "Melanie knew?"

"Calm down. She didn't have a clue either," Mike said with a look at his own mother who was, apparently, having heart palpitations.

"We didn't want to hurt anyone," Patrice added, looking at her mother and Mike's in turn. "We were just going to elope, but thought it would be a more fun and romantic if all of you were here."

"Your daughter is an angel," Bubba's mama announced. "She knew it would hurt you if she ran away and got married, so she didn't. She planned a wedding with a priest and a reception in your home, but took away the burden of planning and paying for it. She's a true angel. There's some who wish their daughters were as thoughtful."

"Now, Mama," Rochelle scolded. "It's water under the bridge."

"I've six sisters," Bubba explained.

"Oh," Roy said in empathy.

"Now," Father McDaniels said, smiling at each in turn. "Perhaps the bride and groom would like to freshen up while their parents decide on just where the couple should stand as they exchange their vows."

Mike led Patrice out of the living room before hugging her.

"What a mess," Patrice groaned, burying her face in his shoulder.

"It'll be all right," Mike soothed, caressing Patrice's hair.

David joined them, carrying the box. "You were very smart to do this as you did. Just imagine what a year of that would have been like."

The couple shuddered and laughed.

"Now, about this dress..." David said, lifting the box.

Patrice turned to him, smiling, "Oh, thank you, David. What does it look like?"

Mike narrowed his eyes at David. "That's what I want to know. What does it look like?"

David smiled slyly, snagging Patrice's arm. "It's bad luck for the groom to see the bride in her dress before the wedding."

"And it's bad luck for the best man to see the bride undressed before or after the wedding."

"I thought Randy was best man," David said.

"I kind of hoped I would be," Randy said, joining the group in the hall. "Did you want one of Bubba's sisters to act as bride's maid?" he asked Patrice. "I could get one."

"No. Actually, David will be my bridal attendant."

Randy shrugged.

Mike sighed. "But maybe the sisters could help you with the gown," he suggested.

David laughed. "Better get the moms instead. It'd make their day, and then they can give wedding night advice."

Patrice groaned.

****

The gown was perfect—long sleeved and off the shoulder made of blushed-cream watermarked silk. The fitted neckline dipped slightly in the line from mid-shoulder to mid-shoulder, and the bodice hugged her curves to her hips before cascading in yards of heavy silk.

"Where did you get this?" Mike's mother asked, staring at Patrice.

"David brought it," Janice said.

"It fits like it was made for her," Melanie said, exchanging glances with Janice. "Just how close are you and David?"

"She's marrying Mike," Janice reminded her friend.

"I know."

"David will just keep him on his toes, make him appreciate Patrice more. It's a good thing." Janice talked to Melanie as if they were alone.

"As long as it doesn't go too far. Mike won't stand for anything untoward."

"I'm marrying Mike. David is just a friend," Patrice protested.

"Of course, dear," Melanie said. "Your mother and I were just commenting on what a near thing it is. Mike needs to realize just how lucky he is."

"He does realize it. Really," Patrice insisted.

The mothers nodded. Janice picked up a brush. "Shall we put her hair up or leave it down?"

Melanie plugged in a curling iron.

"Down," Patrice said. "I want it down. Mike likes it down."

"Up in a bun with spiral tendrils brushing her shoulders," Melanie said, as if she hadn't heard Patrice. "What do you think, Janice?"

Patrice sighed, and gave herself up to their maternal ministrations.

Chapter 58

"It's my sister's," David said when Patrice asked him about the dress. They stood alone together outside the living room waiting for their cue.

"I knew it looked familiar." She looked down at the dress, loving the way it made her feel beautiful and desirable. She swished the skirt several times, enjoying the feel of the silk as it brushed her legs. Her eyes returned to David. "Tell her thanks."

"I already did. She said she married the man of her dreams in the dress and was glad to loan it to you so that you could do the same."

Patrice's eyes filled with tears even as she smiled. "She's so sweet."

"She's so sappy. She gets that way after she has a baby. But enough about her—did your mother give you the talk?"

Patrice laughed. "The go-ahead talk? Actually, no."

"I'm shocked. Let me call her over." He took a step toward the living room.

She grabbed his arm. "Don't you dare. But wait. Get my dad. He's supposed to be here with us so he can walk me down the aisle."

"I don't think he wants to give you away," David said, looking into the living room. "Are those tears in his eyes?"

Patrice peeked around David. Her father was talking

to Mike's father and looked perfectly normal. "Are those tears?" she repeated sarcastically, stepping back behind the wall. David chuckled, and she backhanded his arm.

David motioned for her father to come. Roy raised one finger before walking over to Mike.

"Uh, oh," David said. "He's giving Mike a little premarital advice."

"Stop it," Patrice scolded.

"No really." He continued to watch, giving Patrice a play-by-play. "Mike's blushing. Now he's shaking his head, denying something." David turned to give Patrice a quick glance. "I'll bet he's asking Mike if this quick marriage is because you're expecting. My advice would be to use protection for the first couple of months, assuming you aren't pregnant, that is."

Patrice hit his arm, hard.

"Ouch. What was that for?"

She said nothing, turning away from him.

He turned her to face him. "You're mad."

She glared at him, feeling foolish and angry. "And you're making it up, about my dad confronting Mike. I'm getting married in two minutes, and you're acting like a jerk."

"I'm sorry, Pet. I shouldn't have done that, but I didn't make it up."

As if to prove his point, Mike stormed into the hall, dragging Roy by the arm.

"Tell him," Mike insisted. "Tell your father that you're marrying me because you love me and not because I trapped you."

"Dad?" Patrice couldn't believe it. David hadn't been lying. Her father stood before her, his face red with anger and embarrassment. "Please don't do this on my wedding day."

"I have to or it will be too late." He shook his arm out of Mike's grasp. Clearing his throat, he continued in a calmer, more loving voice. "You don't have to marry him, honey. Not unless you really want to."

She put her hand on her father's sleeve. "I really want to, Dad."

"I just wanted to be certain that you weren't being pressured into this. Your mother and Melanie...and if he..."

"I know about Mom's plans, Dad, but no one is pressuring me into this. I love Mike, and he loves me."

"But," he protested, still looking unconvinced.

"I want this," she said. "And Dad, he's not making me." She leaned close to whisper.

"What?" Roy asked, disbelieving.

Patrice blushed, but repeated herself in a louder whisper. "I'm still a virgin."

Roy blushed crimson. "I...um, you...um. That's inappropriate, young lady," he muttered stiffly.

Patrice was crimson as well.

"Well..." David broke the awkward silence. "If that's all taken care of, let's get this wedding started. We've got us a virgin bride to give away."

Patrice buried her burning face in Mike's shirt.

Mike wrapped his arms around his mortified bride, rubbing her back to soothe her. "Don't worry, honey, it might not happen all that often any more, and it usually isn't announced before the ceremony, but the bride is supposed to be a virgin."

David laughed. "I'll bet more would be if the truth were announced before every wedding." His voice dropped into a lower register as he continued, "Mary Ellen comes to this marriage having had thirty-six different sexual partners. The groom has had forty. The couple is expecting their second baby in six months."

Lifting her head from Mike's chest, Patrice smiled at David. "Thanks."

Mike hugged his bride. "Let's get married." He looked at his future father-in-law. "You okay walking her down the aisle?"

"I'm sorry, Mike. I..."

"Forget it. If she were my daughter..." He stopped cold as the thought of a future daughter occurred to him. He shot a panicked look at Patrice.

"Worry about it later," Patrice said. "Our children haven't even been conceived yet."

Mike nodded. Roy grinned, knowing he was truly forgiven. A man who looked that pole-axed by the mere thought of a daughter wouldn't hold a bit of over-protectiveness against the father of his bride.

Chapter 59

The wedding was short and simple. All the mothers cried, including Bubba's.

Afterward both Bubba and David kissed the bride.

"No tongue," Mike warned David, alerted by the mischievous twinkle in David's eyes.

"I was saving that for you," David teased.

Mike looked stunned.

Patrice laughed, giving David a kiss on the cheek. "Mind your manners."

"Spoil sport."

The food was wonderful, of course. Mike filled a plate with the riblets he loved so well and sat in a corner next to an end table with plenty of napkins.

David joined him, sitting on an adjacent chair. He had an equally laden plate balanced on his knee, but seemed more interested in watching Mike eat.

"Ah," David sighed.

Mike raised a questioning eyebrow.

"Don't mind me," David said, smiling wickedly. "I love watching a man...eat ribs."

Mike choked, putting his plate on the end table. "Shit, David. Is this going to be a constant thing? I thought you owned a closet."

"Sorry," David said, his grin showing that he wasn't

sorry at all. "Don't let me spoil your dinner."

"Too late." Mike wiped his face. "Was there something you wanted other than to ruin ribs forever for me?"

"Actually, yes. I've got a little wedding gift for you and Patrice." He reached in his coat pocket and pulled out a present the size of a package of nylons.

"What is it?" Mike asked, taking it from him.

"Lingerie for tonight."

"It's not a very big package."

"There's not much material in there."

Mike nodded, trying to keep a straight face.

David grinned. "She deserves the best, but she's got you. Try not to disappoint her."

"Should I take it personally that all the men in my wife's life keep telling me I'm not worthy of her?"

David shook his head. "We're men. We know what we're like. None of us is worthy."

"Worthy of what?" Patrice asked, joining them.

"Worthy of eating like this every night. Mike is going to get fat."

"I don't think so." She eyed Mike's plate. "Is there something wrong with the ribs?"

"No." Mike said, looking uncomfortable. "It's just..."

"A change in outlook," David finished for him, smiling wickedly.

Patrice pursed her lips, nodding sagely. "You've become a vegetarian."

Mike shook his head. "Uh, no."

Patrice nodded again, picked up a riblet and slowly licked the sauce from it. She had a rapt audience as she held one end of the bone and slid the entire riblet into her mouth. She met Mike's eye before closing her teeth on the bone and pulling it from her mouth, scraping off the tender meat in the process.

Mike swallowed convulsively.

She chewed and swallowed before sliding the bone back into her mouth for a final polish.

Mike tugged on his collar.

Finished with the small, pinky-size bone, Patrice held it aloft."Yum! I love these little suckers," she told her rapt audience. "They're almost as good as the full-sized ones." She added the bone to the small pile on Mike's plate then turned to walk away. "Oh, honey," she said, over her shoulder. "I'm ready to go as soon as you've finished eating."

Mike surged to his feet.

David stopped him with a hand. "Better eat something. You're going to need the strength."

Chapter 60

Later, in her apartment bathroom, Patrice put on the scrap of red satin that David had given Mike for her. Two narrow triangles of material came over her shoulders, barely covering a third of her breasts as they plunged to meet south of her navel in a skirt so short it wasn't even worthy of the name. She thought maybe it was on backwards, but there was even less material there.

"Are you ready yet?" Mike called from the other side of the door.

Patrice poked her head out of the bathroom. "I can't wear this."

"Why not?"

"There isn't enough of it to actually wear."

"Let me see," he said, grasping the doorknob.

"No!" She tightened her grip.

"What happened to the seductress with the ribs?"

"That rib had more sauce than I have material," she complained.

Mike grinned in anticipation. "I forgive David everything."

"I don't," Patrice pouted. "I can't wear this. I'd feel more comfortable nude."

"I'm sure I can take care of that," Mike assured her. "But just let me see it first."

Patrice sighed her resignation and let Mike open the door.

"I see what you mean." He grinned like a madman, the evidence of his desire tenting his boxers. "There isn't much material, but you sure make the most of it."

"What does that mean?" Patrice asked, blushing ferociously and looking down at her body. Seeing herself nearly naked, her hands automatically went to cover key areas.

Mike shook his head and gently replaced her hands with his. "Mine."

Wisconsin author Laurel Bradley believes that wishes really do come true. After 11 years of writing, Bradley has finally achieved her dream of seeing her stories in print. Her first novel, the romantic time-travel **A Wish in Time**, was released February 2007 and was a finalist in the 2007 National Indie Excellence Book Awards. Now, she enjoys sharing the lessons she has learned about new technologies, networking and the importance of savvy marketing with other book enthusiasts and writers. **Crème Brûlée Upset,** a contemporary romance, is Bradley's second novel.

For more information on Bradley's books or her upcoming appearances, visit www.laurelbradley.com.

Thank you for purchasing this Wild Rose Press publication. For other wonderful stories of romance, please visit our on-line bookstore at www.thewildrosepress.com.

For questions or more information contact us at info@thewildrosepress.com.

The Wild Rose Press
www.TheWildRosePress.com

Printed in the United States
202922BV00001B/1-105/P